To Harold &

Enjoy.

L Shana Torra

06

IN SEARCH OF HENRY

IN SEARCH OF HENRY

Arnold Powell

Book Guild Publishing
Sussex, England

First published in Great Britain in 2006 by
The Book Guild Ltd
25 High Street
Lewes, East Sussex
BN7 2LU

Typesetting in Baskerville by
Acorn Bookwork Ltd, Salisbury, Wiltshire

Printed in Great Britain by
CPI Bath

A catalogue record for this book is available from
The British Library.

ISBN 1 84624 027 1

This love story is dedicated to my wife
and to our grandsons that they might learn that a flower
should be the prelude to every date with a lady.

As important as light and water to a plant, the most essential ingredient in this book does not appear on any of its pages. Namely the encouragement received from others. I would like to express my gratitude and thanks to the many who have assisted me, often unknowingly, in the production of this story. In particular my thanks go to: June, critic, friend, my love and partner of many years, for her suggestions, great forbearance and unfailing support in all my endeavours, never doubting me when it mattered. Almost as important, her fantastic cookery recipe for the sour cream cake.

My cousin the late Louis Cheslock, Peabody Conservatory stalwart, teacher extraordinaire and musician and his wife Elise, for the friendship extended to my wife and me during our stay in Baltimore many years ago.

Flora Gursky, our wonderful distant transatlantic cousin who graciously taught me so much concerning genealogical research. Jeremy Balcombe, my son-in-law, and his cousins Jean Balcombe and Margaret Weyler of PA who were all, unsuspectingly, the inspiration for the original research and this love story. Ivan Hartog, friend and long time boating companion, who challenged me in January 2005 to write a book. Frederick Powell, grandson and poetry-reading companion, whose enthusiasm when he read a few pages of the first draft and wished to read more, encouraged me to continue writing more than any thing else. Liam Rand, cousin, both for his encouragement and for drawing to my attention that this was not simply a 'how to genealogy book', but a love story that needed to be told. Thank you Liam, I am eternally in your debt. Milton Kaplan, friend and Baltimore MD attorney. Eunice Kaplan who through her marriage to Milton, a Baltimorean, ensured the early years of my marriage were spent in that magnificent city. Harold Ellis, Professor Emeritus of Surgery at the

Westminster Hospital Medical Faculty, London, a great surgeon, with a wonderful sense of humour. A marvellous surgical teacher, whose lectures were always instructive, amusing and inspirational, particularly on the Battle of the Somme. Tessa Uys, friend and concert-pianist whose Bach transcriptions are a remarkable revelation. Michael Powell, Jan Porter, Michael and Melanie Williams, and many other family and friends for proofreading and suggestions.

Bless each of you and my thanks.
Arnold Powell, London, 16 April 2005

Look not mournfully into the past.
It comes not back again.
Wisely improve the present, it is thine.
Go forth to meet the shadowy future,
with a bold heart,
without fear.

Henry Wadsworth Longfellow

Chapter 1

Baltimore Maryland 1914

Bewildered, a skinny malnourished ten-year-old boy with long unruly auburn-brown hair arrived at Baltimore's Penn Station in late November 1899 from London, the city of his birth. Henry had accompanied his mother and two sisters across the Atlantic via New York, and standing on the railway concourse he gazed in baffled wonderment at the uncharitably harsh Maryland welcome. The streets, piled high with snow, had been battered by an early winter's storm that had suddenly and briefly swept in from the Atlantic. He watched as gangs of heavily-clad men, breathing out tiny clouds of steam in the cold winter air, tirelessly shovelled ice and snow into teams of horse-drawn carts, clearing roads and sidewalks as rapidly as possible, to keep this great port open for trade.

* * *

In the first few years of their life in America, Henry's mother Rebecca Chiswick sent him to the Edgar Allen Poe Public School, where he grew into a thin gangling youth, with a particularly sunny disposition. Bright and well spoken, he had quickly shown great intellectual promise and natural ability, but in May 1902, shortly before his thirteenth birthday, Rebecca had told him sadly she could no longer afford to keep him at school.

A few days later Henry had returned home with a letter from Mr Crawford, the school principal, inviting her to come in to discuss Henry's future. Two days later, on an overcast warm spring morning, she had hurried down Fayette Street and arrived at the school almost twenty minutes before her appointment. Uncertain why she had been summoned and anxious to show no disrespect by being late, she waited in the corridor, slowly pacing up and down until the large school clock adorning the corridor wall indicated the time of her appointment was at hand. Apprehensively she straightened her outer attire, adjusted her hat and approached the

1

principal's door, where she raised her clenched hand and timidly knocked. Her tap was answered from within by a man's voice with a curt, "Come in."

She nervously pushed open the door to an outer office in which sat a supercilious young man whom she took to be Mr Crawford's assistant. She explained that she had an appointment with the principal. The assistant curtly asked her to wait as he disappeared through a door to an inner office before reappearing some moments later and, with more courtesy than he had shown earlier, requested her to enter the inner office.

In the impressive wood panelled room that she entered was a large oak desk, set at an angle facing the door. Behind it was a window, while in front were two leather-buttoned upholstered chairs. Along each wall was a line of narrow tables and above them was a series of glass-fronted cabinets full of files and books. The principal, grey haired and bespectacled, was seated in a bosun's swivel chair behind his desk. As Rebecca walked through the door he politely rose to greet her, extending his hand across his desk in welcome.

"Thank you for coming Mrs Chiswick; it's a pleasure to meet you again. Do have a seat."

"Thank you." She nodded nervously and perched on the edge of one of the magnificent chairs.

"I'm sure you're a busy woman and I'll be as brief as I possibly can. I've invited you here to tell you that you're a most fortunate parent. We've recognised here for some time that your son Henry is an intellectually gifted child. Now I understand that you may be taking him out of school once he reaches his thirteenth birthday. If I could discourage you from this course of action and perhaps persuade you to permit him to stay on, then should you wish to apply for a bursary, I feel certain I can persuade the school board to grant one to cover his full tuition fees. I might add that unlike many of the other immigrant children we endeavour to educate, he has the enormous advantage that English is his native tongue and as you're doubtless aware, he's a prodigious gift of recall for much of the considerable volume of literature he's so avidly read and enjoyed. We've found this quite remarkable, for a youth of his age."

Rebecca took a deep breath; she hated having to refuse him. "Thank you for your very kind offer, Mr Crawford. I only wish to heaven that my boy could take advantage of your generosity, but

2

unfortunately, I must decline your help. I've long passed the point where I feel shame, or embarrassment when I need to explain that we're very poor. It wasn't always so, but Henry and my other children have been greatly disadvantaged by the early passing of their father eight years ago. Henry and I live with one of my younger married daughters, who every day struggles to put bread on our plates, as well as those of her husband and her growing children. There's simply no way that we can avoid Henry leaving school at the earliest opportunity in order to support himself and assist me. If he has the ability you claim, then one day he may be able to obtain an education to make something more of himself. Meanwhile to survive, we need to eat, and Henry must leave school as soon as possible."

The principal gazed at her with real compassion as well as disappointment at the prospect of losing such an able pupil. "Mrs Chiswick, I fully understand your predicament and I'm truly sorry. I greatly regret the loss of the real contribution your son could make to our society. We must hope and pray that when he's a little older he may be able to exploit his intellectual potential more fully." He stood up and walked around his desk to shake her hand. "But thank you for taking the time to come in to talk to me."

* * *

A week after Rebecca had left the principal's office, Henry, who had reached his thirteenth birthday, started work at $3.00 a week in a small cigar factory not far from the quayside in downtown Baltimore, where his sister Annie's husband Mo Levy, was the overseer foreman.

Baltimore had long been a thriving seaport and industrial centre at the head of the Patapsco River, protected from the Atlantic Ocean by one of nature's greatest sheltered waterways, the Chesapeake Bay. Forty miles to the southwest it was overshadowed by Washington DC, rebuilt to French architectural design following its destruction by fire in 1814 at the hands of the British in the war of 1812. Ninety years later, unrelated to war, Baltimore suffered a similar fiery calamity, but its rebuilding never rose to quite the same heights of architectural splendour as its more elegant political neighbour.

Over the previous century, the port of Baltimore had become the hub of the American tobacco distribution industry, the quaysides

3

crowded with warehouses full of bales of tobacco leaves, gathered from the growing areas of the southern states and Caribbean for processing and distribution to the northern United States and Europe.

In the sweltering summer of 1914 the factory in which Henry now worked could best be described as one of a series of large garages. These had been constructed as cheaply and rapidly as possible in the months following the down town fire of 1904, which over a two-day period had ravaged and devastated the commercial and trading centre of this great, thriving town. The brick building had a pair of substantial wooden sliding doors. Coated in creosote and heavily glazed, they ran along one complete side providing access for staff and the delivery of raw materials, directly from quayside warehouses. Through these same doors crates of finished goods, packaged in boxes, were carefully carried out, to be loaded onto a horse-drawn wagon waiting in the cobbled alleyway.

Daylight filtered through a row of small windows in the doors and from a line of small high-level windows along the opposite wall, while a double pair of gas mantles lit the interior during the late afternoons and evenings with pale amber light. The same wide sliding doors also provided ventilation for the more than two score young men and women working in the building, seated on three-legged backless stools at long wooden benches, rolling cigars.

Work in the bustling premises began at eight a.m. sharp, every morning, and Henry soon discovered that this meant working inside the factory, not just arriving at the heavy door. Woe betide the employee who came in one minute late: the owner, Mr Burch-hardt, would remove his fob watch from a waistcoat pocket with his long grubby hand, and make a great show of looking at it.

"Valkomme. Vot sorta time oft dey iis diss to beginnin voik? Mebbe somvun vas sic? Yew hed mebbe a layte nite und jost got up?" He would enquire solicitously, although intending no kindness. A second infringement that month would draw a similar rebuke, but at day's end there would inevitably be the corollary, unmoved by tears or pleading for a second or third chance.

"Herre's yor geldt an' rimemba nod to kommen beck in ze mornin." Time was money and there was no shortage of eager young hands willing to work from eight in the morning until six in the evening and often later, with a half hour break for lunch and no overtime pay. The unfailing incentive to comply and work was

4

simply the need for a job and at the end of each week, the salary it provided to pay the rent and buy groceries.

During the summer months, the stifling heat and humidity were almost overpowering inside the factory. Even with the doors wide open, the very tobacco leaves appeared to wilt as they were released from their huge bales, while in the winter whatever warmth was grudgingly generated within was immediately dissipated every time the great doors were pulled open. This crude factory was like scores of similarly small operations cashing in on the ever-growing demand for tobacco products. Henry had started his apprenticeship, like most of the young men his age, by sweeping the floor, unloading bales of tobacco and loading boxes of cigars for shipment to customers.

Over the next few years, despite the oppressiveness of the surroundings, Henry cheerfully progressed to rolling the narrow inexpensive cheroot cigars and, later, applying the maker's coloured band with a dexterous dab of glue. Now an able and responsible young man of twenty-five he used the guillotine to ensure the correct length of each cigar and supervised their careful packaging into wood and cardboard boxes.

Henry carried no surplus weight and stood five feet ten inches. He possessed clear blue grey eyes, and with his mop of curly auburn hair and clean-shaven face, had the appearance of an adult cherub. The natural good humour with which he had been blessed never failed him and when he spoke, his almost constant smile betrayed an inner happy confidence while the range and rapidity of his speech confirmed an agile and erudite mind.

He continued to live with his widowed mother in a two-room tenement apartment, all that his weekly wage could provide, while Rebecca supplemented the family income with a little sewing and mending, but most frequently with letter writing. She had pleasingly legible, copperplate handwriting and her services grew in demand as word spread among the more recently arrived immigrants and the less literate that for fifty cents to a dollar, there was somebody who could formulate a letter in acceptably correct English, as competently as any lawyer, and for far less money. She did it for those who needed help, when the need arose to write to legal, immigration and other authorities, particularly the plethora of Baltimore officials requiring written statements of one kind or another.

5

After breakfast she would clear the crockery away, wipe the table clean and then sit down to write her letters in black ink on plain white paper. On some days she might produce up to eight or nine, always providing each 'client' with a copy of the original document, as a record of the correspondence. Her income from this activity could considerably exceed the wage many men carried home from their manual labours.

In their tiny apartment, Rebecca slept in the back bedroom, while Henry slept on a couch in the living room/kitchen. To Henry these basic arrangements verged on luxury living, especially when compared to their neighbours and friends the Rosenberg's, a family of twelve in the same size apartment. When he had first arrived in Baltimore, he had shared a similar amenity with his two older sisters in their eldest sister's home, which in turn was a great improvement on conditions he had known when they had lived in London. There, as the baby of the family, he had been placed in the Norwood orphanage in South London when he was five years old, along with his two older brothers Sid and Alf and his sisters Amelia and Annie.

These forlorn circumstances had come about when their father, David Joseph Chiswick, had gone to America to visit his recently married eldest daughter Rachel in Baltimore, from where, it seemed, one day he had just disappeared.

Henry's eldest sister Rachel, a pretty young woman, employed as a mantle maker in a nearby factory since she had left school, lived in the crowded two roomed family apartment in London's Spitalfields.[1] In 1892 when aged eighteen she had bumped into Barney Romack on the dimly lit stairwell of the busy tenement that provided access to her drab home. Barney, an eligible young bachelor from Baltimore, had just arrived the previous day to visit his family in London, who lived in the same cramped ugly block of flats as the Chiswicks.

Apparently it was love at first sight and within two weeks of their first meeting he had proposed to her. Hastily banns were posted at the local register office and three weeks later they were married in the nearby Great Garden Street Synagogue. The day after the wedding ceremony and nuptial celebrations, Rachel accompanied her new husband, with two tightly packed leather cases, by train to Liverpool. There they stayed for one night in a bed and breakfast boarding house close to the docks, prior to embarkation the following morning as steerage passengers on a White Star steamship, to sail to Baltimore to begin their married lives together in the New World.

The next year Rachel gave birth to her first child, Jonathan, and when in 1894 news was received of their grandson's first birthday, Rachel's father took the decision to travel to Baltimore to see his grandson. Until now he had made a meagre living in London as a master tailor. He wanted both to see Jonathan and check out the prospects for work and establishing a home in Baltimore, which from Rachel's letters seemed particularly encouraging. Should Baltimore turn out to be a good prospect, he would send for Rebecca, with money for her and the children to join him. He set sail in steerage from Liverpool to Baltimore in September of 1894, leaving Rebecca with funds that would barely be sufficient for two months.

On arrival, he had stayed with Rachel and Barney. Not only did he have the enjoyment of seeing his grandson Jonathan for the very first time, but also to his immense pleasure he discovered that Rachel was pregnant and there was another grandchild expected within the next few weeks. He searched for employment and found that he could readily find tailoring work to provide an income for his family's needs. As in London he would be working in the same sweatshop conditions of twelve hours a day, six days a week, but his income would be relatively far better.

He decided that he would remain living in his daughter's apartment until the first of his family arrived, before taking on the additional financial commitment of his own accommodation. He worked out that supporting his wife and family and saving for their fares to the USA would take him at least four years to achieve. He had talked the matter over with Barney, who had agreed to help him with an interest-free loan. He had confided to Barney that he had noticed over a number of weeks a certain degree of heartburn some time after he had eaten his main meal of the day and whenever he climbed the stairs to the apartment. Neither of them thought very much about this, since David Joseph invariably found that if he drank a small draught of brandy, or rested momentarily as he ascended the stepped incline, the pain rapidly eased.

That very afternoon, a few hours after David Joseph had discussed the loan with Barney, his daughter had gone into early labour. Hurriedly leaving her father in charge of the baby, Rachel and her husband had set off for the hospital. Delighted at the imminent prospect of a new grandchild and with the news that he

7

had arranged his finances to bring his family over to Baltimore far earlier than anticipated, David Joseph scribbled a brief note to his wife. Anxious to catch the Saturday post, since there was none the following day, and with his grandson safely sound asleep, he had gone out into the chill November air to post the letter. The post box was situated near the top of a graded prominence that could barely be called a hill, less than a quarter mile from the apartment. He knew it would take him a little over five minutes to walk there and back if he hurried. Fast asleep, his grandson would be perfectly safe for the brief period of his absence.

As he briskly walked up the hill, he felt a return of his heartburn. Ignoring the discomfort in his chest he continued until he reached the post box and dropped his letter through the slot, before pausing to catch his breath. The heartburn appeared to be increasing in intensity and he was somehow experiencing trouble catching his breath. He looked around in panic.

If only there were somewhere I could sit, he thought. He had recently taken to carrying a small hip flask for such an occasion and, pulling it from his pocket, he took a nip. The fluid seared his throat as he swallowed, but did not bring the expected relief.

I'd better take another, and then get back home out of this cold, he thought.

He took a second; followed quickly by a third gulp of brandy, and still the heartburn persisted. Fearful of what this might mean and anxious to return to his baby-minding duty he turned for home and slowly started to walk down the long hill. The heartburn was becoming worse with each step until it was downright agony. He stopped; the top of his chest was hurting and felt as if it were being crushed in a vice. He just couldn't seem to move one leg in front of the other.

He looked back to confirm the meagre distance he had travelled: the blue steel post box was still no more than thirty paces away. He knew he could never make the short journey back down the hill to his baby-sitting duty without help. He gazed around wildly for a hackney carriage, or someone who could help him, but the street was empty. Desperately he forced himself to move two more paces onwards, but the pain was now agonising, rising from his chest into his throat, neck and arm. "Help me!" He mouthed the words almost silently. "Someone, please help!" As he collapsed forward onto the ground, he made no sound. The occasional passer by stopped to help, but then walked on, as the odour of brandy wafted upwards into the cold air.

An hour later a policeman on his rounds noticed a huddled figure on the sidewalk and summoned help to take the body to the city morgue. When the police pathologist examined the dead man, they found no identification in the pockets. Thus for the time being, David Joseph Chiswick lay anonymous and unmourned.

Returning home from the hospital later that evening Barney heard his infant son's loud crying. Searching the apartment he was greatly perplexed to find his father-in-law missing and the baby unattended.

His priorities then and over the next few days were to find a babyminder, visit his wife in hospital and work, leaving him no time to deal with the mystery of what had happened to David Joseph. For nearly two weeks he made no attempt to trace the older man's whereabouts, although he sent a brief letter to Rebecca telling her of the safe arrival of another grandchild and the strange disappearance of her husband, who had mysteriously vanished.

In Baltimore the matter was reported to the police, while in London Rebecca was facing her own winter crisis, trying to feed her family and pay the mounting arrears of rent, without any income. By mid-December, the anonymous body in the city morgue was at last identified. Following a routine autopsy and coroner's inquest, David Joseph, aged 49 years, was buried.

Rachel sent a letter home notifying her mother of her father's death and enclosing the report from the coroner's court. The letter was never delivered, Rebecca and her children having been evicted from their home some days earlier for non-payment of rent. The three boys and two girls had been placed in an orphanage, while Rebecca, in the deepest depths of despair, was allowed to stay as an unwelcome guest with her older married brother.

Nearly a year elapsed before Rebecca was able to summon the inner resource even to write a brief letter to her daughter in Baltimore with her address, seeking news of David Joseph, and to tell her of her dreadful social and financial predicament, with all her children in an orphanage.

In early 1896 Rebecca received a letter from Rachel, who had been writing at regular intervals over the previous year without response, with news of David Joseph's demise in November 1894, confirming her worst fears. She could then see little point in telling

9

the children, who were aware, at least, that their father had somehow mysteriously disappeared. In the series of letters that then flowed slowly between her and her eldest daughter across the Atlantic she made plans for the family to emigrate to Baltimore. Rachel offered to provide the fare money – all that she could afford, by borrowing. The two older boys – Alfred aged sixteen years and Sidney aged fourteen, both now in low-paid but steady employment, would be left in London. Alfred was learning to make musical instruments and Sidney to become a jobbing tailor. They would follow when money could somehow be scraped together to pay their fares to Baltimore.

Henry had never forgotten his tearful parting from his brothers in mid November 1899, left on the platform at Waterloo Station. He could still visualise their tear-streaked faces as they stood waving, afraid and alone, rooted to the platform. He was ten when the heavy London and South Western Railway steam locomotive whistled and began to chug, noisily disgorging pulsating clouds of soot-blackened smoke and pungent grey steam. Henry, together with his mother and two older sisters, waved and called amidst tears and farewell shouts, not daring to guess when they might see each other again.

With barely perceptible acceleration, the dark-green steam engine gathered momentum, pulling the chain of unheated carriages, each noisily and boisterously, bumping and rebounding from the carriage in front, out of the station into the dampening greyness of one of London's frequent autumnal fogs. Still waving, the brothers slid from sight and earshot as the train, with wheels slowly and deliberately clickety clacking, glided by the slate roofs of a thousand terraces of darkest brown brindled brick houses into the suburbs, on the first stage of the family's passage to America.

A little under two hours later they arrived at Southampton and the quayside terminal. This had been newly constructed the previous year, after major dredging operations to deepen the waters of the Solent and Southampton water approaches, which allowed the large transatlantic liners to sail from Southampton while shamelessly robbing Liverpool of its traditional monopoly.

Passing through emigration and customs with small bags tied with string, containing their few possessions, they walked on to the quayside where the huge steamship, the SS *St Paul*, was moored. Henry could scarcely believe the immense white-painted hull towering above them, showing its thick black plimsoll line, a leviathan held captive by giant coils of twisted sisal binding it to the huge black metal mushrooms on the stone quayside. Nervously they climbed the wood and metal gangway to enter the steerage accommodation, their temporary home in which they would voyage to New York.

Rebecca and her children endured eight days of a miserably rough winter crossing, barely able to keep down any food throughout the journey. They were all considerably lighter and paler for the experience, as the ship ceased its pitching when it entered calmer waters to make its sedate approach into New York. With excited bravado they went up on deck, and stood shivering in the cold, clear morning air, dressed in meagre shawls and coats, to watch the Statue of Liberty slowly emerge from the November mist. They stared in silent wonder, teeth chattering periodically, as in the distance across the rippling surface of the grey-green sea, the tallest buildings they had ever seen pierced the lower Manhattan skyline.

Soon they were scrambling into the ship's tender, where a nonchalant sailor drove them to the Ellis Island quayside terminal. Up the worn grey stone steps onto dry land, they shuffled forward slowly, in line with their few belongings clutched in hands and arms amidst a throng of subdued and anxious people, none of who were speaking any language they understood. They arrived at last at the cavernous hall of the Ellis Island immigration centre. There they were questioned by forbidding immigration officers and their answers recorded in a large ledger. This was followed by a brief physical examination, particularly to exclude any eye disease, before being permitted to enter the United States. Once they had been cleared, one of the immigration men, carrying a stumpy stick of chalk, made a large white cross on each of the luggage bundles they carried and indicated with a smile that they were free to go.

Leaving Ellis Island, they boarded the ferry for the docks on lower Manhattan Island, from where they had directions to find the New York Penn Railway Station. Unable to pay for any other conveyance, they walked to the station amidst the horse-drawn hustle and bustle of a modern New World city, buying food from a street vendor to hungrily devour as they walked to the railway terminus. With pre-purchased tickets they boarded a train travelling south to Baltimore.

Three hours later, Rachel, who had been awaiting their arrival for several hours inside the Baltimore Penn Station, met them with great hugs and tears of joy. Henry was thrilled and fascinated.

Rachel was his eldest and only married sister whom he had last seen when he was only five years old and barely remembered. As a treat, they travelled by hired horse-drawn carriage from Penn Station, with their little bit of luggage, through the snow-clad streets to the warmth of Rachel's home.

Rebecca, Henry and his older sisters quickly settled in, delighted at first to be reunited with Rachel and meet her two young children. However it soon became clear that life was no less testing economically in Baltimore than in London. Try as they might, neither Rebecca nor her daughters could earn enough to save any money at all, let alone send anything back to Alfred and Sidney to put towards the fare money they would need to sail out to join them.

Letters were steadily exchanged across the Atlantic although, as the years passed, they would become fewer and fewer, until they dried up altogether and in the end all contact was lost. Meanwhile, Henry, his mother and sisters stayed in Rachel's home until the two younger girls were married and he had left school to earn his own wages, when he and his mother had moved into their own tiny apartment.

Henry had a particular friend, Philip Rosenberg, amongst the neighbours living in the next apartment, with whom he had much in common. Philip, who had arrived in America in 1901, had started work in the same cigar factory some two years after Henry. Henry and his mother were poor, but in comparison the Rosenbergs were impoverished.

Philip was a tall wiry individual who had been born in Poland in 1892, the second of Rebecca and Jacob Rosenberg's children. His father, a shoe repairer and boot maker, had emigrated to London in 1894 with his wife and one child. Life was difficult in England and with financial help from Jacob's bachelor younger brother, Henry, who was living in Baltimore, the family had then, with three further children born in London, travelled to Liverpool and then by steamer to Quebec. There they crossed by train from Canada into the USA. At the border they registered with the name of Rosenberg at customs and immigration, concealing their original Polish name of Cieslak, since the citizens of Baltimore, were known to be predominantly German in origin. They then proceeded to New York and on to Baltimore, fortified both with a new name and the expectations of a bright new beginning.

Jacob Rosenberg's main propensity was to cut and mould leather

12

to make and repair footwear for a pittance by day, and to impregnate his wife by night, while every Saturday he donned his only suit, slightly threadbare, to attend synagogue with his older sons, in suits of similar material, equally worn and threadbare. There, during his head-covered devotions, he would thank his creator for delivering them safely to the land of the free and for the bounty that he and his family enjoyed. The result was that Jacob and his family, free, but somewhat short changed on bounty, remained as poor as church mice, ultimately with a family of ten surviving children to shelter, clothe and feed as best he and Rebecca were able.

All the children worked in some capacity in their spare time, as soon as they were able to walk. Whether selling newspapers, running errands, cleaning floors, they helped in any way possible to earn a few nickels and dimes each day, with little time for recreation. It was a matter of simple economic survival. Work or starve.

Philip's younger brother Lou[2] had a rare musical talent. He had initially taught himself to play a decrepit second-hand violin that he had obtained from a scrap merchant for $1, when aged twelve. He had saved money, a few pennies at a time, from selling, alongside his brothers, newspapers and Christmas cards on the streets. Week after week he struggled to amass the single dollar with which, unknown to parents or other family members, he made his purchase. His parents, having witnessed his determination to master the instrument when he gave them an impromptu tune in their apartment, permitted him to use some of his own hard-earned money to have an occasional violin lesson.

Within a relatively short time, he had demonstrated an ability to play the instrument sufficiently well to enable him to win a scholarship to study at the Peabody Institute, where he enrolled in 1914 when fifteen years old. Such was his ambition and determination to play that his progress enabled him to commence employment there as a teacher just two years later, a year before graduation. He was by that time evolving into a remarkably fine young man who was considered something of a musical prodigy. It was through Lou that Philip and his friend Henry were able to obtain tickets to attend the various concerts and musical offerings that were available at the Peabody.

13

Chapter 2

Baltimore 1914

The mid nineteenth century had marked a golden era of philanthropy in Baltimore with George Peabody[3] donating money to establish a library and the Institute of Music, bearing his name. Enoch Pratt established a free library, Henry Walters, an art museum and Johns Hopkins a university and medical faculty.

A series of weekly recitals and concerts were regularly held throughout the year at the famed Peabody Institute of Music. At one such concert, in mid-September 1914, Henry had acquired from Lou Rosenberg, his friend Philip's younger brother, a surplus, unwanted complimentary ticket for one of these weekly Saturday evening concerts. A performance of Ludwig Van Beethoven's Fifth Piano Concerto, the *Emperor*, was to be given and Lou was participating as one of the second violinists.

Arriving late at the East Mount Vernon Place entrance of the Peabody Institute, breathlessly he dashed, three steps at a time, leaping down the curved marble staircase, with its light scrolled metal balustrade, to gain the entrance to the Miriam A. Friedberg Hall auditorium, just as the audience were applauding the arrival of the conductor. He rushed in and sat in the solitary vacant seat at the end of the nearest row, as the audience stood, to the sounds of the *Star Spangled Banner*, and he again stood, hand on heart, slowly recovering his breath and composure in salute of the flag of the United States, standing proudly at the side of the stage, representing his newly-adopted homeland.

The *Star Spangled Banner* was not at that time the national anthem, although all Baltimore and Maryland's citizens treated it as such. It would not be until 1931, when by an act of Congress this poem and melody would finally be accepted as the official national anthem of the United States. Baltimore had always accepted the flag and Francis Key's poem, set to music, as its very own, since it was the emblem that he had observed that morning in 1814 which

14

confirmed the embryonic United States had withstood the naval might of the British. The same powerful navy that had destroyed the combined naval fleets of Spain and France at the Battle of Trafalgar in 1805 and then sacked, burnt and destroyed the city of Washington in 1814, had been unable to subdue Baltimore. The defenders of Baltimore's Fort McHenry had thwarted this plan, inspiring Francis Keys. The remainder is history, as Baltimore's proud citizens would explain.

With the concluding notes, all were again resuming their seats when the pert and pretty young lady in the seat next to Henry dropped her programme. It slipped from her gloved hand, falling to the floor, between their seats. Hurriedly she removed her glove, which in turn in her haste tumbled downwards. She stooped to retrieve both objects. At the same moment Henry, by reflex, gallantly bent down, attempting to capture the programme and glove, where both lay between their seats. Their heads and hands collided. The opening bars of the *Emperor* precluded any exchange of embarrassed excuse or apologies, as with dimmed house lights gravity's latest captives remained on the floor where fate decreed they must rest.

At the conclusion of the concerto, as the applause diminished and the light intensity within the concert hall increased to signal the intermission, the young lady and Henry again bent simultaneously to retrieve the objects on the floor, with the consequence that heads and hands again collided. Henry managed to grasp the programme and glove. Forgetting his usual shy reticence in front of an unknown woman, he retrieved the young lady's possessions, and blushing, returned them to their owner.

Smiling he extended his hand and laughingly said. "These are yours, I believe. I'm terribly sorry we collided like that. I do hope I didn't hurt you. I think I'd better introduce myself before I knock you out completely. My name's Henry Chiswick, but please call me Henry. I don't usually make a habit of assaulting young ladies in concert halls, unless they're pretty, but if they're particularly attractive, then I usually make a practice of doing it twice."

She laughed, as she addressed Henry for the very first time.

"Thank you for your help. There's really no need for you to apologise. It was really my fault for being a bit careless. I won't press charges for common assault on this occasion, but you may not be so lucky a third time."

15

"I seldom do that sort of thing three times in succession, twice is usually sufficient to obtain a response, but in your case I'd be prepared to take the risk of a third or even a fourth encounter to have you tell me your name."

"If that's to be my lot, I guess I'd better surrender right now. I'm Claire Robins, and I'm a second year music student here at the Peabody studying the piano and organ."

Henry observed that she was well spoken and had expressive blue grey eyes, which were enhanced by the paleness of her complexion and her dark auburn hair. He thought of her as pretty and as they stood to stretch their legs in the intermission he noticed that she was slim and that her figure was enhanced by a tight-fitting pink floral dress. They chatted pleasantly and Claire revealed that she was twenty years old, played regularly at the church of the Holy Trinity, and admitted that she had been told that she had a promising soprano voice. Henry, the young immigrant, whose English accent she found so enchanting, explained that he had a brother in London whom he last saw fourteen years ago, who made and sold musical instruments, and that his friend's younger brother Lou Rosenberg studied violin at the Institute and had been playing second violin in the orchestra.

At the end of the concert Henry offered to walk Claire home. With a captivating smile, she gracefully and shyly declined. She explained that she might have accepted his gallant offer but she was scheduled to play, later that evening, at a midnight mass at her local church, where she would meet her parents. With considerable charm and persuasion, Henry coaxed her into agreeing to meet him at the next concert, a recital, which was to take place at the Peabody the following Saturday evening.

Henry could hardly wait for the time to pass. He arrived early and stood in the small entrance vestibule carrying a small bunch of pale blue violets, which he had earlier purchased at a florist's stall close by. He immediately spotted Claire as she arrived and hurried forward to meet her. Greeting her with a smile, he shyly said "Hello" as he presented her with his floral offering.

"Hello. Oh thank you, they're absolutely beautiful and such an adorable colour, thank you."

"I chose that colour, since they seemed to match the colour of your eyes. I think my memory served me well on this occasion." Flattered, Claire blushed at this compliment. They agreed to leave

16

their coats in the cloakroom and, unencumbered, they chatted together as they proceeded into the hall to take their seats, discussing the previous week's concert and studying the programme for that evening's performance.

At the conclusion of the recital, Claire agreed that Henry could escort her home. They walked at a meandering pace, talking and laughing. Much of the time it was Claire who spoke and with a few minor interruptions Henry listened, as she explained and narrated some of the finer points of the instrumental playing in the music they had just heard. She then spoke of her parents. Her father, whose family origins were Irish and Scottish, was a successful executive, working for Charles Schwab at the local Bethlehem Steel Corporation[4]. She talked of her three sisters, all older and each married when but sixteen years old and living in various parts of this huge continent. She was the youngest, born fifteen years after her elder sister, a surprise arrival for her mother. Unlike her sisters, she was the first to have been permitted to study at college.

Henry with an earnest smile pleaded and persuaded her to meet with him the following week, when there was a charity concert at the Peabody. Flattered at the attention she had received from this articulate and handsome young man, Claire readily agreed and they again arranged to meet in the Mount Vernon Place entrance vestibule at the head of the stairs. As they parted, Henry shook hands and the very touch of her gloved hand, with her accompanying smile, sent his heart racing as he watched her turn to mount the steps to her home and knock on the front door, which moments later seemed to open magically.

He turned and slowly walked away. After a few paces he looked round to wave and noticed to his surprise that Claire had been standing in front of the open door watching his progress. As she noticed him looking back, she hurriedly waved in response and immediately turned to enter her home, appearing, Henry thought, embarrassed to have been caught out staring as he walked away. Henry hurried homeward, again glancing back as he walked, to obtain one final glimpse of her. As he walked home he whistled the melody of one of the themes he had earlier heard at the evening's concert. Happy and light-hearted, he could not previously recall having ever encountered such a pretty, vivacious and intelligent young woman. He acknowledged that something within had captivated and transformed him. Whatever it was, he recognised that it

17

was very much to his liking and he was determined that he wanted to see this young lady again.

He never stopped thinking of Claire as he walked. He was too modest and effacing to consider that the young lady entering her home ascending the stairs to her bedroom was experiencing something similar, as though they had caught some communicable malady, simply by sitting, or talking and walking together. The touch of a gloved hand, the final catalyst, to set in train a host of emotions, which they barely recognised at the outset and which in time, slowly gathering pace and momentum, they would be power-less to bring to a halt.

* * *

The concert on the following Saturday, in October 1914, had been organised by a committee of citizens, who had thought it their civic duty to raise funds to send food parcels to the starving children of Belgium, who had been caught up in the war that had raged in Western Europe since August, as an invading German army success-fully swept in an anticlockwise wheeling movement across neutral Belgium to attack the lightly-defended borders of northeastern France. Henry had purchased a ticket to attend the event, since although an American citizen, he still felt concern for the British forces, among them two unknown English cousins, who with their French allies were valiantly trying to stem the German onslaught.

He met Claire as arranged and again presented her with a small posy of flowers. Smiling they took their seats with the other concert-goers. Following the intermission, with the orchestra awaiting the conductor, a tall grey-haired and bespectacled gentleman dressed in a tuxedo strode on to the centre of the stage.

Claire whispered to Henry, "That's Harold Randolph; he's the director of the Peabody Institute. I wonder what he's doing out front? It looks as though he's going to make an announcement."

"Ladies and gentlemen. For those among you who do not know me, my name is Harold Randolph and I'm on the board of the Peabody Trust. I don't want to take up more than a few moments of your time to detract from this splendid musical evening that this evenings committee have sponsored and organised.

"Many here will have asked the question why we in Baltimore, one of the oldest and greatest city-ports in the country, have to continue to feel like a musical backwater in this great city of ours.

18

Why do we have to travel considerable distances, often at great expense and inconvenience, to hear some of the wonderful works of music performed in this country? Why indeed. We can boast of cathedrals, The Johns Hopkins and other famous medical faculties and colleges, a splendid conservatory of music, with a wealth of musical talent almost unsurpassed anywhere in the world, let alone the United States. We have theatres and halls that can accommodate hundreds of people and my board at the Peabody and I firmly believe that we should have our own Baltimore Symphony Orchestra..." The announcement was drowned by applause and calls of Hear! Hear!

Holding up his hands and requesting restraint he continued. "This enterprise will need support, and not just financial, although every dollar will help. At the end of the concert you will find in the foyer a group of our students with sponsorship forms, which you can complete here, or take for your friends and neighbours to complete at home and mail to us. My colleague Frederick R. Huber, a member of Henry L. Mencken's Florestan Club, of which many may have heard, has met with Mayor James Preston and has persuaded that worthy first citizen to donate the magnificent sum of $6,000 for the start of a municipally-supported symphony orchestra. In addition should there be sufficient support from you this evening, as well as members of the public who have not been fortunate enough to attend this marvellous performance, I am certain that in a number of months, not years, I repeat, in a number of months, we will be able to welcome the inaugural concert of our very own Baltimore Symphony Orchestra."

Again the audience's clapping interrupted him. He held up his hand indicating that he had something further to say.

"I believe, among the Peabody board, our mayor and ourselves, we will be able to claim proudly, in generations to come, that it is we who have been instrumental in the launch of our own orchestra. Thank you ladies and gentlemen for your kind indulgence and support. Please continue to enjoy the remainder of this evening's concert."

With a brief bow, as the audience applauded, he turned to leave the stage. At the same time the conductor advanced to take his place on the podium. As they passed, they stopped momentarily, shook hands with each other, before each continued their short journey. At the conclusion of the evening's entertainment Henry walked

19

Claire home and before parting they arranged to meet again the following Saturday evening.

The following Saturday, Henry waited, with heightened anticipation, to meet Claire, as arranged. Instead of a posy of flowers he carried a small box of chocolates, which he presented to her as she arrived. They talked excitedly of the implication of the previous week's announcement that Baltimore might one day soon have its own orchestra, before entering the auditorium to hear that week's musical offering.

During the following weeks Henry and Claire met at the weekends. Claire was seldom able to accept dates midweek since she had a prodigious course schedule and with the approach of Christmas there were additional musical pieces to be learnt, practised and rehearsed for recitals and concerts that were to take place throughout the festive period.

On the last Saturday in November, the weather had turned considerably colder. A light flurrying snow was caught in the pale rays of the street gaslights, sparkling and glittering, as it assaulted the rooftops and trees and lightly carpeted the ground. At the conclusion of that evening's concert, as Henry escorted Claire home, she slipped on an icy patch, stumbled and would have fallen had Henry not grabbed hold of her elbow to support her.

"Whoops, watch out."

"That was close! Thank you Henry. I nearly went down."

"You'd best tread carefully. I guess it's snow boot time for the next few weeks."

They continued walking and Henry continued to support her, holding her arm, enjoying the closer enforced proximity, until they reached her home when he had no option other than to release his grip.

"See you next week, same time?"

"Of course and Henry, it was a really lovely evening, and thank you for saving me from slipping over."

"Not at all. The pleasure Claire was all mine," replied Henry, smiling gallantly.

"There's the first of the annual series of Christmas carol concerts and recitals at St Magnus the Martyr church, next Tuesday evening. Have you ever been to any of them?"

"Can't say that I have. St Magnus is the church just a stone's throw from the monument isn't it?"

"Yes it is. Well, I'll be singing some Christmas carols with the choir. Two or three people are playing instrumental pieces slotted in between the carols. At the beginning of the term they invited me to play an organ piece and so I shall be one of them. Would you like to attend?"

"I'd consider it a privilege. I've never heard you sing, or play the organ, so yes please, I think it's something that I shouldn't miss."

"It starts at half after seven and will probably last about an hour. They're serving refreshments afterwards and my parents will be there. You won't need a ticket. There's no entrance fee and when you meet my father you just have to remember his bark is far worse than his bite. You'll find he's been house trained tolerably well, and he's really a darling when you get to know him."

"I'll remember that in case he bites my head off when we meet," Henry laughingly replied. "What will you be playing?"

"It's the adagio movement from Marcello's oboe concerto."

"I'll be there, but somehow I don't recall you mentioning that you play the oboe."

"No, I don't play the oboe," she replied laughing. "The concerto was written in 1708 by Alessandro Marcello who was a rich Italian amateur composer. Johan Sebastian Bach transcribed this movement for the organ in about 1720-something and that's what I shall be playing. It's a hauntingly beautiful piece of music, which I simply love and I'm sure you'll adore. It takes less than five minutes to play, so please don't be late, or I'll have practised all these weeks in vain and it's very difficult to find an organ where they'd let me play just for my friends to hear."

* * *

It was not uncommon at the Peabody for students to wander into a performance area. On just such an occasion Lou Rosenberg, who studied music theory with Claire, had been sitting with a number of other students listening to her practising her performance piece, which she was to perform the following day. He had earned the unique accolade of being appointed a music teacher earlier that year.

At the conclusion of her final rehearsal preparation, as she descended the steps from the organ, sheets of music tucked under one arm, he ran over to her.

21

"Hello Claire, can I have a few moments of your time before you leave."

"Certainly Lou."

"Let's sit down here," said Lou indicating the front row of empty seats. "I've something to tell you and I don't want you to take what I'm about to say the wrong way."

"Of course not. Why ever should I?"

"Well I'd like you to do something for me."

"Certainly. If there's anything that I can do to help, you've only to ask."

"I'd like you to go back to the keyboard and play that piece again."

"Of course, I'm flattered that you should ask."

"There's a sting in the tail."

"I don't quite understand what you mean."

"Claire you play beautifully. You play, with clarity and precision, without a single mistake, with every note in the right sequence, but playing with mechanical correctness is pedestrian and boring, and you can do so much better with very little extra effort."

"You're telling me I play correctly and precisely and then you suggest that my performance is boring. What more can I be expected to do to achieve a better presentation?"

"Claire, if only you had learned to play the violin, you would understand the two essential ingredients you have left out, without my needing to tell you. They're warmth and feeling. You play correctly, and that's wonderful, but your rendering is mechanical. It's ice cold and frigid. You know all the correct notes, now learn to love and embrace them until you feel the very texture they can produce. Caress and polish some of those musical phrases, until they sparkle, then your performance will no longer just be very good, it will be infinitely better. It will be thrilling and scintillating."

"If what you're telling me is true, why hasn't anybody previously made comment, or suggested that something is lacking?"

"When learning it's essential to master all the mechanical skills and technique of playing and to memorise scores. There seems too little time to concentrate on interpretation. You've reached the stage in your career where you've more than mastered the mechanical elements. Now you've to remove the thermostatic controls and add some warmth and range of colour."

22

"Lou, I'm going straight back up there. Will you wait and see whether I've added those bits of colour that you're suggesting?"

"No way. I'm going to go with you. I'm going to turn the pages. Forget playing the notes in the correct order, you can clearly do that in your sleep. From here on in, I'm going to yell at you when you're not adding the full spectrum that I know you can produce. I guarantee that you'll be amazed at the difference."

Chapter 3

Baltimore December 1914

The following Tuesday evening Henry attended the recital at St Magnus church. He heard Claire play for the very first time. He was captivated. Both the audience and Henry found themselves breathtakingly moved, and entranced in a way that none that evening had believed possible. Whether it was Bach's transcription, or Claire's improved playing, it just didn't seem to matter, judging by the enthusiastic applause of the audience.

At the end of the carol concert, he joined the choristers, instrumentalists and audience, among which were Claire's parents. Offering congratulations to the various recital participants, Henry congratulated Claire, telling her that he had found her performance enchanting.

"I don't think I can ever be the same person again after hearing your rendering of that music Claire, it was simply fantastic. Well done," enthused Henry.

"Thank you Henry. I don't think I'm really entitled to all your praise. The genius comes from Alessandro's music and Bach's adaptation, two hundred years ago. I'm just a very minor agent who presents it to you, from them."

"Claire, you're being far too modest. I'm no authority, but there can't be many composers around, living or otherwise, who've such wonderful agents performing and interpreting their music."

They continued chatting and then Claire said, "I'd like you to come over to meet my parents."

Claire then introduced a very nervous Henry to her parents for the very first time. He offered them his congratulations on Claire's remarkable performance, and continued to chat very perfunctorily, feeling slightly intimidated and reserved, certain that he was not making any, or perhaps even the wrong, impression on the Robins. He was totally wrong, as Claire would later discover, and relate to him.

After Henry had bid goodnight to Claire and her parents he left the church to return home. A short time after, Claire walked with her parents the relatively short distance to their home on North Charles Street, glowing with happiness at the approbation she had received from the audience, her parents and, in particular, from Henry.

Once inside their home, Mrs Robins ordered the cook to bring hot chocolate and mince pies to the sitting room for herself and Claire, while Mr Robins would be taking his in his study. Seated in front of a log fire, warm chocolate in hand, Mrs Robins said.

"Claire, your father and I thoroughly enjoyed this evening's carol concert. I don't believe I've ever heard you play so well. The main thing I've liked about Christmas is singing and listening to carols. Now I'll have to include listening to our youngest daughter play the church organ. We felt immensely proud to hear you play so well. You made us very happy, and proud parents indeed."

"Thank you mother dear, I'm so happy that you and father could be there with me, it helped make it a more special occasion."

"It makes all your hours of study, and practise truly worthwhile. I know it was hard to give up skipping and playing with the other children when you were younger, but it's all been worthwhile. I wonder that you can play all those pipes, pedals and keys without feeling frightfully nervous, and getting all muddled. By the way, who was that rather handsome young man you brought over to introduce to us?"

"That was Henry Chiswick."

"Did you know him before this evening's recital? Is he a personal friend of yours?"

"Yes, to both questions mother. I first met him at one of the Peabody concerts some weeks ago and I've met him at other concerts. He's never heard me play the organ, or sing in the choir, and I thought he would like to hear me perform, so I invited him to this evening's recital."

"That was very sweet of you. Is he anybody special that I should know about? He speaks with a delightful English accent. Is he English Claire?"

"In a manner of speaking, yes mother. He told me he was born in London and arrived here in 1899 with his widowed mother, but he's now a naturalised American citizen."

25

"Claire, I do hope you won't form any attachment with this young man."

"I'm not forming an attachment, as you so delicately put it, mother dear, but why ever not? He seems very polite and presentable."

"That may be so, but he's English and we're of Scots Irish descent."

"Mother, can you really be serious? He was born in England and was once English when he was a little boy, but he's now an American citizen the same as you, father or me for that matter."

"Claire, your father's grandparents came here from Ireland in 1846 in the second year of the great potato famine. Many of their family died from the terrible privations of those years. The hardships they endured were unimaginable, and your grandparents were the lucky ones who managed to escape, and survive the journey to this country. The English were in large measure to blame, and we've never been able to forgive them, nor ever will. We Irish have prodigiously long memories, and any friendship with the English is truly unacceptable."

"Mother, for shame at harbouring such attitudes. At school they taught us that there were many causes, such as the potato blight that ruined the crops, the terribly small farm holdings, and a hugely increasing birth rate that the economy couldn't support. The only thing you can blame the English for is that they haven't given the Irish the independence to which we all believe they're entitled."

"Claire, they've been filling your head with a lot of nonsense at school if that's what they've been teaching you. I often wondered why your father allowed you to continue at that school, particularly after we had to complain to the school board when they permitted the teachings of that dreadful man Darwin about that foolish nonsense that he called evolution. Just imagine filling children's heads with the ideas that we're descended from monkeys and apes when the Holy Bible specifically tells us that Adam was created in God's own image. You're right however about the English not giving the Irish the independence we need, and will surely have one day. Your father and his friends say that if Mr Woodrow Wilson keeps us out of this war in Europe, and the Germans give the English a thoroughly good trouncing, which they richly deserve, then it's very likely we'll see a free Irish republic very soon."

"My life mother is music, not politics, and certainly not war. I still don't see how Henry who was a little boy when he left

26

London can be held accountable for whatever happened in 1846, or the granting of Irish independence. Anyway, the British failing to give the Irish independence is no longer our concern, we're American, but I hope for Henry's sake the British don't lose to the Germans. He'd feel terribly upset, and so would I, and the poor French and Belgium people don't deserve to have to live under German rule."

"In Europe they're always having their silly little wars. After a few battles they then have a peace treaty, exchanging bits of land here and there, after which they all go home. Then a few years later they start a new war over the bits of land they handed over after the last war, and it starts all over again. Those Europeans never seem to learn how childish it all is. You should be proud of your Irish ancestry. The English have behaved very badly towards the Irish, and you should know that."

"Mother, of course I'm proud of our origins, of the Irish playwrights like Oscar Wilde and George Bernard Shaw, but we're not Irish anymore, we're Americans. Anyway, you adore Shakespeare, Chaucer, Purcell and Handel, and they're all English."

"Well they're completely different. They were writing and composing long before the time of the troubles I was speaking about."

"They were English, Mother, and the same stock as Henry, and all the other English people."

"Claire, your father would be most disturbed to hear your opinions if you speak like that. It was bad enough having you track all the way over to Washington eighteen months ago to join that senseless women's party, and their suffragette parade in Pennsylvania Avenue, shouting, and waving posters saying, 'Votes for Women', when poor Mr Woodrow Wilson was trying to have his inauguration ceremony. The sheer indignity of it. Poor Mr Wilson, all so discourteous to our new president. Whatever do we need the vote for anyway? My grandmother never had a vote. My mother, who lived to be ninety-three, never had a vote, and she'd have lived a lot longer had she not slipped on the ice and broken her hip, poor dear. Please remember what I'm telling you about your friend. He may be a pleasant enough young man, but he's English, and we can never change that. Neither our family, or your father's friends would welcome your English friend; so the less you see of him the better. One needs to be particularly circumspect about who one

27

chooses to count as a friend. Better to simply keep that young man as a casual acquaintance and nothing more."

"You're so old fashioned, mother. Women's suffrage is terribly important, and if needs be I'll go and wave banners and shout at Mr Wilson again, and again, until he gives women the vote. And by the way, that's only the first step. We women need equal pay for equal work. Did you know at the conservatory they pay a woman who instructs us less than half the pay of any one of the men?"

"Well a man has a wife and family to support."

"What of the male instructors who aren't married? They don't pay them less. What if an unmarried woman has an elderly mother to support, or a woman is widowed, and has children? They don't charge father less for my tuition as a girl than they charge for male students. It's the principle that's wrong. If a woman performs the same task as a man in education, or any other endeavour, she has the right to expect, and to be given, the same salary, and not something like less than a half. Equal pay for equal work, should be our motto, like when the founding fathers fought for independence with the rallying cry 'No taxation without representation'."

"Claire, you're quite the rebel. In my young days girls were more respectful when they spoke to their parents, and didn't concern themselves with these matters."

"Mother, I'm not a rebel. I'm an American. You taught me to read, and you framed the copy of the Declaration of Independence on the wall in my bedroom, which I've been reading. There's been no amendment that says a woman should be disenfranchised, or impoverished if she chooses to work."

"Claire, a woman's place is in the home raising a family, and caring for her husband and children. She should not be out there working."

"That's completely illogical, mother. What of the young women who teach, who are nurses, who attend to the laundries and cleaning? Women need to work to earn money and society could not manage without them."

"I should have qualified what I meant by saying married women, not every woman."

"Haven't you been reading the papers recently mother? There are hundreds of young soldiers who are being slaughtered in Europe each day, scores dying on the battlefields, even as we speak. That means there will be a similar number of women who are either widows, or won't be able to marry, because there aren't enough men to go round. What of them? They'll need to work."

"Claire, there have always been wars, and there never seems to have been any shortage of men that I've ever heard about, or seen. So don't you go worrying your pretty little head. You're really quite the little firebrand. It's rather late, and I think it's time you took yourself to bed. You have college in the morning, and you must get your beauty sleep."

With that Claire stood up, heading for the door.

"Good night Claire, sleep well."

"Thank you mother. As for my English friend, I'll think about what you've said, but personally, I find him very sweet, and rather dishy. Goodnight mother, see you in the morning."

Chapter 4

Baltimore November 1914

Henry's employer, Mr Burchhardt, finding that almost every second year produced another young mouth to feed, had decided that with this growing family he needed to expand his business. As an immigrant he spoke German, with some Polish and a newfound smattering of largely mispronounced American. He had sporadically attended the evening American language classes, freely available to all immigrants, but because of the pressure to work all hours available to provide for his family, his attendances were too erratic to provide any real benefit. He could communicate with his workforce more than adequately in German, with some Polish, and a few chosen well rehearsed English expressions.

He felt self-conscious however when speaking to the American store proprietors to whom he needed to sell his produce. Many had invariably been in the country far longer than he, and had acquired greater mastery of the American language. His foreman, Morris Levy, with a family of five young children, was a good solid dependable worker, and honest, but was likewise a recent immigrant with a limited American vocabulary.

He could employ more operatives in the space he had available in the factory, to increase production, but selling his merchandise at a premium price in a very competitive market required that he pay a disproportionately larger wage, including an incentive bonus to a salesman. Strategically he thought that Henry, promoted as his salesman, might provide a less expensive alternative.

Henry worked diligently, and was popular at work. He had a charming nature, with an engaging smile, and always greeted friends and newcomers with a welcoming outstretched hand. He had a natural flare to communicate well. Although not a salesman, he was intelligent, avidly read the books he regularly borrowed from the public library, and had somehow acquired an improved dress sense over the past months. Most important of all, he was well

30

spoken. He enunciated his words clearly with an English accent that never failed to impress, and frequently resulted in having strangers, with whom he spoke, asking him to repeat utterances, simply to hear his English pronunciation. Thus it was that Mr Burchhardt decided to offer Henry a small salary with a large bonus related to sales, commencing Monday 2 November. This he thought might be the chance to increase his market share.

Ever since May 1902, when Henry had started work, Henry's youthful employment ambitions had changed in those first years every few weeks. However, the economic realities of providing for his widowed mother and himself kept him in low-paid servitude as surely as though he had been chained to his workplace. His only escape from his tedious unskilled drudgery was in the words he avariciously and rapidly read in library books every evening and weekend.

Henry leapt at this new, challenging, opportunity. He could break free from his low wage, hand to mouth existence. He would go on the road, become a traveller, a salesman, with boundless opportunities to earn considerably more money. Succeed, and this might be the way to acquire a larger apartment where both his mother and he could live. He would be able to own one of those new automobiles he had recently seen from time to time in the streets of Baltimore. He could move up in the world. Anything and everything was now a possibility.

Henry took to his new employment as a salesman like the fledgling with feathers on its wings, as it first leaves the security of its nest and takes to the air. At the end of the first week, he saw his salary decline. There were no sales to speak of, and therefore no bonus. His salary had been reduced and everything looked as grim and bleak as the cold November weather, with the steely grey sky above presaging rain or even snow. Daily he gave himself a private pep talk, telling himself that failure was not an acceptable option. He had to walk in to see his customers as though he hadn't a care in the world. He had to convince each of them that he was the most successful salesman in the industry, and even though he felt he was failing, he had to keep up the pretence. Had he not had ingrained at school in England the story of the Scottish King Robert Bruce, and the spider[5]? When at first you don't succeed, try, try, and try again?

With each rebuff he felt more dispirited. What was he to tell his mother when there was simply no money to pay the rent and where,

31

and from whom, might he be able to borrow a few dollars for food and necessities? He had to ignore each set back, and must keep trying. *There's only one way to go and that's upwards,* he admonished himself. Henry soon discovered that with perseverance, somehow, with a personable smile and a cheery greeting, he suddenly started to attract potential customers. His optimistic doggedness, born out of sheer necessity, bore fruit in his third week. He made his first major sale, and wrote the order into his order book in pencil. With renewed confidence, the next sale came the following day. No longer was he an unsuccessful salesman. The bird, falteringly falling, hurtling earthwards, nearly crashing to the ground, had simply to extend its wings to soar into the air.

It had been a close call.

Paying Henry his first bonus at the end of the month, his boss realised that he had been unnecessarily generous. He was sorely tempted to renegotiate the bonus package, but realised that he was reaping a twofold benefit in increased sales, and a commensurate increase in profit. When reviewing his increased turnover in trade at the end of the financial year the following April he was astounded that he hadn't thought of employing Henry as his sales representative years earlier.

Within the first month, with a modest bonus swelling his normal pay packet, Henry realised that he could soon afford the larger apartment he had dreamed of. He told his mother that he wanted something a little larger, in the same neighbourhood of course, but with a separate bedroom for himself, with an internal toilet, and separate washing facilities. He would like her help in the search to find this new apartment. He had to reassure her several times that his increased salary was not a temporary flash in the pan. As a successful salesman he was going to continue earning larger bonuses which, added to his previous meagre salary, meant more money from now on. He would never, ever, have to return to the lowlier paid mind-numbing job of making cigars, with the nicotine stains from the tobacco leaves constantly discolouring his hands. His life was changing week by week for the better, and as his life improved, he was determined that his mother's quality of life would likewise benefit.

He told her he intended to scrutinise the advertising boards and papers in his search, and once he had secured an apartment he might set his sights on what had previously been an impossible dream: to own an automobile, which would enable him to see more customers and earn far larger bonuses.

The Saturday following the midweek church concert, Henry met Claire in what had become their usual meeting place. He told her again how much he had enjoyed her organ playing and how privileged he felt to have been invited to listen to her performance. He had a surprise for her. He had bought two seats at the Variety Theatre, in celebration of his new promotion at work and of her splendid organ recital. They would need to hurry to take in the show if they weren't to miss any of the acts. As they rushed through the streets he teasingly declined to tell her who the main acts were on the bill of entertainment, but as they approached the entrance the posters announced 'Bojangles' Robinson, the great black American tap dancer, and the main act, the magician and escape artist, Harry Houdini.

Inside the theatre the atmosphere was warm, crowded, and noisy, the audience far less well mannered than the sedate concert hall, with its more genteel clientele. They were given programmes with the price of admission, and bought a large package of popcorn to share as they hurriedly took their balcony seats. The orchestra in the pit struck up George Cohan's melody 'Give my regards to Broadway', the house lights dimmed and one after another the variety acts followed until 'Bojangles' came on stage, tap dancing to another hit Cohan melody 'I'm a Yankee Doodle Dandy', with a dance routine that they found spellbinding. In the intermission they laughed and talked, and Claire told Henry verbatim what her mother had said after the concert when she had arrived home that evening.

Henry expressed his amused surprise to realise that his British ancestry was for the first time to be considered an impediment when all his previous conflicts with boys in the orphanage and at school had been related to his Hebrew lineage. As a consequence of his English birthright he was being held accountable for the thwarting of Irish emancipation and the famine of seventy years ago, which now made him an unsuitable companion. At least he wasn't to be held accountable for the foray at Bunker's Hill and the colonial fight for independence from King George.

"Do your parents know that I'm also Jewish and my ancestors were responsible for the walls of Jericho tumbling down?" he lightheartedly enquired.

33

"Not yet." Laughed Claire. "I think we should let them get over one shock at a time."

"Do you think this will create any additional difficulties?"

"I'd hardly think so since you don't play any trumpets or musical instruments I'm certain the houses in Baltimore might withstand the shock any time you should choose to serenade me. Mother is terribly staid and straight-laced. Father is also a bit old fashioned and he's the important one, but given time, I'm certain I can twist him round my little finger. I've watched mother do it often enough."

At that point the lights were again dimmed and the audience were treated to a roll of drums as the curtain rose to reveal the great Harry Houdini, famed escape artist and magician. Deep within, Henry felt a kinship to Houdini, as he perceived that he in his turn, through his own industry as a salesman, was on the threshold of shedding the shackles of poverty that had held him captive since earliest childhood.

Chapter 5

Baltimore February 1916

Henry had known Claire for a little under eighteen months. They dated by attending concerts and the occasional vaudeville show, in one of the better downtown variety theatres. Often they would go for walks, and enjoy a soda at one of the soda fountains in one of the many stores they passed as they returned home. There were visits to the cinemas where Claire recognised Peabody students who, to supplement incomes, played to provide music, both to entertain and drown the soft clatter of the projector as audiences watched the silent screen offerings. At other times they would enter one of the five- and ten-cent stores where music was promoted by some of her fellow Peabody students who played some of the new sheet music the store-owners wanted the public to buy, as they earned funds to pay tuition fees. Occasionally, for fun, Claire would join one or more of her college colleagues at one of the stores for an impromptu music session, while Henry had fun as he assisted in the sale of sheet music. The owners and managers never objected since at no additional cost this invariably attracted far more customers, with a resultant increase in music sales.

Early in January Claire and Henry had obtained discounted gallery tickets to attend the inaugural concert to be given by the Baltimore Symphony Orchestra on 16 February. There had been a great demand for tickets, and ultimately many potential concert-goers were disappointed. Henry called at Claire's home to escort her to the concert at the Lyric Theatre, dressed in his only formal outfit, a dark-grey tweed suit, a clean white shirt and magenta tie, over which he wore a heavy navy-blue topcoat to protect him from the biting cold wind. He knocked at the door, which was soon opened by the ebony-skinned family butler, and announced he had called for Miss Claire. He was not invited in, and was requested to wait for her, as she would shortly be down. Fortunately, although cold, it was dry, and the sidewalks had been swept clear of snow.

Claire appeared almost immediately. She descended the steps and, greeting Henry, graciously received the small box of candy he had brought her for the occasion, before they hurriedly walked the relatively short distance to the theatre.

The cream of Baltimore's society was there, including Claire's parents, who sat in the second row of the stalls. The entire Peabody faculty were present along with the politicians, industrialists, entrepreneurs, professionals and those who were as interested in being seen as in listening to good music, together with news and media reporters from as far afield as New York and Boston.

It was a glittering occasion. The conductor was the former assistant conductor of the Boston Symphony Orchestra, Gustav Strube. An Austrian, he had moved to Baltimore the previous year to join the Peabody faculty where he taught Claire and her fellow student's music theory and composition, and also conducted the student orchestra. Many members of the orchestra were faculty staff, as were some of the more talented students, including Lou Rosenberg, all of whom Claire excitedly indicated to Henry. Lou was the youngest member of the orchestra, and was playing in the second violin section. Dressed in his first tuxedo, Philip had earlier confided to Henry that such was the parlous state of Lou's finances that he had purchased the suit second-hand from a retired waiter for ninety-five cents.

Following the 'national anthem', the house lights dimmed, and the orchestra commenced their first public performance with a large ambitious repertoire of music. The main symphonic piece, prior to the intermission, was Beethoven's eighth symphony. The audience were enthralled. At the conclusion of the short intermission the mayor and other dignitaries made brief speeches before the concert orchestra could continue with the programme. There followed various operatic arias, a piece by Saint-Saens, and then a rousing finale with Wagner's *Tannhäuser* overture. Henry and Claire stood to applaud, as did the whole audience, at the evening's conclusion. As the applause diminished and faded a cheerful audience, chatting animatedly, slowly exited from the theatre to hurry home through the cold February night air.

The following Monday, H.L. Mencken, Baltimore's own famed literary luminary, wrote a glowing review in the *Baltimore Sun*, which was then syndicated across the USA. Not to be outshone, John Oldmixon Lambdin, literary and music critic for the *Baltimore*

36

Evening Sun wrote a similar glowing critique, eulogising that Baltimore, which boasted the Peabody Conservatory of Music, now had its very own symphony orchestra, placing it on a roster of musical excellence among the finest in the United States.

Normally the major English, French and German newspapers would have noted this event, unique in the annals of classical music, but no mention appeared at the time. In England the public was still stunned and subdued from the appalling news of the atrocious behaviour of the Germans in executing as a spy by firing squad in Belgium – an English nurse called Edith Cavell[6] – in October of the previous year.

The English and French, reeling from horrific manpower losses, were introducing military conscription, while the Germans were ferociously attacking the military gateway to Paris, guarded east of that great city by a series of fortresses at Verdun. As a consequence of this prolonged assault, the French demanded that their British allies must mount some form of major diversionary attack to save the forts and prevent the capture of Paris. The British commander, General Haig, responded by planning an attack along the Somme to commence in the early summer, thereby orchestrating the bloodiest and most costly battlefield orgy of human death and destruction the world had ever seen: the Battle of the Somme[7].

The following weekend, Claire, and Henry met as they had arranged, avidly discussing the concert and the newspaper reviews. Henry felt comfortable and at ease in Claire's presence, and she with him. Any intimacy had been restricted to holding hands or linking arms since she had nearly fallen on the icy sidewalk the previous winter, and more recently the occasional fraternal kiss on the cheek when greeting or parting, nothing further, never an embrace.

They became closer through words, through thoughts, ideas and a common interest in literature, and music. They occasionally discussed religion, and the similarities between his Jewish faith and hers as a Catholic, and the manner in which the differences had evolved from a common stem, but no more. They learned from each other. He was impressed by her musicality and avidly learned to understand many of the finer points of music. Henry's unschooled intellect, and the breadth of his literary knowledge and understanding of the great classics impressed Claire. She particularly enjoyed the times he read poetry to her, especially their

37

favourite, Longfellow's *Hiawatha* which, with his English enunciation, she found as captivating as he found her piano playing of Bach, Beethoven and Schumann entrancing.

To any observer with time to watch or listen, there could be little question or doubt that these two sensitive young people, from such different socioeconomic backgrounds, were 'soul mates' in the truest sense. Articulate and intelligent, they had as yet to awaken to the realisation of their common destiny, nor to the attempts that would be made to wantonly and capriciously destroy such harmony, simply because it was considered that their friendship did not conform to their parents', or their co-religionists', accepted norms.

Henry had taken Claire up the four flights of stairs passing through the intermingled odours of stale foods and seldom washed bodies to the two-roomed apartment to meet his mother in their meagre, sparsely furnished home without any sense of shame or loss of pride. She had accompanied him over the months more than once, meeting Rebecca, who was always hospitable and pleasant, and provided a cup of English tea and a biscuit. However, she was formal in a manner that made her distant.

Henry had made no secret of the fact that Claire was not Jewish, made patently obvious by the small gold crucifix she wore on a fine golden chain round her neck. Rebecca had an ingrained sense of the immense historical and emotional gulf that separated a Jew from their chief persecutors, the Catholic Gentiles. Jesus may have been Jewish, but his followers behaved as abominably as in the sibling rivalry of Cain and Abel for their creator's affection, as though their deity, the creator of the universe, had some deficiency that precluded an ability to love two children equally, and simultaneously. This being the case, it became essential for the child who more urgently craved that love to kill, and destroy anything that competed for that deity's love.

Henry's sister Amy, with whom he was closest, remonstrated with him following Claire's visits. Was it not bad enough that mother, an impoverished widow for all these years, bringing up five of her six children unaided, must now be confounded by her youngest son befriending a young woman who, regardless of musical talent, was a Gentile, and a Roman Catholic at that?

Furthermore, were Henry to remotely consider marriage at this stage, who would then support mother? Henry's action was selfish, and absolutely intolerable. Annie sided with her sister, chiding her brother that she and her husband had barely enough to care for their brood of children, and could do little to support mother. Marriage at this time would be financially difficult for the family. To marry a Gentile was unthinkable and completely out of the question. It would bring embarrassment and shame on the family. He must surely realise that all connections with his family would be severed. He should stop seeing this Catholic girlfriend, at once, before matters got out of hand or became too serious, and in a year or two the family would introduce him to a Jewish girl from a good family, who would make a far better match.

Such admonitions made Henry miserable. He spoke to Claire of his modest ambition for the future, and the larger apartment he and his mother would shortly be moving into. He never discussed his family's opposition to his friendship with her. Claire however mentioned to Henry that while his mother was always very formal and correct there seemed to be no real cordiality or friendliness.

"Henry I just don't understand why your mother seems to entertain me in her home almost under sufferance. She seems so formal and distant. It makes me feel very awkward and unhappy. Have I inadvertently done something, or said something to offend her?"

"Claire I don't think this is anything that you've done, or said. It's much more who you are. Most mothers feel that no woman is really good enough for her son. However, there's a further dimension to her opposition. Dare I mention that it's because you're not Jewish, and ever since the ancient Hebrews returned from Babylonian exile some twenty-five hundred years ago tradition has required that a Jew must marry a person of the same faith."

"Surely we're simply friends, aren't we? We've never talked of marriage and it's never even remotely, been a consideration."

"That may be so, but mothers will invariably regard any of their sons' adult female friends as potential marriage partners. Being deliberately aloof and indifferent, even at times hostile, the parent sends out a straightforward message that can be clearly interpreted. *You won't be welcome if you step beyond the bounds of simple friendship.* It's like a lighthouse, or a warning buoy, marking rocks which imperil a ship at sea in the vicinity, thus far and absolutely no closer at your peril. Such parental behaviour is a caution, a clear deterrent signal to both of us."

Henry did not say that while he had met and spoken to her parents at her church on a number of those occasions when he had

39

attended to hear Claire sing, or perform on the keyboard, he had never met them formally. He had always been one among many in the congregation, but he realised that he had never been invited to meet her parents at home because, as Claire had tactfully and laughingly attempted to explain, they would be aghast to find their daughter dating an Englishman, or anyone but a Roman Catholic. She concealed that worst of all; they would be horrified to learn that her companion was of the Jewish faith. She was willing to spare him that dubious accolade.

He in turn deliberately made no mention to Claire of the certainty of his mother's and sisters' increasing ire and hostility. He was certain he could in time overcome his mother's resistance should their friendship evolve into anything more serious, but as Claire had said, and he readily agreed, "We're simply friends. Marriage has never been a consideration." Wiser heads might have disagreed, and with the benefit of hindsight would have been correct, but at that time this was precisely the state of their slowly evolving friendship.

Once Henry's sister Annie had married, and set up home, Rebecca and Henry had celebrated the first Passover evening, known as the *Seder* night supper, in Annie's home with her growing family. In March, just before the Passover, Henry had asked Annie if he might bring a friend to the supper. Imagining that he meant his friend Philip or Philip's younger brother Lou, she had readily agreed and thought no more of it other than needing to set cutlery on the table for one more place.

The weekend before Passover, following one of his Saturday evening dates with Claire, Henry asked if she would like to accompany him to a Passover supper service the following Wednesday evening.

"That sounds very interesting and I'd love to go, but you must surely know that as a Roman Catholic I'm not permitted to attend any place of worship other than a Catholic Church."

"Perhaps I've put that rather badly. This Passover *Seder* is not conducted in a synagogue or place of worship, it's a traditional supper held in an individual's home. It's a private family supper not unlike some form of Thanksgiving, except it's celebrated around Easter, and historically it's far, far, older. I think you'd find it rather interesting, and great fun. My mother and I usually join my sister Annie's family at her home, and she has agreed that I can

40

invite a friend."

"When you put it that way, how can I possibly refuse? Of course I'd love to accompany you. Where, and what time shall we meet?"

"I'll call for you at six-fifteen. We'll be able to have a slow walk over to my sister's apartment, and I can then do my best to explain the ceremony, and all that you will see happening during the evening."

"It sounds as though it will be a very mysterious, and intriguing event."

"Claire I'm only inviting you because I think you'll thoroughly enjoy yourself. You'll find it very interesting, and it's something I'm certain you'll always remember with fond memories. I promise you'll find it an inspiring occasion especially when you realise its historic significance."

Some days later, at the arranged time, Henry knocked on the Robins door carrying a small bunch of Lily of the Valley, and a larger wrapped bunch of flowers. When Claire appeared, he presented her with the Lily of the Valley, and noticed that she was carrying a large box of chocolates.

"Claire, if those chocolate are intended for my sister I think I should explain that we mustn't take them, and you must leave them behind."

"Are you being serious? Why ever shouldn't I take them?"

"I'm taking flowers which will be more appropriate, and as we walk I'll explain why we mustn't take chocolates this evening."

Claire knocked on the door, and when it reopened she handed the chocolates to the butler, together with her flowers.

As they set off walking happily arm in arm in the spring evening air, Henry explained that the *Seder* night was like a traditional thanksgiving family dinner but far older and with many significant differences.

"The Passover *Seder* night is a family supper. Probably the longest running show on earth, it's some four thousand years old. We read the story from a book called the *Haggadah*, and there are probably more editions of that book than any book that's ever been published. We retell the story of the ancient Israelite escape from slavery in Egypt, how they gained independence and freedom, and the importance of this event on our lives as their descendants.

"In the second book in the Bible it describes the manner in which my ancestors settled in Egypt, and their ultimate escape. This escape

41

from slavery was an event of such magnitude that among the first verses in Exodus Chapter 12 we are instructed that the Jewish years are to be counted from this seminal event, as are the months of the year. Further, the anniversary of the Passover is to be celebrated for eight days every year, in perpetuity, and every Jew in future generations is obligated to celebrate this escape to freedom, as though they personally had been freed from slavery.

"Every Jewish head of household is commanded to tell his children of the events of the Passover. We're specifically instructed to imagine that we've been released personally from slavery, and aren't simply celebrating an event that happened to unknown ancestors thousands of years ago. These were our ancestors from whom we're descended, and this is part of our family history. This makes us more aware of the value and importance of freedom and democracy, the importance of human life, and the need to help all people, Jew or Gentile alike, who are deprived of their civil rights and liberty, or are being persecuted.

"When the ancient Hebrews left Egypt they did so in such haste that in the process of bread-making they had no time to add yeast. There was no fermentation, and the bread remained flat, just like a wafer, which we call *Matzo*. During the eight days of the Passover festival, this is the only form of bread we're permitted to eat. Any food containing yeast, or that has been in contact with the process of fermentation in any way, is banned for those eight days. That's why we didn't take your chocolates with us for this evening, since they wouldn't have been considered *kosher* for the Passover."

"What do you mean when you say something is, or isn't, *kosher*?"

"That's easy to define, but it'll take me some while to explain all the rules relating to the term. As a word it simply means something that's absolutely correct. It's strictly according to a prescribed and proper method. There won't be sufficient time for me to explain the meaning of *kosher* as it applies to dietary regulations, if I'm to be able to tell you sufficient about this evening's *Seder* before we arrive at my sister's apartment."

"All right, but you must promise to tell me later."

"Now one of the most important parts of this *Seder* is recounting the story of leaving Egypt to become a free people. Almost at the very beginning of the procedure, the youngest child present asks the father of the house four elementary questions, to which he must respond. The questions are very simple; such as why do we eat

42

matzo, why do we dip green herbs in salt water, and why are we permitted to lean at the table when normal good manners dictate that we sit up straight? The answers are those that one gives to a child, and I think you'll find it enchanting to hear the explanations.

"Each of the men will keep their heads covered with a small hat, not unlike the skullcap used by a cardinal, but this rule will not apply to the ladies, and while some of the proceedings are in English, a considerable part is in Hebrew. When Jesus and the disciples sat down to the last supper, apart from the absence of English, the ceremony itself would have been recognisably similar."

"Do you mean to tell me that we're going to witness what our Lord's last supper would have been like?" Asked Claire in some surprise.

"Nineteen centuries ago, absolutely."

"I somehow always imagined the last supper was some sort of farewell dinner with his disciples because he knew he was going to be arrested."

"No, not at all. I think somehow you've muddled your facts a little. I believe the story is that the Romans knew where Jesus would be at the Passover supper, and lay in wait to ambush him when he left the supper, using Judas, who they'd earlier bribed, to identify him. As I was saying, during the early part of the ceremony, after the child has asked the questions, and during the response, there's an interesting part in which we all participate. Everyone has a glass of wine. As the head of the house reads out the ten plagues that were inflicted upon the Egyptians, everybody takes one drop of wine from the glass as each plague is mentioned, and deposits it in a saucer."

"Why on earth do you do that? Why not just pop it in your mouth, I know I might have, had you not warned me."

"The reasoning is very simple. Drinking wine is deemed pleasurable, as I think you'd agree, particularly if it's a good vintage. During the exodus from Egypt certain dreadful things happened to the Egyptians. The last of the ten plagues was that God arranged the killing of the first-born children of the Egyptians, including pharaoh's son. As the Israelites fled across the Red Sea the Egyptian army, in hot pursuit, was overwhelmed by the rising tide, and the soldiers drowned.

"While commemorating our escape from captivity we're not permitted to celebrate the death of any Egyptian since we're all

43

God's children, and taking human life, for whatever reason, is considered inhumane and unacceptable. To detract from our happiness in our escape from slavery to liberty, we reduce our pleasure by reducing our intake of wine by a token measure of ten drops. Not much I'll grant, but symbolically its there. The life of one's enemies, including their animals and livestock, must be considered as precious as the lives of one's family and friends. Even when one's enemies are killed, one is never permitted to gloat or celebrate. There must be no triumphalism."

"That's a really remarkably humanitarian concept."

"It's certainly a wonderfully humane model on which to base one of the pillars of our ancient religion."

At that point they arrived outside Annie's apartment.

"Here we are," announced Henry, "But before we go in, I must warn you about something. You'll hear and see something mentioned as 'a bitter herb'. You'll be given some to eat as a token reminder of the bitterness in the lives of people who lived in, or still live in, slavery. This bitter herb is horseradish, and it's usually very strong, so don't take too much, or I guarantee you'll be wishing you hadn't."

Entering the apartment Annie, her husband Moe and Rebecca, greeted them. There was a large central table set with wine goblets and plates with chairs set round for ten. As Annie chatted with Claire, Rebecca invited Henry to follow her into one of the bedrooms. Once inside, she firmly closed the door, and angrily turned upon her son. In a low voice so as not to have the sound carry she almost hissed, "Henry, what right did you have to bring this non-Jewish interloper into our midst like this, embarrassing your sister and our whole family? Tell me who gave you this right?"

"Mother, I asked if I might bring a friend to the *Seder* night celebration. I was told that I could, and that's all that I've done."

"Well we thought you meant Philip Rosenberg or maybe his brother Lou, not a Gentile. Don't you see how upset you've made Annie? We all feel that this wasn't necessary. You're completely out of order."

"Mother, you're so wrong, you amaze me. I never thought you of all people could be so old fashioned, and narrow minded."

"Whenever a parent makes a stand against something a child wants, we're described as being old fashioned. I said it about my own mother, and she said that about hers. 'You're old fashioned' is a basic childhood cliché like 'I want my mummy!', except you're supposed to be an adult, an intelligent man, Henry, who should know better than to condemn me in this manner."

"Mother, I'm not insulting you. I simply want you to understand my reason for doing this."

"Very well, I'm prepared to listen. Convince me if you can, and if you succeed then I'll sort this business out with your sister and her husband as best I can, but make haste, they need to get started and the children want to ask their questions."

"Mother, we've witnessed, and learned to our cost that most Gentiles have been sustained with a diet of anti-Jewish propaganda for centuries. These same people, either through ignorance or with a flawed misdirected education haven't been permitted to express opposition to the tyrannies, the book burnings and excesses that have kept them downtrodden. They've been encouraged, particularly where there's economic discontent and no freedom of information, to direct whatever energies they're permitted to express towards removing the Jews, the unwanted evil interlopers, from their midst. If there's a shortage of something, blame it on the Jew. should there be a flood or an epidemic or some natural disaster which causes some food or power shortage, identify the Jew as the cause of the problem. Our kinsmen have always been singled out as the interlopers, because these Gentiles have been unable to recognise the lies and falsehoods doled out to them by anti-Semites for centuries. To our sorrow, and cost, we've been our worst enemies."

"How can you possibly say that we, the victims, have brought this upon ourselves? Have you taken leave of your senses? It's like saying that a housewife walking innocently in the streets one afternoon, and who's robbed, has brought this upon herself by carrying a shopping bag."

"Mother, nothing is quite that clear cut. In an ideal world your housewife should be able to walk along the quietest of lanes without harm or hinderance. But this, for all our longing, has never been, nor ever will be an ideal world.

"She could however reduce the likelihood of being robbed with a little thought, and a few simple precautions. Only walk where others are present; avoid walking alone in poorly-illuminated places, or in the dark. She should attempt to walk with a companion, or have a large dog on a lead. We could go on, and on."

"I understand the point that you're making, but do get on with

45

what you want to tell me. How do we avoid the excesses of the anti-Semites?"

"I believe our non-Jewish neighbours see us as some type of mysterious secret society, to be held in awe and suspicion. Most of us behave differently, and some even dress differently. We refuse to eat the food that they eat. We conform to different customs and traditions. We pray in an ancient tongue, which the people round us just don't comprehend, and for that matter the vast majority of our co-religionists don't understand either. They suspect, and the anti-Semites encourage them to believe, with rumours and lies, that there's some evil conspiracy afoot."

"That may be true Henry, but what would you have us do? Give up the beliefs and traditions of nearly four thousand years because our neighbours don't understand us? Because they eat Chesapeake Bay soft shell crab, and lobster, are we to be condemned for not eating our share, and leaving more for them? As a matter of fact our Gentile neighbours should be pleased that crab and lobster are not *kosher* and are prohibited foods for us. If that weren't the case, so many of us would be competing to eat them that the price would rocket upwards. Each lobster would then cost a small fortune and then the anti-Semite's would at last have a genuine cause for grievance."

"Please be serious mother. Your housewife walking with her shopping bag is seldom if ever robbed at night because she doesn't walk out alone at night. She doesn't walk alone at night because she can't see, and quite rightly, she's frightened, and wary of that which she can't see, or understand. People are seldom fearful of things they understand. We need to be more open in what we do. We must be obliged to show as many Gentiles as possible why we do the things we do, and how we do them. We've become too introvert and opaque. More transparency is needed. Remove the darkness and let the daylight in so that others need not be afraid of what we do, and can see what we proudly represent. We must invite our non-Jewish neighbours in to observe and even participate should they wish in some of our beautiful, timeless traditions. We have an obligation to show them how some of their own ceremonies and customs have evolved from the Jewish origins they seemingly despise.

"We should be required to show them, and explain exactly what we're doing, and our reasons, not because we want to convert them, but because we realise that with understanding, and transparency

46

they will no longer be fearful of a Hebrew conspiracy hatched by people who use secret signs, and an incomprehensible written and spoken language which none other than scholars can understand."

"You certainly have a valid argument Henry, but how do you propose doing this?"

"By inviting Claire, and others like her, into our synagogues. Encourage them to witness our rituals, and explain their meaning. We have to invite them to the various ceremonies that take place throughout the year, and particularly to Friday-night suppers in our homes."

"Are you sure that you don't have some ulterior motive so far as this young lady is concerned?"

"Mother, that's immaterial. The principle is the same. There will always be the idiotic fringe minority that hates something, some fundamentalist group whose adherents, intoxicated with their own self-righteous ideas, believe that only *their* way is correct. They will hate somebody because they have a different colour skin, speak with a different accent or for simply no explicable rational reason at all. It's the majority that we can influence, and must influence. If we fail to do this then we have only ourselves to blame. To prevent recurring tyranny against Jews, we must of urgent necessity expose every part of our religious practice to our neighbours. Let them see the innocent truth of what we stand for and who we are.

"Should we fail to do this, then heaven help us when the next tyrant king or potentate appears on the scene, as he will, somewhere in the world. It happens as regular as clockwork, in every generation. He'll randomly change laws, disenfranchise people and burn more books. He'll tell the masses, as in centuries past, that Jews are the real villains who need be hunted down, punished, driven out and, heaven forbid, even annihilated. In the same way a thermometer is used to measure temperature, one could say that a community's treatment of their Jewish minority measures the democratic process within that culture. The measure of anti-Semitism is inversely proportional to the democracy within a society.

"We the victims will be responsible in great measure for this anti-Semitism. We will be guilty, because we haven't created an environment in which the masses, including our neighbours and even our Gentile friends have not had their eyes and senses opened to the reality that they have nothing to fear from us, and are being duped by these tyrants. Not simply because we tell them so, but because

47

we've become more transparent in sharing our traditions and customs with them. It must be an obligation, as much as truth, honesty and upholding the laws of the land, that we invite them into our meeting places to see and participate in our celebrations of every festive occasion. None of these celebrations should be considered complete, particularly Passover, without half the participants being Gentiles as onlookers or even participants."

"Henry it's getting very late and we can't stand here talking all night. You've put your case very clearly and discussions like this should always have a place round the Passover table as in past generations. I'm proud that you should think this way and I'll try to explain this to Annie. Perhaps later on you can speak to her yourself. We can't change everything in one evening, but we can make a start with your friend. Now let's go and enjoy the *Seder*. I'm certain everyone's very hungry and the children are waiting for us to begin."

Chapter 6

Baltimore June 1916

Henry was a handsome bachelor, and although he had no musical prowess he was intelligent and well read, with a great interest in music and the arts. He had periodically submitted poems and short literary articles to local newspapers and magazines over the previous year and had enjoyed some minor success with the publication of two articles, which had produced a modest income of $12 for each and more importantly the accolade of family and friends seeing his name in print as a writer. He was kind, attentive and best of all had a bubbling, effervescent sense of humour. Henry only saw himself as a poor immigrant, just one step removed from a cigar maker, without realising that as a salesman with a good personality, and rapidly improving economic status, others, particularly of the opposite sex, regarded him as a worthwhile catch.

Claire had revealed to Henry that she had at times been dating other young men from her college. This was only natural. She was both pretty and musically talented. A well-dressed intelligent young lady, she made no secret of the fact that eligible young men at college were frequently in attendance and flirting with her. What was Henry to do? Such was his modesty and shyness with young women that he never considered that he might hold some attraction for Claire, or for that matter any other attractive young woman.

He did not feel confident enough to tell Claire of his increasing fondness for her. He needed to explain his secret ambition to meet her father with the object of obtaining his consent, one day, to marry his daughter. He dreaded that he might be rebuffed, and might even lose her altogether, which he would find unbearable. She had never indicated that she sought anything other than a simple platonic friendship where each enjoyed the many varied and cultural recreations that were available in Baltimore. This apparent competition, revealed from the attention of other potential suitors, created the dynamic spur Henry needed. This was a wake-up call.

Henry realised that if he did not say something to Claire, make some commitment very soon, then some other suitor would pip him to the post to claim his prize.

His intentions, his feelings, his thought processes were short-circuiting, and in a tumult. He no longer felt himself capable of any rational thought process. He felt compelled to talk with someone in whom he could confide.

However, he had no close family member, such as an older brother, to speak with to unburden his heart's yearnings. Among his friends there were none closer than Philip Rosenberg ... Could he reasonably burden his friend with this information, and expect from him the help that he might need to breach the existing religious divide? Such was his growing attachment to this beautiful and talented divinity that he was determined he would overcome these differences in faith, for failure was completely unthinkable.

Every minute of his waking day he was distracted, thinking about Claire and the possibility he might lose her. He started to write love poetry, none of which he sent her at the time, and incessantly wrote the name 'Claire', or sometimes just the capital letters C.R. on scraps of notepaper. He daydreamed of her, and the only portions of the day when he was able to banish any thoughts completely were when he was either submerged under a tepidly cold shower, or when he was avidly talking to one of his customers, and even then he found his thoughts wandering back to Claire. Even in his sleep, he would either dream of Claire or awaken with her on his mind. He was becoming completely and helplessly besotted.

He resolved he must speak to someone, or go completely insane. Philip, he feared, might laugh, and mock him, or humiliate him. Could he be trusted, never on any account, to reveal Henry's inner-most desires and longings to others?

It had to be Philip. There was no alternative. He would feed information to him, drop by drop. Seeming casual and nonchalant as they spoke, he could then assess whether, depending upon his response, he would either stop, or continue, and reveal the totality of his longing. It had to be very soon, but when? The rollercoaster torment of his longing for Claire was making life intolerable. It had to be as soon as possible.

The following day, as they walked together, heading home from work, Henry casually broached the fact that he had been dating the same girl for several months.

"Good for you. You've kept it very secret, you dark horse. Is it anyone I know?

"I've fallen head over heels in love with her."

"That's terrific," said Philip, "What's her name?"

"Philip this is all very private. She's a student at the Peabody. Before I tell you anything else, swear you won't breathe a word of this to anybody else."

"Of course I won't."

"No, that's not good enough. You've got to *swear* you'll not breathe a word of this to another living soul. Not ever; until I tell you you can."

"OK. I swear, on my mother's life, I won't breathe a word of this to another living soul," replied Philip.

"It's a girl in your brother's theory and composition class at the Institute."

"There aren't many girls at the Institute. What's her name?"

"I've been dating her for well over a year and a half, but she doesn't know of my feelings for her."

"Who is it? Come on, you rogue, tell me."

"It's Claire Robins."

Philip gave a whistle. "I've seen her. She's a beautiful-looking girl with a great figure, and my kid brother tells me she's very musically talented. Best of all, Lou says that her old man's loaded."

"Philip there's a dilemma. Our friendship has so far been entirely platonic, and she's no idea I'm in love with her. I want to..."

"You've got to be kidding me Henry. Platonic? I bet! You've been dating a fantastic-looking girl like her for months and months, and it's platonic? No way, I just don't believe you."

"Philip can you please be serious for a few minutes. I said platonic, and that's what I meant. I've never kissed her. Maybe once or twice on the cheek in greeting, never more than held her arm or hand. I would like to marry her, if she'd have me, but first I need to ask her father's permission. Although I've met her parents from time to time, it's always been in a public place. Any time I call for her, I'm left on the steps with the front door closed, like I'm some kind of a salesman, until she joins me, and I've never been invited in..."

"Henry, I'm no expert in these matters, but if the girl didn't like you then she'd just tell you to go, get lost! So, what's the problem?"

"There are lots of problems as I see them. She's a smart, sophisticated and talented, full-blooded, third generation Scots Irish American girl, while I'm just a poor English *schlemiel* of an immigrant, who only knows how to make and sell cigars. Her father, as your brother says, is loaded. He's a director on the board at Bethlehem Steel. They have a cook, maids, servants and even a butler to open the door, and heaven knows what else. . ."

Philip interrupted. "Henry, for heaven sakes. If you play your cards right, you've got it made!"

"If you could just stop interrupting for a minute, and let me finish. Those are not the only problems. The real difficulty is that I'm Jewish, and she, and her parents, are staunchly Roman Catholic."

"Henry, old boy, if that's the case, have you got tzures and problems. Let's just go into this diner on the next block, and get us a cup of coffee, and talk this thing out."

They entered the small diner, The White Coffee Pot, ordered two cups of coffee at the counter, and with the steaming beverage sat at a small table in the window, where they could watch passers by, and the bustle of the trolley cars, and traffic in the street.

Philip asked, "How were you able to persuade the daughter of one of the foremost Catholic families in this city to even talk to you, let alone let you date her?"

Briefly Henry described the way in which he had met Claire, and the manner in which his friendship with her had developed. He spoke of their mutual love of literature, music, and the arts, which had kept the friendship on track.

"I didn't deliberately set out to fall in love with her, or to take advantage, or elope with someone who might be an heiress. On our first couple of meetings I knew she was a student, not unlike your brother, and we simply appeared to hit it off. We just seemed to like each other's company, and now I can't think or dream of anyone else but Claire. It doesn't seem to matter whether I'm sitting down to a meal, working, walking, bathing, I only seem to have thoughts for one person, and that's her. It's as though I'm hooked on drugs or something. I know I should try to get away, but I not only appear not to have the strength, but strangely I really enjoy being in this euphoric state. When I meet her, it's heavenly, as though I'm floating on cloud number nine. Life takes on a whole new perspective. Colours look brighter, sounds are clearer. Everything seems enhanced. . ."

"Boy, oh boy, have you got it bad," interrupted Philip. "You're either in love or you've an incurable malady, called an obsession. Whichever it is, as I said before, you've got it bad, and you've got problems."

"Philip, if I propose to her, that is, if she'd have me, I'd marry her tomorrow. My family will never forgive me, and I guess the same will apply to her family. If I don't marry her, each day will be like a living torment in hell, without her. Help me; whatever am I to do?"

"Tell me Henry, are we friends?"

"Of course we're friends. We've been neighbours, and I've worked alongside you for more than ten years. Sure we're friends."

"But are we really friends? Are you the sort of friend I can tell the truth to, even though it may hurt, and we can still stay friends?"

"Of course. I don't want some kind of sycophant who's just willing to tell me what they think I want to hear. I genuinely want your help and advice because we're buddies, and because we're committed to remain friends for life."

"If I were to tell you you'd be a prize idiot to marry this girl, I don't think you'd want to be my friend for much longer."

"Don't be ridiculous. I've said I want your honest opinion, and whatever that may be, it will never affect our friendship. Do you really think I'd be an idiot to marry her?"

"No. I didn't say that. I'll give you my opinion in a minute, but first I have a little story I heard some time ago to tell you. A young student goes to his college professor, and says, 'Prof. I'm in a dreadful dilemma. I have found this stunningly adorable young woman. She says she loves me, and wants me to marry her. I can't sleep nights; I can't concentrate on my work; I simply can't get her out of my mind. Please advise me, whatever should I do?' The college professor immediately replied, 'To marry, or not to marry? It sounds almost like Hamlet's soliloquy, but that's your question, and the choice is remarkably simple. If you don't marry her, she'll almost certainly go away, and find some other partner. You'll probably never see her again, and you'll doubtlessly be heartbroken and for the remainder of your life you'll berate yourself for not marrying her. If you do marry her, then you'll have her as your companion, and wife for the rest of your life. Now I'm unable to advise you what choice to make, but of one thing I'm absolutely certain. Twelve months from making your decision you'll return

53

telling me that you believe you made the wrong choice.'"

"Philip, that's great, but it's a story, a joke. I'm serious. I've a real-life dilemma. Claire doesn't know of my intense feelings for her, and it's me, your best friend Henry, who feels he can't live without her."

"Henry, I don't think we've sufficient time to discuss this thing as fully as we might..."

"Well we could talk some more tomorrow," interposed Henry.

"Henry, what I just said doesn't apply to a few minutes. We could talk for months, and never discuss this thing as fully as we might. You're the book reader. You must know of some of the untold numbers of volumes that have been written on this subject, so forgive me if I tell you I'm not the most learned individual to give you advice. To begin with you're going about this the wrong way. Hear me out, and I'll tell you why. Imagine that you are a knight at King Arthur's round table. You're given the task to go off in search of the Holy Grail. 'Go bring it back to Camelot,' orders King Arthur. Assuming you knew where to search wouldn't it be a good idea to know what this thing looked like, and if it were available for you to buy, borrow or even steal? After all, this grail might not be an object. It might be a fable, an idea, something intangible. It might be frozen, and as you travel, it slowly drips away in the warm air, or evaporates, so by the time you return home all you have is absolutely zero.

"No my friend. You tell me you're madly in love with Claire. Now let's assume you're Claire's father, and a young man comes knocking at your door asking for permission to marry your daughter. Surely you're going to ask him a few pertinent questions. The first question would have to be, does she want to marry you, and the next, how long have you known each other? You can't possibly consider asking a father for his daughter's hand in marriage until you've determined whether the daughter fully reciprocates your feelings.

"You tell me it's a platonic relationship. The first thing you must do is ask Claire does she want to marry you, or don't you believe she has any say in the matter? If she says no, then you must either sling your hook, or try to persuade her with your American wit, English charm, good looks and Jewish *chutzpah* to accept you. I guarantee she'll find the combination irresistible. If she then says yes, you have to ask her father for his permission, and that's when your problem really starts."

54

"Philip, I know you're right, and of course I have to ask her. It's simply that if she says no I don't know how I could go on with my life. I might end up throwing myself off some bridge."

"Henry, let's have none of these histrionics about jumping off of some bridge, or certainly not a high one in winter, when it's freezing, and you could maybe slip off accidentally, and hurt yourself, or catch your death from hypothermia, if you're not dressed warm enough. You can't *make* someone love you. Take my advice, and go and see her. Take her some flowers. No, forget that. Just one single flower, preferably a rose. You may be in love, but you don't have to be madly extravagant. You've got to work within a budget, and anyway, believe me, one flower's always more romantic than a whole bunch. Make it a red one, even if it costs a couple of cents more, girls always think a red one's more romantic, though heaven knows why. Go down on your bended knee. Make sure you've cleaned your hands and fingernails beforehand; you have to make a good impression. Say something real smooth, and complimentary like," Philip imitated in a high-pitched squeaky voice as they both laughed, "When you smile, you've got the best little dimples in the world that I've ever seen, or your eyes sparkle, and captivate me when you smile. Girls always believe that kind of smoochy nonsense. Go on two knees, and grovel a little if you think it's going to help; make sure you do this on the sidewalk. Grass will stain the knees of your pants, and your mother will never forgive you ruining your best suit. Ask Claire the one simple, essential, question, 'Will you marry me?' And preface your question by saying 'Darling', so that it sounds like you might mean it. I guarantee she'll find you irresistible. Once she tells you yes, come and tell your old friend Phil, and then we'll take it from there, one step at a time. Believe me; those steps are going to be like climbing a mountain without oxygen. You'll then have to speak to her father, and you'll have to think, would it be worthwhile?"

"Before we leave here Philip, let me organise another cup of coffee, and explore this thing a bit further." Henry indicated to the waitress that they would like more coffee.

"I suppose as much as advice, I really want a sounding board, because I think my mind is made up. I have to marry this girl, and if I can't then I might as well kill myself."

"Henry, you're at it again. You're talking melodramatic stuff like a kid. You've been reading too many classic novels where people die of love. One girl is very much like another. If you were to stop seeing this one for a few weeks, you'd get over your puppy love, and find somebody else just as pretty, and just as smart."

"Of course Philip, you think you're right, but I believe you're confusing infatuation with love. Maybe in some instances what you've said might apply, but let me give you an example of true love, and we'll see if even you can tell the difference."

"If I'm going to receive some Talmudic dissertation, please spare me, or we'll be here all night."

"Philip, this is no joking matter. I'm trying to illustrate a point, to show you the difference between what you believe is infatuation, and what I tell you is love, and how I love Claire. Imagine a woman goes into a hospital where she has a baby. She leaves the hospital, and unknown to her there's been some kind of dreadful muddle, and she's handed the wrong baby. A couple of years later the infant suddenly falls sick with diphtheria, or whooping cough, or something, and dies. She's totally bereft. The very next day she receives a letter in the post from the hospital admitting there's been a mix up, and that her baby is alive, and well, and asking her to bring the child she's been nurturing for two years, and which isn't hers, back to the hospital. What does she do? Well I believe that while her husband might later institute legal proceedings against the hospital for negligence, she will grieve for the rest of her life for that dead baby with whom she has bonded, and won't even want to know her own genetic infant. An animal bonds immediately with its young. A new-hatched duckling will bond with a hen, and follow it around everywhere if that's the first animal it sees.

"You take a child of two or three, or twelve or thirteen, away from its mother. There may not be any tears for a little while, but just you wait. The young child will keep breaking down crying it wants its mummy, and will become depressed, and withdrawn. With the older child, we call it being homesick. In the American Civil War you read in book after book how those young soldiers were 'homesick' for their mothers, or their girls back home. Were you to go to France, at this very moment, you'd find millions of fine men in the trenches, and when they're not firing guns, they'll be thinking only of one thing, the girl back home. The allied Generals Haig and Foch will call it building morale; I call it breaking bonds that can't be broken, in other words, love."

56

"Henry, you're describing mainly long-term relationships."

"Philip I agree, but my relationship has been going on for months. You see I think I've found somebody very special in Claire, and I think if I had to let her go now, something within me would die. At this moment of time I genuinely feel that I couldn't go on with the rest of my life if that were to be the case. I've dated girls before. Not many it's true, and I'm no innocent child, but with Claire it's completely different. I feel as though I've found myself slipping down the bank into a mighty river, and once caught in its current I'm powerless to oppose it, as I'm swept, regardless how I might struggle, out to sea."

"Henry, has it ever occurred to you that love is a two-way street? In the same way you've bonded with her, she may have emotionally dovetailed with you."

"You could be right, but you're not. I only wish that you were, but we're simply good friends, and were you to hear her sing, or play the piano or organ you'd realise I'm just not in her league. She's elegant, beautiful, highly intelligent and talented, her background is as blue-blooded American as it gets, and economically in comparison it's like the princess and the pauper, and you can guess which category I'm in."

"Henry it's getting late. As I see it you're hopelessly in love, and you're just selling yourself short. I bet the girl's mad about you, and she's just too shy or timid to tell you. Girls are brought up that way. They're taught it's unladylike to make the first move. I reckon she'd elope with you if you just happened to snap your fingers. I think you haven't begun to scratch the surface of the real problem."

"Which is?"

"Haven't you ever noticed that when we ride in the tramcars we're white, and we sit in the front, while the coloured folk, our Negro brothers and sisters, have to sit in the back? When you look at water drinking fountains, some say white only, and the same applies to toilets, waiting rooms, cinemas, theatres, restaurants and coffee shops. We're in 'The White Coffee Pot', and you don't see any brown or black faces. It applies to schools, tennis clubs, hospitals, cinemas, theatres waiting rooms and country clubs. In the armed services Negroes aren't permitted to bear arms, and there are no black trolley or train drivers, police officers or newspaper reporters. Do I need to go on with a disgraceful list that's longer than the arm on the Statue of Liberty?

57

"Just think of it. This state, our own adopted state of Maryland, maybe most of the United States, founded on liberty, and justice for all, is riven with colour prejudice and bigotry, from top to bottom. A prejudice, by the way, which works both ways. I sat in the back of a trolleycar last week, and this coloured guy tells me to go down the front, which is where I'm supposed to sit, and belong. If you were sick, and they took you to Mercy Hospital, they'd take one look at your lily-white skin, and tell you to go some place else, 'cause this here hospital is for us coloured folk. Just imagine that.

"Now instead of coloured and white, substitute the words Jew and Catholic, or Episcopalian and Catholic. We're talking about race and religion, not colour, and unhappily this applies to some extent in every country in the world. I've seen signs at a country club just in the suburbs of our city that say, 'No Niggers, No Jews, No Dogs'. I bet that's the sort of club your girlfriend's father belongs to, and if not him then many of his friends. That Henry is the problem you will have to face now, and every day for the rest of your life with her, and that my fine friend will be the obstacle to your romantic happiness."

"Philip, I know Claire is Roman Catholic, and I'm a Jew. But I seldom go to synagogue, and while my religion is important it's not an overriding thing in my life."

"Henry, I understand what you're saying but what of the opinions of your mother, your family, and your friends? They're the ones who'll condemn you for selling out to the 'enemy'. And don't forget the guy on the trolley who pushed me down to the front, even though I had no objections sitting with him, a fellow human being. In the same way your family will condemn you, and try to isolate you so that the contagion of intermarriage doesn't spread. Exactly the same thing will be going on in Claire's family, and it'll be equally as difficult, possibly even worse for her. They'll abhor the idea of her marrying a Jew and do everything they can to prevent it happening.

"As the Bible's commandments tell us, 'Your God is a jealous God'. That's to say, we all believe in this deity, but every group believes that only theirs is the correct path, and they're prepared to commit mayhem to make you accept only that route. In my opinion these religions always seem too insecure to stop and consider that there's no completely wrong or right path, because they're too damned scared. They're scared as hell that the members of their

58

religious sect might start thinking for themselves, and will defect *en masse* to the other side. Jews would be converting to Christianity, Christians to Islam, Muslims to Hindus to Episcopalians, and back again. Everybody would keep changing religion like in musical chairs. It would be heresy to the religious leaders who wouldn't be able to budget their finances. We could have a new religious group the Heretics, but I think they tried that one once before, and the members found it too hot, with the Inquisition some time back. So come on Henry, it's late and I'm tired. Let's go home."

"Philip, I'm going to take your advice. I've decided I've absolutely got to ask her to marry me as soon as I can. When she says yes I'm putting you down for best man."

"That won't scare me one little bit providing I don't have to sit next to your future father-in-law. Just remember what I told you. If you accidentally snap your fingers, you'd better watch out. Wear your running shoes in case you get caught in the stampede, and you need to make a run for it to avoid being trampled to death."

Chapter 7

Baltimore June 1916

As the weeks passed the weather grew warmer. Henry and Claire were able to take longer walks in the park, where floral tributes to the season were in profusion, their colours and wafting fragrances attracting hosts of butterflies and other winged insects, adding to nature's colourful displays. The day after his talk with Philip was just such an occasion. It was on Tuesday of June 1st that Henry discovered his opportunity. Carrying a small bunch of yellow primroses, he had met Claire in the early evening. He had never once met her without some small floral or gift offering, and as he presented the delicate yellow flowers to her, she smiled, admired her posy, and thanked him.

As they started their evening stroll, they walked side by side slowly along the path, a paved grey ribbon through the fragrance of newly-mown deep green grass. In the pleasant warm evening air Henry felt awkward for the very first time in her company. In spite of a prodigious command of the English language he felt unusually tongue-tied. He wanted to ask Claire to marry him. Whatever was he to say, and how was he to approach this delicate subject? When would be the most favourable moment? His conversation started awkwardly.

"The primrose was always said to have been the favourite flower of one of our most flamboyant English prime ministers."

"Which prime minister was that?"

"Benjamin Disraeli. He was a favourite with Queen Victoria, particularly since her husband Albert had just died, and he made her the Empress of India, and arranged for the British government to buy a controlling interest in the Suez Canal."

"They're such beautifully delicate yellow flowers. It always seems such a shame to pick them. They never survive for long out of water."

Henry decided that he must first confront her with his sense of her apparent faithlessness. As they walked he said.

60

"Claire, I know you've been seeing somebody else these past days, and I would prefer that you didn't."

"Whatever do you mean you would prefer that I didn't?"

"Quite simply I mean we've been keeping company for a little under two years, and I feel unhappy and a little jealous to think you're seeing anyone but me."

"Henry Chiswick, I'm unaware that you've ever proposed to me. Why, we're not married, nor even engaged to be married are we?"

"No we're not."

"Well, that being the case, I'm a free agent, and I'll do whatever I please; I'll see whoever I please; I'll go wherever I please and with whoever I please, without any by your leave, thank you very much."

"But Claire, you know you mean the world to me. I think you're the most beautiful girl, the most wonderful I've ever known. I just can't stand the thought of you walking out with another fellow, let alone holding hands with another man."

"Well that's too bad," She retorted angrily, and she strode faster along the footpath. "I admit I care for you, but no more than any other friend I've known for all this time. While I'm a single free agent, I can walk out with, and date, whoever I wish, and whenever, so you can take it or leave it, just as you please."

Henry felt that this was a pivotal moment in his relationship. His best friend Philip, that maven of love and romance had told him he only need snap his fingers, and he risked being trampled underfoot in the stampede. Some advice; some maven; an authority; what did he know about these things? At this rate it seemed that Claire could end her friendship with him right now, and he would be left staring into the abyss, not knowing how he might survive the empty void confronting him, without her. The words of Robert Burns kept going through his mind. 'Faint heart ner won fair lady', which seemed more appropriate than Philip's finger-snapping strategy.

Firmly taking Claire's hand to restrain her progress, he stopped, and as she attempted to stride angrily onwards he blurted out, "Claire, I love you."

"What did you say? Did you say what I thought you said? I always thought ours was a platonic friendship. You've never spoken to me this way before," replied Claire angrily, as Henry restrained her further progress along the path.

And then again more gently, his words spilling out in a desperately hurried rush he said, "I said Claire, I love you. But that's a

61

half-truth. Darling, I love, and adore you is what I really meant to say."

Claire had ceased her angry progression and now stood to face Henry. "Are you telling me you want us to become engaged?" responded Claire, in a more conciliatory tone.

"Claire I've explained my family's expectation that when I marry it must be to someone of the same faith. 'Marrying out' would be seen in most quarters as an act of treachery, a never to be forgiven crime. I would experience almost insurmountable opposition from my mother and sisters should I even think of becoming engaged to you. And anyway, I've yet to meet your parents formally, who you've told me wouldn't be enamoured with the idea that I ask your father for his daughter's hand, so I can't see how we can ever announce our engagement at this juncture."

"Well Henry, whatever's a girl to think or believe? You suddenly announce you don't like me dating other young men, and then you say you love me. The next moment you tell me you don't want to be engaged to me since your family would object. Is this some kind of marriage proposal or are you in some bizarre way telling me you want to put an end to our months of friendship? You're making me quite dizzy with your changes and I don't know what to think."

"Claire, of course I don't want to end our friendship. I'm trying to tell you in the only way I know how that I love you."

"Henry you profess you love me, and don't want me to date other boys, yet you don't wish to become engaged or to commit yourself. In other words you want to have your cake and eat it, is that it?"

"Claire, it's not like that at all. I'm just trying to explain why this is not an appropriate time for us to become engaged, particularly since I've not spoken to your father."

"I simply can't agree not to date others, unless you commit yourself to become engaged to me. So that's an end to the matter isn't it; unless..."

"Unless what?" Henry urged, like a drowning man, clutching at straws.

"If you love me as you say let's just get married. We can skip the formality of an engagement and parental disapproval. We could put up banns and marry in a justice's office with just two witnesses. Later we could tell our parents, and they would have to face up to the truth. That you and I are married and there's nothing they can possibly do about it."

"But what if they don't accept our marriage?" *She hasn't told me that she loves me, how am I to know?*

"Henry, of course they'll come round to our way of thinking when they see how deeply we love and care for each other. My parents couldn't fail to adore you just as I do, and you could always agree to accept instruction from father Shaugnessy to become a Roman Catholic."

"Now wait a moment, hold on. I never said anything about converting to become a Catholic," exclaimed Henry, who now realised she had spoken the words he had been longing to hear: '*I adore you*'.

"Then you certainly don't love me. How can you possibly say you love me?"

"Of course I love you. I love you more than life itself, but I can't renounce my religion just like that. I'm not setting any precondition that you become a Jewess. Let's each follow our own religious precepts, as in the past, without trying to convert the other. In the same way that I'm a man, and you wouldn't wish to change me into a woman, nor would I wish to change you into a man. Let's accept that we are diverse, have different views on religion, and accept and respect these differences."

"Then there's nothing further to discuss. My parents would be horrified to see me marrying anyone, but a Catholic, a true believer."

"Claire, look at me. You've never spoken this way before. I love you as you are. I've never asked you to convert, and adopt the beliefs of my ancestors. I don't ask you to change your religion to become a Jewess. Although I might wish it, I don't expect it, or make it a precondition. I don't think though that I could ever betray the inheritance of thousands of years by converting, and I don't feel that you should demand this from me. Mary and Joseph, Jesus and his disciples were all Jews by birth, and in their practice, and you find that quite laudable. I dress, and speak differently, since we live in a different era of time, but tell me how else do I differ from those Jews that I should be found so unacceptable?

"In all that's holy, why in heaven's name can't we be who we are, each with our own religion? We would respect each other's beliefs, in the same way we accept the likes and dislikes we may each have for a food, a fabric, or a colour, or even the music of Mozart or Mahler, and simply be two of God's children, facing the future as two upright honest American citizens? If you continue attending mass or playing the organ in church I would have absolutely no objection or reservation, and the same should apply when I attend synagogue or observe the Passover or Day of Atonement, just as Jesus and his family did scores of years ago. There must be more than one road through which we find God's grace."

"Henry. Would it work out? I love you, and want you more than anybody in this whole world, but I love and respect my parents, and I wouldn't want to hurt them. What will we do when we have children? How will we educate them?"

Henry appeared outwardly calm although his mind was in an excited turmoil. He noted that she had at last said those three magic words, '*I love you*' and had dissipated all her anger. He felt his heart beating like a steam hammer within his chest. Within his mind the thought screamed out at him, *Robbie Burns was right!*, *Robbie Burns was right.*

"We will see that they're educated to respect all religions, and to fear God, but without being specifically Jew or Gentile. When they become responsible adults they can then make up their own minds which religion, if any, they wish to follow. They would be emotionally and morally richer for their unbiased exposure to both religions."

"Henry, I want to believe you, and belong to you, and none other, but do you think it can work?"

Henry somehow managed, with a superhuman effort, to appear calm as he replied.

"If our love for each other is determined, and strong enough to accept and live with our differences, it's bound to work. Our differences will provide us with interests that will add viability to our relationship. Claire, my darling, I do so love you. On those terms, will you be my wife? Will you marry me?"

"Henry Chiswick, ever since that day at the concert when we bumped heads, I've been waiting and dreaming that you might one day ask me. On those terms, I would belong to none other. I will marry you, my darling."

With Claire's reply and quivering with excitement, Henry placed his hands around her waist and drew her close. Terrified lest anything might end this first magical moment, he lifted her almost effortlessly into the air, swinging her round and round, and she with her arms round his neck permitted him to find her eager parted lips, as they sealed their intentions with a kiss.

"Henry, put me down this instant. We have plans to make."

"I know, but first I demand another kiss to seal our agreement."

"Not here Henry; people will think we're very badly behaved. Even if it's dusk, it's so public."

"Well let's away from the path, and go over to that tree copse where we'll not be seen."

They walked hand in hand as lovers will. Upon reaching the shade of the trees, dusk rapidly falling, and partially hidden from moon and stars, Henry turned to face Claire. She tilted her face upwards, the starlight reflecting in her eyes, as the mild fragrant warm evening breeze gently rustled the canopy of leaves above them, as Henry gently kissed her lips.

"Claire, my darling, a Jewish bride and groom are always married under a *chupah*, traditionally a canopy of leaves beneath a further canopy of the stars in their heavenly orbits. So I shall ask you once more." And then using a voice that he imagined a judge might use, he intoned, "Miss Claire Robins, talented music student, daughter of an accounts executive residing in Baltimore, midst the whitest of white stoops, do you still wish to marry this handsome Anglo-American salesman, recently come to these Maryland shores of the Chesapeake Bay from London Town?"

"Yes Henry, I do."

"No mumbling. Louder miss, if you please. Are you still certain Miss Claire Robins that you wish to marry the said handsome blue-eyed Henry Chiswick esquire, and no other?"

"Yes my darling."

"Do you have any doubts that you might be marrying in haste, and may repent later at leisure?"

"None at all," replied Claire, laughing. "A courtship of almost two years is hardly to marry in haste in anyone's estimation."

"Miss Robins a little attention please, if you don't mind. To love, and cherish each other, in spite of parental and family objections?"

"Yes, yes, ten times more than the million stars we see overhead. Yes."

"Then I shall pass sentence. Would you please listen carefully and take note.

Miss Robins, you are sentenced that you shall live happily forever and a day with the said Henry Chiswick, who you have made the happiest man the world has ever seen."

Laughingly they embraced and kissed; first once, as lips firmly

65

pressed on lips, then a second time, lips gently parting, and then again, standing in the shadowy moonlight, before Claire sat on the grass, pulling Henry down beside her.

"Henry, I don't think I shall ever forgive you for taking so long to propose to me. We've known each other just three months short of two years. I thought you'd never want to kiss me, or ask me to marry you."

"And I think you're absolutely right. I've been an absolute jackass, and idiot to keep you waiting this long. What penance do you think I should be required to provide?"

"This," as she lightly kissed him, "And this." They kissed again. As they did so, each started to experience a strange, minute and unfamiliar tingling tremor within the other's embrace. They clung together, hugging and kissing more closely, lips separating, permitting tongues to embark on those tiny rapid voyages of exploration in the passion of their love, happier than at any time that either could remember.

Tremulously they embarked on a previously hidden and forbidden journey of exploration, neither one bidding the other to cease. Within each lover's breast, hearts heaved and bounded joyously. Each heart pumped furiously, to circulate their libations to Aphrodite's calling. An emancipating circulation, overloaded with a cornucopia of hormones, liberating all conditioned reticence and restraint.

He was startled but delighted by the awareness that from rejection and his despair of only minutes earlier, both he and Claire had ascended to the heights of unabandoned human ecstasy. Claire's response overwhelmed him in the intensity of her sheer, passionate abandon in his embrace. He found her riposte to his love exhilarating, and an amazing revelation, which left him incredulous at the intensity of her warmth and love that he had never before considered remotely possible in Claire, or indeed in any woman.

Their embrace continued, as each caressed hitherto unknown, forbidden areas of love. Henry became aware of a soft mewling sound within his ear, mounting and crashing, and mounting ever higher to a thrilling crescendo of sound as their ardour of longing for each other blended in a blaze. The passion of his love had kindled and stoked a fire not all the waters in the Chesapeake Bay could ever quench.

At last like any consuming blaze its fuel and intensity spent they

66

lay wrapped, still panting and warm in each other's arms. As the young always do, they laughingly protested eternal love for each other, deliriously happy. In love, blissfully contented, as in no time previously; with their happiness, challenging, even defying fate and the world to break their bonds of love asunder.

And fate, that unseen, knowing, fickle mistress, accepted the gauntlet thrown down that June starlit night, and determined to test their metal to fatigue and breaking point in the most dreadful manner possible in the years to come.

Chapter 8

London 1999

It was shortly before six a.m. when I awoke to the sound of an infant crying. Hastening into the adjacent bedroom in our two-bedroom first floor flat in Islington, I went over to the cot to pick up Edward, our five-month old son.

"Morning puddle, had a good night have we?" I said as I bent down, picked him up, placed him on the bassinette and proceeded to remove his saturated nappy, all the time smiling, cooing and speaking to him, and very pleased there was nothing more solid to deal with. As I finished fitting his clean, new nappy and clothing I announced, "Up we come. Let's go see what mummy has that's different for breakfast this morning. Never mind if it's the same old diet of warm milk, I bet you'll never see it delivered in better packaging."

I carried him into our bedroom, handed him to Laura, who had just woken up, and hurried off to the kitchen to retrieve the two glasses of freshly squeezed orange juice I had prepared the night before and placed in the refrigerator. Carrying the juice back to our bedroom, I handed one glass to Laura, who was contentedly engrossed in breast-feeding Edward, and sat next to her to drink my own juice at the leisurely pace I enjoyed at this time of the morning.

Sitting there I watched this extraordinarily beautiful, primordial sight, of a mother suckling her infant, and the child, our firstborn, contentedly feeding at his mother's breast, with eyes closed. I gazed, as I had each day for the past five months, feeling a happiness and contentment that had never before existed in my life. Here was Laura, my wife of almost five years, with whom I was more deeply in love than ever, nurturing our son. It was easy to understand how through the ages so many artists had attempted to capture on canvas tranquillity and contentment, such as this moving sight.

As I watched, realising that soon I would need to prepare breakfast for Laura and myself, before rushing off to work, I thought

68

that my own parents would have experienced these same, all too fleeting minutes of contented happiness, as would parents everywhere.

But wait. Unfortunately parents everywhere did not all fall into this category. Whether through poverty, war, disease, work, or a myriad of reasons there were many unable to enjoy this most wondrous and beautiful, of all experiences. My own father's father Paul fought in 1942 with the Allied Eighth Army in North Africa, where in the course of action against Rommel's Africa Corps he lost his life, and was never able to see his infant son.

I had a picture in a photograph album of Grandpa Paul as a soldier, a corporal in General Montgomery's army, taken somewhere in the Libyan desert. He was part of the force engaged in fighting Rommel, 'the desert fox'. Grandpa was about my age and I could see the photograph in my mind's eye as I dozed off and imagined him talking to me, asking me to begin a search to find where his family had come from.

"I don't know how to find where your family came from grandpa, and anyway, I don't have the time to go searching for your roots."

"Alf, all you have to do is to find the time. It's a bit like being your own Sherlock Holmes. I bet you'd even find it fun once you made a start."

"No grandpa, sorry. If you were that interested, why didn't you do your own research back then, instead of leaving it?"

"I always meant to Alf. Kept putting it off and never had the time. I guess I simply procrastinated, if you want to know the truth, but you should make the time. Make the t...i...m...e."

"Time to wake up! Alf wake up! Sleepy head. Alf, wake up! Look at the time, you'll be late." I suddenly became aware of Laura calling me.

Without mentioning my imaginary encounter with grandpa to Laura, I resolved that something had to be done to search for grandpa's roots, which were of course my own. From this point, I wondered where my grandfather's parents and grandparents might have been living, to enjoy this same basic human pleasure of watching ones own newborn infant being nurtured by its mother.

Who were they, what were their names, where had they lived? It seemed incredible that having spoken with and quizzed my father about these things periodically over so many years we knew nothing more than the name and occupation of his own grandfather, who

69

lived in London. It was common knowledge that in 1290 all Jews were expelled from England, and were not permitted to return for almost four hundred years until the latter part of the seventeenth century, some time after the French Huguenots arrived in London as refugees. This being the case, one of my great-great-grandparents must have arrived in England from abroad. Who was this ancestor, when did he arrive, and where had he lived previously, were questions my father was unable to answer.

Father had earlier suggested that the wife of a cousin he had met at a family wedding last year had been preparing a family tree. He gave me her phone number, indicating that I should speak to her, since she might be able to help. It was now, after my encounter with Grandpa Paul, that I decided to telephone this woman, Janet Chiswick, with the object of preparing the gift of a family tree for my son, and discovering grandpa's roots. Grandpa had asked me, and I believed that I owed him that much.

That evening I telephoned Janet, and in my best-cultured voice, enquired, "Is that the Chiswick residence?"

"Yes, it is."

"Is that Janet Chiswick?"

"Who is this?"

"My name's Alf Chiswick, and I'm trying to do a little research into the origins of my father's family, so I'm trying to contact Janet Chiswick. I understand that you've been doing some research on the Chiswick family."

"Well it might seem apparent from my voice register, that I'm not she. Janet is my wife, but if you don't mind, I don't think I know you. Could you please tell me who you are?"

"Oh I'm sorry, let me start over again. My name's Alfred Chiswick, Alf to my friends and I believe we are second, or maybe even third cousins."

"If you say so, but I still don't know you, and I'm not prepared to call my wife to speak to a total stranger."

"My father is Edward Chiswick, and his grandfather, my great grandfather, after who I'm named and your great grandfather who, if I'm correct was Sidney, were brothers."

"Sounds as though you might be right, except Grandpa Sid was my grandfather, not my great grandfather."

"You're probably right. It depends on your age. If you're closer to sixty, well over the hill so to speak, which is my dad's age, then

70

he would be your grandfather, but if nearer thirty, which is my age, then it would be your great grandfather."

"Look I'm rather busy, and I don't find your ageist comments at all funny. You seem to be trying to confuse and blind me with your genealogical nonsense so I'll say goodbye."

"Please don't hang up, I didn't mean to offend," I hastily exclaimed in as conciliatory a tone as possible, wondering why the over fifties are so touchy about age.

"Father said he met you last year at the Minchin's wedding and that you had told him that your wife Janet was working on a Chiswick family tree."

"I seem to recall meeting your dad, Edward Chiswick you say, last year at some family get together. Wasn't he connected with the film trade?"

"He was in the radio trade. It was cousin Jonathan who was connected with films."

"Well I'm the wrong side of fifty if that's any help, and which you seem to find so hilariously amusing, but if you hang on for a bit, I'll call my wife. These family matters are more her cup of tea."

There followed a brief pause as I heard some faint distant conversation, which I could just pick up and included the words,

"...Janet, do help me. It's another of those lunatic ancestry people wanting some help or other. Says he's related, and I simply can't get rid of him."

A few seconds later, through the handset, once again reinvigorated with electronic life, I heard: "Hello this is Janet Chiswick here, can I help you?"

"Yes, I'm Alf Chiswick. I'll start at the beginning. We're second or third cousins, and in our case it's through marriage. Five months ago, I became a father for the very first time."

"*Muzzletov*, how wonderful. Was it, a boy or a girl?"

"Thank you, a boy."

"What do you call him?"

"Edward when we're in company and puddle when we're not," I replied laughing.

"Alfred or whatever your name is, if you're going to maintain this juvenile sense of humour of yours, which neither my husband nor I find in the least bit amusing, I shall certainly hang up."

"No please don't. I promise to be serious, without any joking." There followed a brief pause as I reviewed my options with these

71

obviously oversensitive, middle-aged people, silently praying that I might maintain a better sense of humour in my dotage than this lot.

"Thank you. Are you going to proceed?" said Janet, in what appeared to be a condescendingly exasperated tone.

"Well, I thought it might be a nice idea for little Edward if I made a family tree, going back as far as possible, so he could see his roots and origins."

"It sounds as though we're both trying to do the same thing for different people. I've been attempting to help my young grandson create a family tree."

"I heard that you had done some research. I seem to have come up against a brick wall when it comes to the ancestors of my great grandfather Alfred Chiswick and his brother Sidney, and I wondered whether we could exchange any information."

"Alf, that seems a grand suggestion. Let me fill you in with what I've been doing," she replied in a brighter tone. "I've likewise been unable to go back further than Grandpa Sid, who was Alfred's younger brother, but I've recently made contact with an elderly cousin of my husband's grandfather, who lives in Wimbledon. She's in her late eighties, and has apparently been hoarding letters, photographs and other family memorabilia and data. I've spoken on the phone with her. She doesn't get out much these days and she has agreed to meet me. I've been invited round to have tea with her next Saturday. If I can wrangle an invitation, would you like to join me?"

"That sounds a great idea." I thought to myself, Arsenal will be playing away and I'm certain Laura wouldn't mind if I go absent for one afternoon, other than for football.

"You can drive down with me, in my car. We can chat *en route* and get acquainted."

"Fine. If you give me your address I'll see you next Saturday, once you've confirmed with the old girl that I'll be there as your assistant."

"Right, I'll call you back, if you give me your phone number, providing you agree to refrain from upsetting our older female relatives by calling them 'old girls'."

"All right, no harm meant." I gave Janet my number and said, "Before I say goodbye, could you answer one question. I know the family came from abroad sometime in the nineteenth century; have you any idea who it was, where he came from, and when he arrived?"

"I'm sorry Alfred, that's three questions and the answer's still the same for each. I haven't a glimmer, and nobody I've spoken to seems to know either. I guess that's part of what we'll have to investigate."

"Then I'll be waiting for your call and shall look forward to meeting you. Goodbye."

* * *

I really should have started this story at the beginning, but when you're dealing with genealogy just where is the beginning? I could tell you about me, and I suppose I shall have to. There might be somebody out there who might want to know, even if it's only to avoid meeting me in the unlikely event we belong to the same golf club, or bump into each other at the Arsenal football ground, or in our local pub down the road.

But I put it to you once again, where does one start?

The whole object of genealogy is to find out who your ancestors were, where they lived, perhaps what they did, and how many kids they had. According to Darwin, if we go back in time, we would each find some early Neanderthal types as our ancestors. Earlier still, there would have been ape-men, and before them we came from orang-utan type animals. This makes me wonder that if we're descended from some early gorilla kind of animal, how come they're still around, chiefly in zoos and how is it we made it, and they didn't?

My name is Alfred Chiswick, as you've read, and I'm married to Laura, my beautiful wife who thinks the world of me. She doesn't seem at all bothered that I snore prodigiously at night or have lost most of my hair. I put these attributes down to an excess production of testosterone, a male hormone, which makes me more virile. It's a simple trade off. I'm better in bed than most, and women can identify with this, because I've got less hair. It not only makes me better in bed, but when the wife forgets to take her pill, she's far more likely to conceive, and make baby boys like our Edward, than girls. It's something technical to do with the little spermatozoa with the XY chromosomes being stronger swimmers. They certainly appear to enjoy better teamwork, which enables them to score more often. Anyway that's my theory, and if I ever win a sufficiently large sum of money on the national lottery, I shall see that research is funded somewhere, to prove my theory right.

73

Not only do I have a slender beautifully elegant wife, I've had lots more going for me. From the start I had a great education at Harrow School, in northwest London. That's the public school where Winston Churchill was once a student and got all those terrible school grades and reports. Those are the two things he, and I had in common, which is where the similarity ends. He smoked huge Havana cigars, went into journalism, and politics, and his father was a lord. I smoke the occasional cigar, half the size of those Winston smoked, my father made radios, and I've got one of these fantastic nine to five jobs.

It's in advertising, and more recently management consultancy, where we con as many large international companies as we can find into spending a fortune using the few ideas and slogans we make up to sell their stuff. They sell more of their products, which keep's them happy. The public buy more of their merchandise, because there isn't much choice anyway. We convince these corporate clients that without our help they would lose market share. It makes them highly anxious and neurotic, and we feed their neuroses, taking in return an outrageous commission on all they spend in marketing and advertising. We never let on how fantastically simple it is, always encouraging our clients to believe it's a tough decision-making job. It's so remarkably uncomplicated. The press barons and media moguls are ecstatic with the revenues they see rolling in. The corporations, which are our clients, see their sales and revenues increase year by year. The public find a constant array of new innovative products to purchase. We in advertising, marketing and parasitic management consultancy are the enzymes, vitamins and lubricants of industry, commerce and consumerism. It's as though we've reinvented the wheel.

There's a downside to this consultancy, advertising, and marketing stuff. I have to spend too much of my time networking. In plain English this means time and effort wining, dining and playing golf or the occasional game of tennis with these corporate fellows. I do this so conscientiously, five days a week, even giving up the occasional weekend when Arsenal aren't playing at home, that last year my handicap went down ten, from twenty-two to twelve over eighteen holes, while my belt needed to be loosened two holes. I enjoy these business meetings over the golfing greens, except occasionally the golfing score and my skimped business notes closely resemble each other, which at times my colleagues have found a little confusing. In my opinion I'm a regular martyr to my job, and that's how I convince myself that I deserve the relatively huge bonus at the end of each corporate financial year.

I sometimes wonder during the year, particularly in winter when it rains or snows, and golf is off, if the sacrifice is worth it. That is until I have the bonus in my hands, and before the wife and Inland Revenue get hold of it. What little I then have left still makes me feel it's all been worthwhile, and justifies my annual eight weeks laying off the booze and wine before Lent, until when standing straight I can safely see my shoes without bending when I look down.

I drive, wait for it, a six-year-old dented and knocked out of shape in places black Saab, which is washed once every third month outside, and cleaned less often within. When I drive it, other motorists, particularly those with newer cars in pristine condition, show me deference, usually reserved for royalty, as they give me the widest berth possible. When I entertain clients, or drink, which is most working days, I use a black cab.

Most of my mates judge you by the car you drive, and among the more juvenile, by the decibels sprouting from the exhaust when the engine is revved, or even the engine size. With that listing, I'm considered little more than an impoverished student. But I don't care. Of course I could afford a better set of wheels, really I could, but I don't want them. Not that I'm modest, or lack ambition, and don't want to make my mates at the local envious. It's just that I've had enough wheels, number plates and radios nicked. As many as two radios in a single week, and once even a pair of bumpers borrowed from my Jag in broad daylight, which at a replacement cost of £1,000, without labour charges for fitting, wasn't funny, or in the slightest bit as amusing as some of my friends believed.

I had reached the stage that I felt I needed to place a card inside the front window of my car, inviting any would be villain to leave my car alone, and in return for knocking at my front door, and not taking my radio, or whatever, I would contribute the forty or fifty quid they needed for the next day's cocaine, opiate or heroin fix. Realising that unaided I could not help smiling Mayor Ken Livingstone resolve London's drug-related crime problems, I decided a fundamental change of strategy was needed. I must learn to play it cool, and low key.

Now when I go out in the morning, the wreck – as Laura and I both fondly call it – is still there, completely intact. I no longer have to waste hours of my time calling the police, who are rarely anywhere to be found. I no longer have to fill in an incident report at the police station because something else has been knocked off my new two-litre, latest model driving machine. The car insurance premiums are at an all-time low, and now we're laughing. We've learnt to play it cool.

As my dad put it, giving me one of his frequent bits of fatherly advice pep talks, "Alf my son, wisdom comes with age. In your case you're ageing too slowly, which is why in your special circumstance being bald is an asset. It'll make you look older and more sophisticated, providing you stay sober."

I don't agree. It's the testosterone level that's high. Judging from some of mother's innuendo about dad giving Viagra a try, I think that he may have been a little envious of his young son's virility. To give him his due he is an extremely tall handsome man, taller and thinner than me, intelligent and modest. I must count myself blessed that while a little squatter in stature, just a little under six feet tall and with less hair, I have however genetically inherited most of his better qualities and can even hold my wine better.

* * *

Janet phoned and confirmed all was set to visit Dorothy. Janet would be driving, with me doing the Boy Scout bit of map reading. I was to later find, almost to my peril, that her driving skill matched her sense of humour, which in my opinion didn't add up to very much.

A few days later, on one of those balmy, hot, dry, late English spring days, I found myself as navigator, cowering down in the front seat of a Jaguar saloon car, held by a seat belt which appeared far too flimsy to judge by Janet's driving abilities. As I recorded in my diary later that evening when a couple of glasses of red wine had calmed my sensibilities, without causing offence, her skills needed considerable honing to approach anything that might be an acceptable standard.

We drove fitfully along, with abrupt stops followed by a too rapid acceleration and then another abrupt stop. This progress was hindered by a manual transmission which had it been a soldier might have been awarded a military cross for bravery. The return journey would have merited the inclusion of a bar, or at the very least, a mention in dispatches. We progressed round the North and then South Circular roads and entered Wimbledon, heading for a small, white, stuccoed post-war block of flats, which was to be our destination. Once in the labyrinthine streets of Wimbledon, with my navigational assistance, we approached our cousin's apartment block from the opposite direction intended. We drove down a one way street, going in the wrong direction, having needed to stop to ask directions twice, as we found ourselves trapped in a one-way system which seemed intent on propelling us out of Wimbledon onto a coastal route to Portsmouth via Guildford. Each time we neared our turn off I warned Janet of the approach, only to find she somehow speeded up by thrusting her foot on the wrong pedal, thereby missing the appropriate street. In the vanity of pursuing style, women ruin their feet with high-heeled shoes, choosing to ignore the resulting middle-age bunion deformities. Why must they also hazard lives by driving in fashion accessory shoes? There should not only be a law to stop people driving when intoxicated, or while holding a mobile phone, but women should be banned from driving unless they wear appropriate footwear that enables them to control most, if not all, the foot controls.

By the time we reached our destination I was beginning to understand how a kamikaze pilot must have felt as he progressed on a mission, as arriving at our destination my companion brought the car to a juddering halt just microns from the brick front wall. Janet leapt out, holding a bunch of fresh spring flowers she had brought for the occasion. I followed, knees a-wobble, carrying a small box containing a cheesecake made by my wife as my offering for our first meeting.

I now appreciated the need to wear a seatbelt as never before. With Janet's driving, a crash helmet and goggles should have been obligatory with ejector seat and parachute thrown in for good measure.

After several minutes of focused searching, Janet found and rung the doorbell. In true English fashion it was well hidden under three or four years' growth of an overhanging pale blue blossoming wisteria branch. Finding the number on the flat had likewise taken an interminable time.

Janet appeared completely unaware of the shattered state of my nerves after our journey and of my private innermost thoughts that Arsenal's away game in Sheffield would have been preferable to

77

this, and maybe my son could one day do his own research, once he had grown up and found his own wife.

A short pause was followed by a voice calling from within,."I'm coming, I just can't move as fast as I once used to." A gentle soft shuffling sound from somewhere within followed this, before the front door was slowly opened to its full extent, to reveal cousin Dorothy.

"Hello. For me?" she exclaimed in delight as Janet, smiling, gently thrust her colourful floral offering forward.

"What beautiful colour tulips, they will brighten the place up. Thank you, thank you, they're absolutely delightful." With that she held out her hand saying,

"My name's Dorothy Monkton, you must be Janet, do come in." Introductions were made at the door as she bade us enter and "Follow me."

We found ourselves in a small brightly illumined ground floor lounge, the walls painted a pale lemon yellow, with the afternoon sun streaming in to reveal a large central table, covered with a white linen table cloth on which were strewn several piles of documents, while on a nearby couch, lying open, was a small light brown suitcase filled brim full with a disarray of photographs and newspaper cuttings.

"Have a seat, pull up a chair, make yourself at home," she wheezed. I handed her the opened box, revealing the cake. Her eyes sparkled as she pursed and licked her lips,

"Oh you shouldn't have!" her facial expression giving lie to her words. "Why don't you set it in the kitchen over there, and we'll have it shortly with our tea."

We sat round the table, chatting about the beautiful weather, Dorothy expounding upon her love of the garden, and myself relating the appalling traffic conditions on the increasingly antiquated London road system which had so impeded our journey. Why, at considerable expense, do Camden, Brent, Islington and a host of other London boroughs build all these raised mounds of silent policemen in the roads to slow us down every few yards when there are sufficient axle-breaking unrepaired potholes that do a better job at no expense to the taxpayer? On a motorway one finds a plethora of signs changing maximum speeds from 50 to 40 to 50, then to 30, then up to 40 all within a few hundred yards of each other and 'speed cameras' to catch the unhappy speeding motorist

78

driving without sufficient care and attention. Our highway advisers have just taken leave of their senses and there's no one willing to tell them how crazy the system has become. This political correctness pendulum has gone too far, but we will need to wait years for the correction before we can sit back and laugh at the foolishness of these attitudes? Suddenly I realised Dorothy was speaking to me.

"So tell me Alf. Whose son did you say you are? Edward's you say. Don't think I've ever heard of him. Are you sure you're related?"

The boys at Harrow school, through jealousy of my athletics, on and off the rugger field, often called my paternity into question, but I didn't expect this from an octogenarian, even though she was my great grandfather's cousin.

"Of course I know I'm related to my dad. He's told me often enough. In a dumpier sort of way I'm said to look a bit like him and without any DNA testing I just know we are."

Janet came to the rescue. Giving a 'leave it to me glance', she quickly took the initiative and in a firm but kindly schoolteacher voice replied.

"Dorothy, they're all a bit after your time. His great grandfather was Alf, that's who he's named after."

"Are you really certain? He doesn't look a bit like my Uncle Alfred."

"Yes I'm quite certain, Joe's grandfather and Alf were brothers and Joe has met and knows this Alf's father".

Then began our genealogy education.

Lesson number one. Always start by questioning as many older members of your family as you can find. Have some writing materials to hand, preferably an exercise book with lined paper, so that you can date and record the information you receive, or use a recording machine to record everything.

Lesson number two. Try to obtain help from an experienced genealogist, who can invariably point you in the right direction.

If there were two Alfred Chiswick's, or two Edward Chiswick's, which there were, how would we differentiate between them without getting confused and what if they found three or four of us with the same name? Dorothy suggested that we give each generation a prefix G1 for first generation, G2 for second. By no means a perfect system, but in the opening stages it was a great help. My great grandfather received the temporary prefix G1 – Alfred

Chiswick. His son (who was also my grandfather) became G2 – Paul. My father became G3 – Edward Chiswick. I became G4 – Alf Chiswick and my infant son G5 – Edward Chiswick. Alf's brother, or should I say G1 – Alfred's brother, became G1 – Sid Chiswick. Sid's son became G2 – Sam, and my companion Janet's husband G3. A bit confusing until we got the hang of it, after which it made life far easier.

"Dorothy, our first question is, do you know anything about our family origins?"

"I didn't until I went to the Family Records Centre in Kew. It used to be in Somerset House, but that was some time ago."

"Quite so, but where did the family come from?"

"As I was saying, I had no idea until I communicated with cousins of my father and your father who live in Boston. I knew about them because one of them was in the American air force during the war. He told us he was stationed near Oxford when he visited us in London. He looked a very handsome fellow in his uniform, but he was reported missing in I think it was 1944. So many of those handsome young men in their fine uniforms, bravely flying out to fight the enemy, never to return. Terrible, such a dreadful shame.

"I actually visited the family shortly after the war, lovely people, but somehow we've lost contact since that time. They told me their family went out there in 1892 straight from Eastern Europe after all that trouble and those simply dreadful pogroms which followed on from the Russians' assassinating their tsar. They didn't know where they had fled from in Europe except it was somewhere in Russian Poland. They were able to tell me that the family had first settled in New York before going to Boston, which gave me my first major clue.

"Most of the immigrants tended to enter New York through Ellis Island. A good number of details were recorded, among which was the ship they arrived on, port of embarkation, town and country of origin, full name and age of every immigrant and a good many other details besides, even including some aspects of their appearance."

"I hate to interrupt, but is there any way we can access this information without going to New York and taking a boat ride to Ellis Island?" I enquired.

"Yes there surely is a way. They've established a very interesting museum there, which I understand to be well worth visiting, although I haven't been there myself. They have spent a fortune on advanced information technology to create a database and a website, where you can access information, at no cost, on any person who entered the United States as an immigrant through Ellis Island since 1890."

"What if they didn't enter through Ellis Island; is there any other way of establishing where an individual was born before they entered the USA?" asked Janet.

"That's a very interesting question to which the answer is yes. There are a number of ways, but the two I would recommend for ease of access would be the federal census, and the individual's death certificate. The federal census is very similar to our UK census, and takes place every ten years. The British one takes place in the year with a one on the end. The last one was 1991 and it's due to take place next in early 2001, but it's only available for public scrutiny after a hundred years. The American census takes place every ten years, in a year with a zero on the end and is opened to the general public for scrutiny after seventy years. This will similarly provide information concerning where each individual in a family was born and their age at the time of the census."

"Yes well where did the family originate?" At this stage I was convinced I should have been watching Arsenal playing away in Sheffield and left the geriatric interrogation to Janet, who showed more demonstrable skill and infinitely more patience than me.

"As I was saying, a third major source of information is an individual's death certificate. In addition to the information that can be obtained from a British death certificate, which in comparison with the information found in the American version is pretty sparse, one can also obtain information concerning the father of the deceased, occupation and where the individual was born, which can be most helpful in one's research."

"Yes Dorothy, but where did the family come from?"

"Well my dears it seems the American cousins, who, by the way, have a different spelling of their family name, originated in a small town called Konin, which was in Russian Poland."

At last, our first major clue and we'd only been asking the same bloody question for the past hour and a half. In reality it was twenty minutes, but in my mind's eye, with those vivid red shirts of the Arsenal forwards advancing towards the Sheffield United goal line, it seemed like an eternity.

Our family came from Eastern Europe, from Konin. A major piece of a jigsaw had been found, but where to place it? Why couldn't she have given a straight answer immediately? We could then have said goodbye and I could have headed for the car radio to hear *Match of the Day*. Janet was not only a dependably erratic driver, neither could she read my thoughts, and she was now assisting Dorothy in the preparation of the obligatory cup of tea.

As we politely sipped our tea, from delicately floral patterned china teacups, Dorothy passed round old letters, newspaper cuttings, yellowed with age, and other documents. She had no photocopier and would not lend them to us, since as she explained, "Some years earlier I loaned some documents to a distant cousin, against my better judgement. He promised faithfully to return them and never did send them back."

Well, I thought, she should have asked him for a fifty quid deposit, which would have soon set him straight. We had therefore to content ourselves by writing furiously on sheets of lined paper given to us by Dorothy for the occasion.

An hour later, thanking Dorothy for her hospitality, we promised to keep in touch and to let her know of any progress that we might make. I silently mused that attempting to obtain information from any four score and ten year-olds required patience and skill akin to repeatedly buying a weekly lottery ticket in the hope that a lucky series of numbers might one day come up to provide an unexpected win. It now explained how never having won on a lottery number I must accept the reality that it was a skill that I lacked completely and that I must from now on resign myself to thinking of each purchased lottery or raffle number as just one more charitable donation.

On our return journey we resolved to seek out and ask questions of other older family members, after which we would go to the Family Records Centre, in Myddleton Street, Islington, to find all G1 members of the family with the objective of tracing at least one descendant of each. A secondary goal would be to trace the earliest member of the family to have arrived in England.

By visiting cousin Dorothy we had observed lessons one and two in our genealogy class for beginners, except we had failed when it came to arming ourselves with writing materials prior to our meeting. But then, we all make mistakes.

Our family tree at this time looked something like the following:

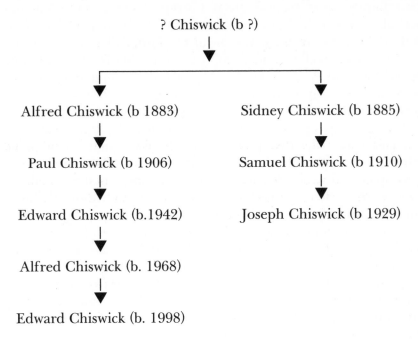

? Chiswick (b ?)

Alfred Chiswick (b 1883)   Sidney Chiswick (b 1885)

Paul Chiswick (b 1906)   Samuel Chiswick (b 1910)

Edward Chiswick (b.1942)   Joseph Chiswick (b 1929)

Alfred Chiswick (b. 1968)

Edward Chiswick (b. 1998)

Chapter 9

London June 1999

Janet and I had decided to meet, armed with pencils and lined writing pads, at the Family Records Centre in Myddelton Street, Islington, considerably closer to home than Kew, when it opened at 9.30 a.m., to see what further we could learn. I had resolved that in future if we were to travel by car I must either wear 'eye blinker shields' or insist on driving. Fortunately the Centre was close enough for me to walk the distance from my home in less than fifteen minutes. We met inside where we discovered on the ground floor, signs that pointed us in the direction of births to the right, marriages in the centre and deaths to the left. We knew my great grandfather's age when he died, so decided to look in the appropriate year for a record of his birth.

There were row upon row of heavy large hard-covered bound books in chronological order, each being slightly more than twice the height and width of a phone book. There were four books in every year, taking in the periods March, June, September and December. We decided to explore those books with years covering the period one year either side of the year in which we believed he had been born. Gently taking one volume at a time and setting it down on the central reading desk we started our search commencing in March 1880, meticulously turning every page and then carefully replacing the book back on the shelf where it had been found before taking another and repeating the process.

Heavy volume after heavy volume was taken from its shelf, placed on the viewing desk, opened, scanned for the name Alf Chiswick and returned to the shelf, without success. Once we had arrived at and scanned December 1884 without finding the name, we realised that we had a problem.

"Where do we go from here?" I whispered to Janet.

"Well, there are loads of possibilities. The easiest to consider is that the age that we have is wrong and that he might have been a number of years older or younger."

"All right, let's scan the volumes from March 1878 to December 1879 and from March 1887 to December 1888. At the same time we can look for his younger brother Sid, just to make certain that we have the spelling of the family name correct."

We again carried volumes to the desk, one at a time, checked and returned them. Suddenly we found a 'Sidney Chiszyk' in 1885, but not Chiswick and still no sign of Alfred.

"What do you think we should do?" I again whispered. But this time I could barely make myself heard and had to repeat my question, speaking more loudly.

The research area had rapidly been filling with members of the public. Some like me were amateurs showing some revered deference to these mammoth volumes, but not for long. The majority were professional genealogists to whom time meant money. They nimbly turned pages at a fantastic speed, deftly handled each record book untiringly with consummate ease, but the noise! The place felt and looked like a library, but with the noise of these heavy cumbersome books being thrown by dozens of researchers with tremendous bangs and clatters onto the central reading desks in rapid succession, it sounded more like a war zone to my ears. I now found myself speaking almost as loudly as I was able without shouting and at times could barely make myself heard above the exhilarating staccato clatter.

"I'll make a note of the location to secure a birth certificate and then we can check the 1871 national census records for London, looking for the family name with the changed spelling," said Janet.

With this decision we filled in an application for the copy of a birth certificate for Sidney Chiszyk, paid our £7.00 fee and filled out a blank envelope with Janet's home address safe in the knowledge that within four working days the appropriate certificate would be in our hands. We then made our way to the much quieter first floor area.

We obtained, with staff gladly helping us to locate it, the appropriate reel of census film. We checked it through the viewing chamber, again staff assisting us in demonstrating the loading and working of the simple controls. After an hour of searching we could find no trace of Alfred Chiszyk or Chiswick.

"Maybe we can't find any reference because he was born after 1870 or perhaps he was born outside the United Kingdom."

"He may well have been born after 1870, but I know for certain that he was born in the UK, because I can remember some years back hearing my dad tell me, when we were listening to a Beatles recording on the radio, that the Beatles were born in the same city where his grandfather Alfred was born. I'm certain he wouldn't have said that had it not been true."

"It's very disappointing, whatever the reason. I suggest we stop now, wait for Sid's birth certificate to arrive and then put our heads together to see what additional information we can find."

"Let's find somewhere to have a cup of tea, go home and then you can phone to let me know when the certificate arrives."

A week later I received a call from Janet. She sounded very excited. "Alf, you've just got to come round. I've received the copy of Sidney Chiszyk's birth certificate in this morning's post and we need to decide what we do next with the information." We fixed an appointment and I went to her home, that evening, which was located just two miles from mine by car; perhaps less than a mile as the crow flies.

Over a cup of coffee we examined the newly-arrived certificate. Sidney Chiszyk had been born in 1885 in London's Tower Hamlets. There had been a change in spelling of the family name, but best news of all was that it provided us with some completely new and important information. It gave his father's name and occupation and his mother's maiden name. His mother was named Rebecca née Levy and she had delivered her infant son at home. His father was David Joseph, a tailor, who had registered the birth. We had gone back one generation in time, revealing information that had long since lain dormant and forgotten.

"This is fantastic, but we still haven't found Alfred, nor do we know when the change was made in the way the family name was spelt. Where do you think we should go from here?"

"It's quite simple, we go back to the records office," said Janet. "You know how old your grandfather was when he died and the year of his death, so let's take off a year from his birth and see if we can find the marriage certificate of Alfred Chiszyk or Chiswick. If we don't find it in that year, we can go back year by year until we do."

"Fine, but while one of us does that, we could save time if we were to check the national census record for 1881 and possibly 1871."

We agreed to meet the following Saturday morning in the records office. On this sortie we were more confident. To save time, I elected to do the heavier work of lifting the heavy volumes one by one from their shelves, checking and replacing them, while Janet went up to the first floor to examine the census for 1891 covering the address in the City of London where Sidney had been born.

I checked the year for 1901 when my grandfather had been born. I checked backwards to March 1895 without a sighting of Alfred Chiswick or Chiszyk. Perhaps there had been an illegitimate birth and Alfred was married after 1901, so I checked forward to 1903 without a sighting. I was just giving up in despair when Janet appeared at my elbow.

"Alf, I've just left the census film open. I've found something exciting and I'm certain it's something you'll want to see for yourself, so come on."

I started to ask, "What is it?" But she was no longer by my side but striding towards the door that led to the first-floor staircase. I hurriedly replaced the June 1903 volume I had been checking and ran after her. I caught up as she approached the viewing screen at which she had been seated.

U.K. National Census 1891

Address. 23 Fournier Street, London.
Head of Household; David Joseph Chiszyk. Aged 36 years;
Place of birth; Konin Poland. Occupation, Journeyman Tailor;
Rebecca Chiszyk, Wife, born 1851 in Aldgate London.
Children: Rachel, born 1873 in the City of London,
              Annie born 1879 in London,
              Amelia born 1882 in London.
              Abraham born in 1883 Liverpool,
              Sidney born 1885 in London,
              Henry born 1889 in London.

"There it is!" she whispered triumphantly, pointing at the screen.

Initially I found it very difficult to adapt my vision to the small thin white writing on the black background, but there it was. In the enumerator's copper print writing of almost a hundred and ten years ago were the names of the entire household living in

London's Spitalfields. There at 23 Fournier Street we had found David Chiszyk, head of household, his wife Rebecca and the names of their six children. The eldest son was called Abraham, born in 1883, not Alfred, and there were two other boys, Sidney two years younger, born in 1885 and Henry the youngest, born in 1889. "That's solved the mystery. Alfred was named Abraham and his surname was spelt differently," I whispered excitedly.

"I'm going downstairs to find that marriage certificate."

Within a few minutes I discovered that Alfred, using his original name Abraham, had been married in the summer of 1903. I hurriedly filled in the appropriate form to obtain the marriage certificate and for good measure we decided to obtain birth certificates for each of the children, and the marriage certificate for David and Rebecca, their parents. We left the records office in high spirits and decided to have a small celebratory lunch at 'Ask', a newly opened Italian pasta restaurant, in nearby St John's Street.

Over lunch we decided on our further strategy. We had no knowledge of a Henry in our family. We immediately agreed that our first priority should be to discover what had happened to Henry, the baby of the family, and if he had survived, to endeavour to trace at least one or more of his descendants. We also agreed that having retrieved one generation we should attempt to go back in time to discover the parents and if possible even the grandparents of our ancestors David Joseph and his wife Rebecca.

I hurriedly drew our revised information on some paper:

"That's fine and dandy, but I would prefer to find out what happened to their children, and their children's children. Apart from Alfred and Sidney who constituted a third of David and Rebecca's children we've lost trace of all the others, and they of us. There might be hundreds of second and third cousins out there somewhere."

"Is that really important? If there are any unknown relatives living out there, they must have known about Alf and Sid, so why haven't they tried to trace or contact us?"

"Who knows? Maybe there aren't any."

"Maybe someone among them might have become quite famous or wealthy," I suggested.

"Or just as likely notorious, and infamous," rejoined Janet.

"This is really likely to take some time, which I don't think I can spare from my commitments at work and obligations at home with

Laura and Edward."

"As a housewife with a grown up family, I don't have the same work commitments, so I don't mind coming up here midweek if needs be. In addition I bet there's probably lots that we can achieve simply by using the internet."

"That's fine with me, as long as you realise that at times you may be doing more of the work, with no increase in the share of glory," I said, in as disappointed and reluctant a tone as I could manage, thinking of the football games I could watch while she dutifully struggled with the research.

"Don't be silly, of course I don't mind. One particular avenue I would like to explore is the family who went to America, to learn precisely how we're related."

"I seem to recall when we visited Dorothy she had a side table with an open suitcase full of old family photographs and documents. Although she won't let them out of her sight I wonder if we, or perhaps you, could arrange to visit her again to go through some of the letters and documents to see what she might have that could give us a few leads."

"Sounds like a promising idea. I could phone her to give her an update on our progress, and ask if I could visit again. She also said, if you recall, that one of the most helpful places to go for research is The Mormon Church of the Latter Day Saints."

"That's terrific, but the Mormon church is located in Salt Lake City, and I wouldn't have the time or money to go there."

"Alf, you're perfectly correct except that they have a magnificent branch in London's Exhibition Road, just opposite the Science Museum, which I shall visit later this week, if I can find time."

"Marvellous, I think you really do deserve an honorary degree in psychology. We should also try to find the family on the 1901 census when that becomes available. In 1881 Rebecca would have only been thirty and might have had a few more children."

"Yes, and in those years there was a high infant mortality rate, so some of the children we've identified may not have survived."

"Let's meet up again when we receive the latest batch of certificates I've ordered, and perhaps one or both of us can return to the records office to check the 1891 census records."

"Shall we say my place again next Saturday for coffee at ten? And by the way Alf, thanks for the psychology award. You don't really know me, but I gained my Ph.D. in psychology some years ago, as well as an MBA from Columbia New York, so thank you for noticing."

So saying, we paid for our meal and left, with me feeling six inches tall, a complete, red-faced condescending idiot. I decided that I would just have to make amends, and show that I could also pull my weight, which with a lapsed health club membership, business lunches and domestic bliss, was with alarming belt loosening regularity rapidly climbing.

I was determined to return to the record centre, to search for further records and pleasantly surprise Janet. 'Strike while the iron is hot' is my motto, providing there isn't a good football game to be watched. I had been discussing my latest family tree research project with all and sundry, which was becoming not just interesting, but bordering on addictive. In the records office I started to chat with a matronly woman who was standing next to me, as we each leafed through the huge record books.

It turned out that she was a professional genealogist, and regularly used the facilities to provide details for her client research. She explained that she was too busy to chat at the moment, but that she shortly intended to take a ten-minute coffee break in the basement refectory where she could talk to me if I wished.

I felt that this was too good an opportunity to miss, and proceeded down to the refectory, where I bought a can of Pepsi Cola for 50p in the vending machine and took a seat facing the door. A few moments later I spotted her coming in. I waved, and smiled. She approached, pulled out a chair, and as she sat down she retrieved a thermos flask from a small case she had been carrying, and poured out a dark steaming liquid into a red plastic cup.

Hurriedly introducing myself I explained that I had been researching my family, and that I had found ancestors married in 1872 in London, but since we were Jewish I would sooner or later need to look abroad for earlier ancestors in view of the fact that Jews had only been permitted to return to London at the time of Oliver Cromwell. I wondered if she could give me a few pointers to direct my research efforts.

"Alf, I think you're giving yourself an impossibly difficult task unless you can identify the country of origin of these ancestors. What did you say your surname is?"

"Chiswick, but an earlier spelling I've just come across is Chiszyk" I replied, as I spelt the name out for her.

"Well that might give us a real clue. Many immigrants had the spelling of their names changed in some way as they came into this country, and quite a few were even allocated names by minor immigration officials at the port of entry. In the case of your ancestors it is probable that the name was the original name, or had no more than a minor spelling distortion".

"Oh I see. Well if that's the case, where do I look next?" I enquired, hoping to encourage her to divulge more information before she finished her coffee.

"In my experience the majority of Jews came into England from very few countries. The earliest were the 'Sephardim', who came to our shores predominantly from Holland. The 'Ashkenazim' were mainly from Germany. Lesser numbers followed from France and Italy. And by the way, we're speaking of merely a few score of people. The largest numbers, several tens of thousands, came from the Russian dominated parts of Eastern Europe. They started coming over during the nineteenth century. A handful each year until the assassination of the Tsar Alexander II in, I think, 1881, when there were pogroms, and Jewish people left in larger numbers. They went mainly to the USA, and about a hundred thousand or so entered Britain before the turn of the century. Now some came to England from India, like the Sassoon family, some from the Austro-Hungarian Empire, the Ottoman Empire and even from America, but most during the nineteenth century arrived from Russia."

"That's most helpful. How would you suggest I go about furthering my research?"

"If we assume your original name Chiszyk was the correct, or close to the correct, spelling, the *szy* might suggest a name with a Russian origin. Assuming this is so then my bet would be that your family originated in Poland, and if not there, in one of the Baltic states. The Russians were expanding westwards during the eighteenth century, and by about 1795 had occupied most of Poland. They would not allow Jews to live in Russia, especially not in the cities, and having acquired sovereignty over Poland they herded the local itinerant Jews to live in the area which they designated 'The Pale of Russia'. Furthermore they made the whole population accept the use of surnames, something we did in this country just after the Norman conquest of 1066, and in China they started in the year 2852 BC."

91

At that moment she looked at her watch, exclaiming, "My gracious, time's up!" She replaced her plastic cup and thermos flask in her case, and standing up said, "I have to get back to work. I would suggest young man that you contact the Jewish Genealogical Society, or the archivist at the London Beth Din, or the archivist at the Bevis Marks Synagogue. You'll find their numbers in the London phone book. They will be able to assist you with further advice on researching sites in Russian Poland or anywhere else outside the UK."

I expressed my thanks. Before I could even tell her she had confirmed the information I had been given by cousin Dorothy, that the family had arrived from Russian Poland, and which I had seen on the 1891 census return that very morning, she was scurrying towards the door, through which she rapidly disappeared, back to her research.

I followed her advice, and managed to obtain the information with a phone call to the Jewish Genealogical Society. I was courteously informed that if I wanted to research Russian Poland, I could do so on the internet through visiting <www.jewishgen.org/jri-p>. They were really very helpful, and suggested that once I had been able to identify the village or town in which my ancestors had lived I could then go to the Church of Jesus Christ of the Latter Day Saints in London's Exhibition Road. There I could order for a modest nominal charge microfilms under 'Jewish record indexing, Poland'. These microfilms would then be available to me in Polish, for several days, to be used in research in the Church of the Latter Day Saints' research room.

* * *

Later that week I received David and Rebecca's marriage certificate. It showed the names of their parents.

Hurrah!! We were slowly on schedule with one of our objectives; we had gone back one further generation. I decided I would give this information to Janet, asking her if she would visit the Mormon temple to continue our research by ordering the microfiche films for the Russian Polish town of Konin. It was then that I began to wonder why the Church of the Latter Day Saints had adopted the name Mormon.

I decided that before sending Janet to a church in the heart of London, we should at least know something about this religious organisation which was about to provide us with help in our research. I felt that by providing her with this information, she would be better prepared for what lay ahead. Forewarned would be forearmed, and I might further redeem my standing with her after my lunchtime restaurant *faux pas*.

1872 UK Marriage Certificate (Summary)

Marriage took place on: 17 January 1872. In the Parish of St. James London.

Groom: 'David Joseph Chiszyk' a bachelor Aged: 25 years.
Occupation: Tailor
Address: 9 St Anne's Place, Catherine Wheel Alley, Bishopsgate, London,

Father: Joseph Chiszyk, Occupation, Tailor,

Bride: 'Rebecca Levy' a spinster Aged: 20 years.
Occupation: Seamstress
Address: 17 St Anne's Place, Catherine Wheel Alley, Bishopsgate, London,

Father: Henry Levy, Occupation, Musical Instrument Maker.

Marriage performed by the Chief Rabbi, Dr. N. Adler,
at the Great Synagogue, Dukes Place, London.

Certificate signed by Bride and Groom and two adult witnesses.

Back home I almost resisted the temptation to watch the sports results, but common sense and a love of soccer won the day. I later checked into the Mormon Church, and found some interesting revelations that I could give Janet.

It seems that the Mormons and we Jews have a number of things in common. In addition to a belief in God they have slightly fewer members – at nearly eleven million followers worldwide with more than half their members living in the United States – than we do, and they also adore choirs, choral and classical music, and give generously to charity. One major difference is that Jacob's followers gave up on polygamy during the first millennium. My theory is that a contributory cause may have been a prolonged period during which real estate prices going through the roof made the accommodation costs of a large family of wives too costly. Being far sighted, and realising that a ghetto existence might one day become compulsory, when living with more than one wife and one set of in laws in close proximity in a small apartment would make life far too stressful. Mormons believed that the old tried and tested ideas were better, and having large open spaces in the midwest on which to build real estate, they opted in favour of polygamy.

One of our original patriarchs, Jacob, who was a successful sheep breeder about four thousand years ago, give or take a couple of centuries, had a dream in which he had a nocturnal wrestle with a nameless angel. At the end of the last bout, with no clear declaration of who might have won, Jacob arranged with the angel for a name change to Israel, which is possibly why our lot, seeing a precedent, have constantly been changing names, ever since.

Way back in the autumn of 1823, Joseph Smith, whose father was a less than successful Vermont farmer in the north-east of the USA also had a nocturnal wrestle with an angel. He was living in upstate New York at the time, and his angel was called Moroni, not to be confused with Giovanni Baptista Moroni, the talented Renaissance painter, or Marconi, the Italian fellow who first transmitted radio signals.

Angel Moroni read him some of the facts of life about the Bible, clean living and the plains Indians possibly being one of the ancient lost tribes of Israel. Maybe it was the same angel Jacob had wrestled with, who now had acquired a name. If it was, after four thousand years, with no known recorded bouts in between, he might have been a little rusty and out of practice, since judging by the outcome of the contest, he hadn't in any way improved his wrestling skills.

It seems that Joseph Smith was so impressed with his tussle that he hurriedly put pen into ink. Being somewhat illiterate at the time, he then had his wife Emma a former school teacher liberally apply the said pen and ink to copious reams of paper, as he dictated his revelations in a darkened room, obtained from a 'Golden Plate' using an instrument called a 'Urim and Thummim' before publishing the *Book of Mormon*, as revealed by the angel Moroni. Some seven years later with his newly-revealed versions of the New and Old Testaments he started the Church of Jesus Christ of the Latter Day Saints.

Unfortunately Joseph somewhat blotted his copybook by failing to curb his interest in some of his younger impressionable lady followers. While married to Emma, he acquired a number of additional wives, allegedly marrying 33 while still married to her. Not usually a jealous woman, this did upset her a little. His conduct also created a few too many enemies along the way. He was shot and killed, together with his brother, in an Illinois prison cell in 1844.

Book publishing has never been a risk free enterprise. At the best of times it is difficult to predict what any literary reviewer might write about any publication. It seems the reviews were sufficiently positive for the movement's followers, each with polygamous numbers of fair damsels as their wives, to head west into Missouri, then Illinois, where success went to Joe Smith's head, and he decided to put himself forward as a presidential candidate.

The voters in those frontier days were at times difficult to impress. Success was not the only thing to go to Smith's head, and when he died from a surfeit of acute cerebral lead poisoning, his younger associate, Brigham Young, led growing numbers of followers into the Salt Lake Valley of Utah where they settled.

The head or supreme council of the Mormons, and their twelve apostles, banned polygamy in 1890 and some years ago ruled that a simple baptism into their church was a mandatory requirement for entry into heaven. Benevolently they accepted that since the vast majority of us are not Mormons we could squeeze through into heaven if a type of posthumous visa requirement is fulfilled. This is achieved when they record the name of any persons in a ledger, whether they are alive or deceased, irrespective of religious belief, which will then act as a surrogate baptism.

By so doing, they have at great expense, munificently undertaken to inscribe the names of all and sundry non-Mormons into this book. This enables more of us than are perhaps entitled to enter the post-life, magic kingdom of heaven.

In addition they have liberally provided access to this database at either no charge, or the most modest charge imaginable, in record centres throughout the world. They certainly have my vote, every time, for their good works in the field of benevolence and genealogy, and like those of us descended from Jacob, they are charitable, almost to a fault.

Chapter 10

London September 1999

It finally worked out that with a small division of labour Janet and I were able to trace the ancestors of David Joseph Chiszyk, a bachelor aged twenty-five years who married Rebecca Levy in London in 1872. The marriage certificate revealed David Joseph's father was Joseph Chiszyk, whose occupation was that of a tailor.

We accepted that there were invariably differences in how names were spelt and ages recorded. At the records office we meticulously checked the birth records to find David Joseph, from 1837 to 1850, without success. From 1837 births were legally required to be registered. Although there was a legal requirement to register a birth, penalties for failing to register were not introduced until later, in 1875. Consequently some births might still not have been registered. The absence of a birth record, assuming he had been born after 1837 and there had been no adoption, indicated the likelihood that he had not been born in the UK.

We checked www.jewishgen.org and found references to the Chiszyk family in Konin, Russian Poland. We next visited the Mormon Temple records office and ordered three of the appropriate microfilms to cover the years we wished to explore at a charge of £2.70 each for four weeks and were told that we would be notified when they arrived.

Within seven days we were informed by telephone that the microfilms had arrived. Two days later we travelled by underground to South Kensington and walked the short distance to the Mormon Temple in Exhibition Road. Entering the building we signed the visitors register and proceeded by lift to the record department located on the third floor, to collect and examine the microfilms.

The staff were extremely helpful and demonstrated how to check the microfilm. Examining the contents of the black celluloid reel film through one of the viewing boxes, we discovered there was little difference in format to the census records that we had previously checked. The writing was in Polish, and these were photocopies of pages of the original ledgers recording marriage, birth and death records. We soon mastered the technique of spotting the names we were interested in, and were able to make photocopies of the records in which we were most interested, for a nominal charge of 20p each. We found the birth record of Josef Chiszyk and made a photocopy of the entry. Later that week, with the help of a Polish friend, we found the document's translation to be roughly as follows:

Polish Archival Birth Record of Josef Chiszyk.

It was reported in Konin on 3rd February /15th February 1820 at 3pm. Attending was Abraham Josef Chiszyk aged 48 years, living in Konin, accompanied by the witnesses Abram Karp aged 62 years and Sloyma Hermann aged 58 years, living in Konin.

Stating our baby boy, was born in Konin 26th January / 7th February in the year 1820 to his wife Esther (nee Lewkon) Chiszyk aged 36 years.

After circumcision given the name Josef Chiszyk.

This document was read to the attending father and witnesses who signed below.

The translation of every record approximated to the above format. The dual dates show the Julian calendar followed by the modern day Gregorian calendar.[8]

We had been able to trace our Chiswick family back to 1772 and the birth of Abraham Joseph Chiszyk, and had accomplished the first of our major genealogical objectives.

Our family tree now looked as follows:

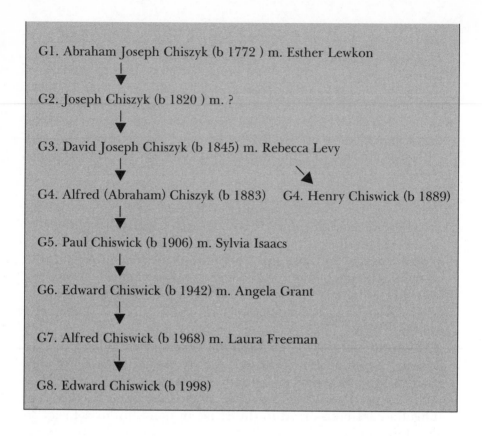

G1. Abraham Joseph Chiszyk (b 1772) m. Esther Lewkon

G2. Joseph Chiszyk (b 1820) m. ?

G3. David Joseph Chiszyk (b 1845) m. Rebecca Levy

G4. Alfred (Abraham) Chiszyk (b 1883)   G4. Henry Chiswick (b 1889)

G5. Paul Chiswick (b 1906) m. Sylvia Isaacs

G6. Edward Chiswick (b 1942) m. Angela Grant

G7. Alfred Chiswick (b 1968) m. Laura Freeman

G8. Edward Chiswick (b 1998)

Our remaining objective for the time being was to discover the whereabouts of the descendants of Henry, the youngest child of my great great grandfather G3, David Joseph Chiszyk and youngest sibling of G4, Alfred Chiswick my great grandfather.

Chapter 11

Baltimore June 1916

They stood, barely visible silhouettes in the moonlight. First adjusting clothing and then helping each other, while quietly telling each other of their love for the other, giggling and laughing like mischievous children, straightening hair, taking it in turn to have the other brush and tug off the odd blade of grass and the unwanted tell-tale hidden leaf, before embracing yet again and proceeding on their blissfully happy way. The two young lovers slowly walked home through the park, overjoyed in each other's company. Having professed their undying love they had joyously and gently crossed the Rubicon of their relationship.

Bathed in the silvery sheen of an almost full moon and the myriad white stars which randomly blinked above them, they meandered in the warm evening air, chattering excitedly like youthful adolescents, arm in arm, hand in hand, in love. Every so often, they would stop in the shadows for one more kiss; the insatiable appetite of their young love needing frequently to be fed and with each further embrace the union of their love grew ever stronger.

Embracing again and again, their conversation became more serious, as they discussed putting up the banns for their marriage as quickly as possible. They spoke of doing so in Washington DC rather than Baltimore, to avoid the possibility of either family discovering their secret prematurely, and then ruled that out as impractical. They would go to Pikesville, on the outskirts of Baltimore.

"We will need two witnesses to stand with us before the justice of the peace who marries us," said Henry.

"Henry my darling, don't worry. I have some friends at the Peabody who live in Pikesville and I am certain they will help us and can be relied upon to keep our little secret."

They spoke in hushed tones of when they should confront their parents with the fact of their marital union. They decided the most

99

opportune time would be the last Thursday in November, on Thanksgiving, with as many of the family gathered together as possible. Claire would tell her mother that she wanted to invite Henry for Thanksgiving lunch, and when sated with the usual turkey, sweet potatoes and pumpkin pie, a warmer, cordial reception could be expected, when she and Henry could together break the news to her parents.

Arranging to meet the next day to make arrangements for their wedding banns and nuptials, they walked more and more slowly, attempting to delay the moment when they would have to bid each other goodnight. Finally, their progress having slowed to a snail's pace, they arrived outside the Robins' house where, briefly embracing, Claire whispered, "Henry my darling, I love you so much. I just can't bear to have you leave me."

Henry gently placed his finger against her lips murmuring softly, "Hush, Claire darling, not another word. We must now say our goodnights and go to our beds. I promise that soon we'll be able to spend every moment of our future together."

"Let it be soon, my darling."

"Claire, we'll soon be together for all our tomorrows. I promise I'll make a home for us, where one day we can raise a family. Our very own little nest, where we'll always be able to talk, read poetry and enjoy music together with our children. We'll watch the seasons, come and go. The winter sunrise, the autumn sunsets, the bright green leaves breaking out of their buds in the spring, or glimpse the autumn dew weave its capricious magic on spider's webs as the foliage changes from green to gold. We'll gaze in wonder as the snow and frost settle on the grass and rooftops each year. You and I will do all these things together my darling. I give you my solemn word that we'll do these things together not once but for the rest of our days, while with the setting sun, I'll hold you in my arms, night after night, and never let you go. We must simply be patient for just a little longer." With that he kissed her one last time to seal his solemn promise, gently saying, "Now no more talking, for we must for the time being go our separate ways. Until tomorrow."

"But Henry..."

"Hush, my precious darling, no more words. Your beauty speaks to me for itself, but now, we must for the present go home to sleep."

100

With that, Claire reluctantly walked up the steps and rang the doorbell, turning, softly saying, "Henry darling, I miss you, just with the merest thought of our parting. Until tomorrow my love, goodnight."

Moments later, the butler opened the door and with one last look at Henry, she walked into her home entering through the doorway as in a dream world, towards the beckoning staircase and her bedroom.

Henry watched her vanish as though she were caressing the very evening shadows. Then, with laggard's steps, he turned homewards, after a few seconds hastening his pace, as his feet seemed to take wing. Each was now a joyful captive to thoughts and love of the other as they went reluctantly alone towards their respective beds.

As Claire ascended the stairs to her bedroom she knew she was climbing, but with such wondrous consummate ease, as never before. She felt she was not really climbing, but rather effortlessly floating, sailing upwards. Once within her room, behind the closed door, she hastily, feverishly removed her shoes, sprang up and wrapped her arms about herself, hugging herself and twirling about the room, pirouetting and softly, over and over again, repeating the incantation, "He loves me, he loves me, he loves me," and feeling that she must burst if she couldn't tell the whole world of her happiness and of her love for Henry.

When Henry arrived home he went straight to bed, his feelings in no less a happy whirl, wondering how he could best break the news of his intended marriage to his mother and family. He was bursting to tell them, to run outside shout his good fortune to the whole world, "*She loves me, Claire loves me; Robbie Burns was right!*" But he must show restraint. He needed to win first his mother then his sisters over to accept Claire as his wife and he needed to achieve this transformation without causing too much distress, for he knew there were emotional battles ahead for hearts and minds, to overcome prejudices, that he must somehow contrive to win.

The following morning he dressed and went to work as usual, his footsteps lighter than ever before, the only outward change. He thought all would notice, yet to his amazement none appeared to, and if they did, made no comment. He felt that he had hit upon a strategy that he would later discuss with Claire.

At the first available opportunity Henry took Philip aside. He excitedly told him, "I'm engaged to be married and I want you as

101

my witness and best man."

"Agreed. Didn't I tell you she wouldn't be able to resist your Anglo-American Jewish charm and wit. What did her old man have to say?"

"We haven't told any parents. We're going to marry clandestinely on the fourth of July and tell them sometime after the event, when they'll have to agree to our marriage. It's still top secret, so keep the date free and I'll talk to you later."

That evening, after college and work, Henry met Claire as arranged, in the small garden of Mount Vernon Place, beneath the Washington Monument. Claire had hurried out of college and rushed towards Henry and wanted to smother his face in kisses. The dictates of modesty forbade such outward public show however. She had to be content with shaking hands and kissing him lightly on the cheek, following which they sat on one of a quartet of stone park benches and talked conspiratorially with heads huddled together, lovers in the closest proximity in public that decorum permitted.

Their very eyes consumed each other. Fingers and hands entwined, locking and unlocking, and with each change of tactile pressure new sensory stimuli were aroused, creating a myriad of new wonderful and unknown erogenous zones. Feet touched ankles, while ankles brushed legs, knee pressed firmly against knee. Fingers, singly and together, caressed hands and forearms.

Claire quietly told Henry of the arrangements she had in hand to place the banns later that week in Pikesville. She would have a holiday that day from college as would her witness and Henry could take a day off from work, as would Philip. Having tentatively agreed these arrangements, Henry expounded his plan.

On July 10th an end of academic year concert was being given, to which parents of students had been invited and at which Claire had been selected as the 'keyboard student of the year' for a solo organ recital. She was to play the Toccata, the last movement from Vidor's fifth symphony and was well ahead in her preparation of the difficult piece. There was to be a sherry reception afterwards for students and parents. Claire's parents would be present and Henry felt that he could arrange for his mother to accompany him, which would give both he and his mother an opportunity to meet Claire and her parents on neutral ground in public in the most favourable circumstance possible. Claire enthusiastically agreed, although they would continue to conceal the date of their marriage from their parents until November's thanksgiving, unless an earlier more appropriate time should present itself.

Little did they appreciate how desperately and badly the best of plans could soon go awry.

Chapter 12

London December 1999

The telephone rang. To my sleep befuddled mind it was either Wednesday night or Thursday morning and until I could find the bedside table clock I was unable to determine which. I picked the phone up and managed a parched "Hullow!"

"Hello, Alf, Janet here. Hope I'm not waking you too early, but I have some surprising news that I just had to call to tell you about."

"My heavens, you're an early riser, just what time is it?"

"It's almost seven and I promise not to do this again, but I just had to tell you my latest news."

"The baby kept us up half the night, but fire away, I'm awake now." I'd also been up late watching football highlights of the month, but didn't intend to let on.

"I don't know if I mentioned it to you, but I have a very dear friend who belongs to the Highgate Genealogical Society. I happened to bump into her at the hairdresser and she gave me some awfully good tips on exploring the internet for information. She suggested that if I was trying to find somebody who had emigrated to America at the turn of the century I should try www.EllisIsland.com and I could purchase records of early immigrants. She also gave me a few other websites to try.

"I checked the Ellis Island website, typed in the Chiswick name and guess what I found?"

"Some of the cousins who emigrated to the US," I ventured.

"Yes, but somebody else as well. Can you guess who?"

"Haven't a clue, do tell me."

"Very well. It was Rebecca Chiswick with three of her children in 1899."

"Never! Was Henry among them?"

"Yes. I've had a copy of the Ellis Island immigration records emailed to me, which I'll show you."

"That's fantastic news."

"Must fly. See you here for coffee Saturday morning at ten."

* * *

That Saturday we were able to exchange notes and take photocopies of the certificates and records each of us had been able to obtain that the other didn't have. We had found genealogical research to be a slow, plodding, often tedious experience. Very little that was truly exciting really happened although it was generally quite interesting. I suppose that had we uncovered a few murky hidden skeletal remains in locked cupboards and closets we might have felt rather differently. That I surmised was why mainly the middle aged and upward found themselves really interested in genealogy. We had concentrated on researching each of the male offspring of David and Rebecca, and had largely ignored following up the female descendants since the continuity of the family name made the task easier and we craved the heady stimulus that a little early success might bring. We knew most of the relatives descended from the elder two sons and the main character we needed to research was Henry Chiszyk or Chiswick

Janet, like a conjurer, triumphantly produced the immigration document she had earlier received from Ellis Island. In November 1899 the family had been proceeding through Ellis Island and we knew, from birth certificate records, that there was a considerable discrepancy in the ages of the two younger children to that given to the shipping line and New York immigration authorities. At the time, Amelia was seventeen and not eleven, while Henry was ten not eight. The most plausible explanation must have been a cost advantage with children travelling when below a certain age.

Our main objective now was to find what had happened to the third brother, Henry Chiswick, and to locate one or more of his offspring. We decided to use the facilities of an internet genealogy site, www.ancestry.com. This site provided a vast number of genealogical services, many at minimal or no cost, including a notice board where an individual is encouraged to post names of ancestors or persons with specific names, whose descendants they would like to hear from and exchange genealogical information.

Ellis Island New York NY.

Immigration Entry Record

Arrival Date: 25 Nov. 1899. Ship: S.S. St. Paul
Embarkation Port: Southampton England.
Immigrant: Rebecca Chiswick. Age; 48 yrs. Widow
Born: London England.
Occupation: Housewife.
Destination: Mrs. Rachel Romack, daughter,
1810 Madison Street, Baltimore, Maryland.
Accompanied By: 3 children.
1) Annie Chiswick. Age: 19 yrs occupation: Cook.
2) Amelia Chiswick Age: 11yrs.
3) Henry Chiswick Age: 8 yrs.

I registered the names of the family ancestors I was interested in researching and left my email address. I then commenced scanning for the name Chiswick. After looking at several pages and scores of entries for this name, I noticed one enquiry which simply said: "I would like to communicate with anybody related to my grandfather, Henry Chiswick, who was born in London England and emigrated with his mother to Baltimore Maryland at the turn of the century. Please contact M. Wilding." A contact email address was given.

I immediately sent an email, suggesting that if this was the Henry Chiswick whose parents were named David and Rebecca, then we were very likely to be cousins. I invited M. Wilding to communicate with me as soon as possible.

Chapter 13

Baltimore July 1916

The days flew by and on the appointed festive July 4th Henry, Claire and their two witnesses sped on their way in a rented horse and trap on the two-hour journey along the picturesque country road to Pikesville. When they arrived, they soon located the justice's office, a white clapboard building on the main street. Henry gave his friend Philip Rosenberg, doubling as best man and witness, the narrow band gold ring that he had purchased for the occasion, while Liz Brady, the other witness, carried a small bouquet of a white orchid spray for the bride together with a petite white Bible.

Leaving the driver to mind the conveyance and wait for their return, the four-person wedding party then entered the office of the justice. Having identified themselves and the witnesses Henry paid the appropriate fee to the justice, Judge Grady. A brief legal ceremony was performed culminating in the placing of the ring on Claire's left ring finger. With a pronouncement that they were now man and wife and with a nuptial kiss and embrace from each of the witnesses they all signed the register and left the wooden building.

Outside in the sunlight Henry announced that to celebrate he had booked a table at Baltimore's smartest and most fashionable restaurant, Haussners, on the 3200 block on Eastern Avenue. They would afterwards conclude the evening by going down to the harbour at sunset to board one of the many pleasure boats plying for hire, taking Independence Day celebrants out into the bay to watch the distant fireworks display at Fort McHenry.[9]

The wedding party proceeded the short distance to the nearby Pikesville Inn, which they entered in jocular mood for some light celebratory refreshment. An hour later each having downed a congratulatory glass or two of white wine, they set off back to Baltimore, chatting and laughing at a merry, slow and contented pace.

Arriving at Haussner's restaurant, they entered through a

splendid double doorway. Once within they washed and refreshed themselves after their dusty journey and then presented themselves in the warm resplendently illuminated and sumptuous interior, with its myriad of oil paintings and mirrors, which copiously adorned almost every available inch of every wall. Once seated at their reserved table, the waiter brought them menus and the meal was soon ordered. A bottle of sparkling white wine was opened and the health of the couple was toasted once again. They drank, perhaps a little too quickly, and a second bottle appeared before the first course of their meal had arrived. It was opened, tasted and then placed in an ice bucket at the side of the table to cool.

Suddenly Claire stood up, announcing to Henry that it seemed very hot and airless in the room and she was going to visit the ladies room to powder her nose. She pushed her chair back, turned and walked a few paces away from the table. She then appeared to have second thoughts, and hastened back. As she approached she reached Henry and said to her husband in a faltering voice.

"I don't think I'm going to make it." As she spoke those few words she attempted to regain her seat, seemed to turn, stumble and then crumpled to the floor with a dull thud.

With a gasp of alarm Henry rushed from his chair towards Claire, now lying very still on the wooden floor. She barely appeared to be breathing, her waxen skin was pallid and moist. Terrified and not knowing what had caused Claire to collapse in this manner, Henry kneeled down besides her, thinking to loosen the neck buttons of her tight-fitting blouse, and struggled to open the topmost button, not knowing what else to do.

"Out of my way, young man, out of my way. I'm a nurse." An extremely buxom matronly figure who had been dining close by with her companion suddenly appeared and brusquely pushed Henry aside. This compelled him to rise and take a step backwards to observe events, greatly relieved that there was a professional person on hand with some medical knowledge.

"Give the girl some air. Give the girl some air and fetch some cold water, fetch some cold water," she instructed, as she bent to feel the fallen girl's pulse, repeating every half sentence as though convincing herself that all were in agreement with her utterances. Henry stood in shock, helplessly transfixed.

After a few moments the nurse straightened up and announced to Henry and all within earshot,

108

"In my opinion she's obviously pregnant, yes obviously pregnant. Now where's the water? Where's that *water?*"

Just then Claire's eyes fluttered indicating she was awakening. As she was saying, "Where am I? What happened?" the nurse bent forward to reassure and calm her. Philip leapt forward to the rescue, a glass jug, more than half full of water, in his hand.

In the urgent rush to provide water, he inadvertently knocked against and tripped over the ice bucket at the side of their table. This disgorged its contents over a lady and gentleman seated at the next table. Suddenly inundated with ice-cold water they simultaneously leapt up screaming as though scalded, rather than deluged with simple cold water, causing a further localised commotion.

"Best to let her lie there for a few minutes, let her lie there for a few minutes," said the nurse bending solicitously even lower over Claire.

"It lets the blood reach the brain, lets the blood...aaggghh..."

With a jug of cold water clasped firmly in both hands, Philip was attempting to correct his balance from his fraught encounter with the ice bucket. He rapidly over corrected his trajectory, compounding one error with another in the chain of events that was now set in train.

His approach towards the fallen bridal figure thus over compensated, he slipped and somehow succeeded in jettisoning most of the contents of the jug both on to the nurse, before she could finish her second anticipated utterance, and onto Claire's head and chest. The nurse screamed unappreciatively as Philip somersaulted past. Vainly he attempted to regain his balance. His forward momentum was completely blocked by the very broad posterior of the flexed portion of the nurse's rear end into which he clumsily and unintentionally bumped. What had been a small disturbance was rapidly escalating into major turmoil and farce.

This unintended collision caused the nurse's protruding posterior to move forward a little too rapidly. Unable to move her feet forward to readjust her centre of gravity and with a further loud unrepeatable feminine squawk, the inevitable happened. She lurched forward and landed sprawling on hands and knees, partly in the puddle of cold water that had settled on the oak wood floor and partly across the legs of her rapidly reviving patient. Philip meanwhile landed on his knees on the floor beyond Claire, holding up the now empty jug with a foolish expression on his face

109

demonstrating that he had saved the situation in that the glass object remained unbroken, though empty.

The nurse's companion had risen rapidly from his place at the dining table, strode over to his fallen wife and was attempting the Herculean task of assisting her fallen form to her feet. He helped her up several inches from the floor, before strength and leverage gave out. He was forced to release his grip and she slipped back to the floor with a thud and a further loud shriek. Amidst the mounting commotion from three soaked women and their companions Philip manfully tried to struggle to his feet, clutching the jug. So did the enraged bedraggled leviathan figure of the nurse. The saga continued as she slipped yet again and went down a third time. Her wet stockinged leg knocked against Philip's legs. He too tumbled back to the floor, and the jug now flew out of his grasp to fall some feet away, shattering with a loud bang, glass flying in all directions.

Claire sat up gasping and shivering, her hair wet and dishevelled, blouse and skirt soaked. The nurse likewise sat up, completely bedraggled. Philip sat up with the most ridiculous grin on his face trying to explain that he was most awfully sorry and was only trying to help. The area round Henry's table was in pandemonium as the head waiter hurriedly approached, and suggested that they might each wish to retire to change into some drier clothes.

Henry arranged that he would immediately escort Claire home to change and that Philip and Liz should dine at his expense, and that they would try to catch up with them if possible to watch the fireworks display later on.

Claire, escorted by Henry, hurried home, shivering and bedraggled, with a tablecloth borrowed from the restaurant wrapped round her shoulders to keep warm. She felt too unwell to venture out again that night. This was certainly an unplanned ending to their wedding night that they would not soon forget. They did not know what had caused Claire to faint. They conjectured and agreed it had probably been the result of too much excitement and the effect of an excess of wine on an empty stomach. Surely the nurse who had gone to her aid was wrong. Her period, merely a few days late, could not have produced this effect.

The concert was in six days time. Claire felt that she had better rest, rather than risk catching a chill. Retiring with a hot drink

110

before dusk arrived would enable her to rise and get an early start the following day.

Reminding Claire to remove and conceal her wedding band lest her parents should see, Henry, in front of the white stoop of her front door, fondly bade her a tender and lingering, if hungry, goodnight.

Chapter 14

Baltimore July 1916

The day of the concert had arrived. Henry had bought both his mother and Claire a small corsage for the occasion, a single white orchid. Claire's was delivered to the concert hall with a simple message placed in a small white envelope, which was somehow inadequately sealed. 'Good luck my darling, see you after the concert, I love you.' Henry and his mother arrived in good time and took their seats near the front of the auditorium. Unknown to Henry, Claire's parents, who had arrived at the concert hall at the same time as the corsage, were mystified when they read the envelope's contents as to who their daughter's ardent admirer might be.

Claire's solo student performance was scheduled in the first part of the concert as the penultimate recital prior to the intermission. Her presentation on the organ[10] was brilliantly crisp and scintillating. The sounds blazing forth sparkled as though the very heavens were thundering into the hall, completely taking the listeners' breaths away. Rapturous applause flowed round the hall following the performance and the Robins felt the magnificent glow and pride of parenthood, amply justifying and repaying the commitment placed in their daughter's nurtured upbringing and education. They were nonetheless greatly intrigued to know who their youngest child's suitor might be and resolved to question her on this non-musical theme once they were home.

Rebecca for her part knew and now understood how it might be that this young lady had captured her son's attention. As the applause continued, she leant towards her son, whispering,

"I'll grant you that this friend of yours has great, absolutely outstanding talent, but mark my words Henry, she's not one of your own, she's not Jewish. At the first whiff of trouble she'll be calling you a dirty Jew or some worse epithet. How will you feel and what will you do then? My son, I beg of you, for all our sakes, give this

112

one a miss. Give her up. It may break your heart for a few days, maybe two or three weeks, even a month, but a few days is nothing compared to a lifetime. Your mother knows something of life. Give her up and find yourself a nice Jewish girl."

Before Henry could offer any reposte in rebuttal, the concert had resumed, but he had, at last, firmly resolved what his course of action must be.

At the intermission, instead of searching for and locating Claire, he took his mother aside. Taking her down to the entrance foyer they found a bench seat overlooking the garden outside, enchantingly bathed in pale amber light from overhead gas lamps, as twilight approached.

"Mother let's sit down. I have something I must say to you and tell you right now." As they sat down he turned towards Rebecca and taking her hand in his, he continued, "You may not have noticed, but last May I turned twenty-seven years of age. I am eternally grateful to my late father, and especially to you, for all that you've done for me, but I'm no longer a child. I'm an adult, a man, and must have a life to lead which is my own. I didn't propose to tell you this just yet, but first let me explain. I've known Claire for almost two years, a time in which we have grown very close together. I felt more than a little privileged to believe that a talented American girl such as Claire would even talk to me, a poor immigrant who along with his brothers and sisters was raised in an English orphanage because we were starving, we were so poor."

"Henry, stop that right now. Your parents might have been poor, but we've given you a priceless heritage and the best education we were able, even though you had to leave school too soon. Don't squander it and undersell yourself. We may have been downtrodden for centuries, but believe me, we're a proud people who are emerging into the light."

"Mother will you please give me a few moments without interruption to tell you something? Something which is very important to me, to you and to all of us."

"All right, I'll not say another word. Even if it breaks your old mother's heart I'll not say one word more. I'll just listen."

"Thank you mother. Claire is my wife. We were married six days ago."

"What did you say?"

"Claire is now Mrs Henry Chiswick."

"Oh my godfathers Henry. Why ever did you do this? Have you taken leave of your senses? How could you marry out and do such a thing to me, and to your family?"

"Mother we love and care for each other very deeply. I tell you quite candidly life wouldn't be worth living if I can't live with Claire as my wife."

"Henry, look at me son, is it because you've made her pregnant? Is she with child? You know things can be done to deal with these situations. This doesn't mean you have to marry the girl."

"No mother. Of course she's not pregnant; we want to be with each other because we love each other very deeply and wish to spend the rest of our lives with each other."

"Henry this is going to be difficult for you and for all of us. I'm not going to tell you that I'm not extremely vexed and upset. I'm saddened by your action and greatly disappointed, but you're my son. I'll put on the bravest face I can and do the best for you that I'm able, but thank God your late father, may he rest in peace, wasn't here to see this happen."

"Mother, once you stop being so angry and hurt you'll see what a priceless and magnificent gift I've made to you in your new daughter-in-law."

"Maybe yes, maybe no, in time we'll see: but first tell me, surely you didn't marry in a church? Henry, at least tell me it wasn't a church."

"No it wasn't in a church, we were married by a justice, in his office."

"Thank heavens for at least that one consideration for your family."

Claire had been searching for Henry and seeing him with his mother waved her hand and started to walk towards them, a warm smile illuminating her face as she approached.

"Hello Mrs Chiswick, how lovely to see you. Are you enjoying the concert?"

Ignoring the question and indicating the seat next to her she said, "Claire, I want you to sit down my dear." Then turning to Henry, "Perhaps you could fetch your mother a glass of cold water and maybe one for this beautiful young lady."

As Henry left at his mother's bidding, Rebecca turned again to Claire who had blushed at the unexpected compliment.

"I thought your playing was remarkable and you are a very gifted

114

and talented young woman, who is to be congratulated and encouraged in her studies and furthering her musical career."

"Why thank you very much Mrs Chiswick that's very kind of you."

"My son has just told me that you two were married six days ago. I won't deny I'm in a state of total shock and confusion."

"I'm sorry you should feel this way Mrs Chiswick, it's just that we love each other very much and felt there was no other approach to gain parental agreement other than to present them – you – with an accomplished fact."

Taking Claire's soft slender hands in her own, coarsened by time and work, Rebecca interrupted her and said, "Now stop. Please listen to me for a minute before Henry gets back. I want you to know right at the start that I didn't want Henry to marry you. I think you've both made a very basic and grave error. In my opinion, you've made a terrible mistake. I know you tell me you love him, well so do I love him, as a mother, and I'm entitled to my opinion. What I have to say is important. You must try to understand that this antagonism on my part hasn't been personal. As a young woman you're slim, pretty and attractive. You have all the attributes I once had when I was a smart young girl and these are the things that men most desire in a woman. In addition you're very talented. You're full of love, hope and optimism. That's natural, but believe me my dear young lady, life's a long hard unrelenting road, full of hazards at every step.

"You'll have children, you'll put on weight, and you'll get wrinkles as you grow older. Should you ever experience poverty, it weakens and impoverishes and can eat you up. I should know. I had to raise a family as a widow for many years. Poverty when you have nothing with which to feed your own little ones, real poverty, with no coal, or kindling wood for a fire to stay warm, or to heat the bits and pieces of food we were given in the streets. I had to watch my family go barefoot in the wet and cold. I saw them beg for leftovers, night after night, going to bed without supper, almost starving. I had to put all of them into the Norwood orphanage and it broke my heart. I had no choice if they weren't to starve and freeze to death. That was my poverty in London twenty years ago. We found ourselves trapped. We weren't rich, but we were always able to put a little something by, for a rainy day. We never planned to be poor. It was entirely unforeseen, and believe me it was hard, horrible and degrading.

115

"There's a terrible war in Europe at this time. Who knows how and when it will end? Unemployment, poverty and famine together with disease and social unrest often return, hand in hand, after a war. It's bad enough when no one has money. At least your family can help out and support you emotionally, even though they can't help with nickels and dimes.

"But listen, my dear. Once you cross the boundary of colour, of race or even of religion then you're throwing yourselves to the bigots who are the hyenas and wolves of this world. These animals in all their human forms, across all colours, creeds and religions, rich and poor, will band together. You'll hardly ever see them, but they'll always, always be there. They'll tear at your heartstrings, trying to rip them and you apart. They're unrelenting and will cause you nothing but misery and sorrow. I've seen it happen too many times. It's very difficult to survive like that, let alone live, or bring up children.

"You're married to my son. There's no going back. You're now my daughter-in-law. So here's what I propose you and I will do. You must be strong and together we'll build up our relationship. You must start as you mean to continue. From now onwards you must call me mother and I'll call and treat you as a daughter. You'll be to me as the biblical Moabite, Ruth, became to her mother-in-law Naomi, the great grandmother of our forebear, David, the slayer of Goliath. This, you see, won't have been the first time a Jewish son has married a Gentile daughter. It can work, although it'll be a hard struggle. Together we can, and we will, make it work.

"Henry's my youngest child and while I can't help you with money I promise, in the remaining years the good Lord gives me, I'll help you in any and every way possible."

"Mrs Chiswick. Oh I'm so sorry, I meant to say mother. Mother, I'm truly overwhelmed, I hardly know what to say."

"Claire we've lots of talking and arranging to do. Hopefully there are lots of days and years ahead, but one can never be certain how many. First I'd like to meet your dear parents. Tell me, my dear, what have your parents said about your marriage to Henry?" After a brief silence Rebecca again enquired,

"What do your parents think of their new son-in law?"

At that moment Claire and Rebecca spotted Henry approaching with two glasses of water.

"I can see and hear from your response; or rather shall I say its

116

lack, that you haven't yet summoned up the courage to tell them. Thank you for the water Henry. In your absence Claire and I have reached an understanding. We have a lot more woman-to-woman things to discuss, but now I hear from the bell we must resume our seats. Perhaps at the end of the concert you could introduce me to this talented young lady's parents. I think it's time we met, don't you agree?"

At the conclusion of the concert, the last strains of music died away followed by the rapturous applause of the audience. Slowly family and friends of the performing students filed into one of the larger classrooms where small glasses of sherry and savoury snacks had been set out on trays, on a long table in the centre of the room. Entering, Henry and Rebecca spotted Claire talking animatedly to her parents. First obtaining a drink of sweet sherry for his mother, he asked her to excuse him for a few moments and leaving Rebecca temporarily alone, strode over to Claire and her parents.

Henry extended his hand smiling to Mrs Robins.

"Ma'am, my name is Henry Chiswick and I want to congratulate you on the brilliant performance your daughter gave in the concert hall this evening."

"Why thank you very much indeed."

Turning Henry faced both Claire and her father.

"Sir, my name is Henry Chiswick. We've met before. I'm a very good friend of Claire's and I want to congratulate you and Mrs Robins on the superb performance she rendered in the concert hall. You must be a very proud father indeed."

"Well thank you Henry. We're very proud parents this evening. She played remarkably well and it's our hope that she may one day be able to explore and develop this gift. You say you're a very good friend of our daughter?"

"Certainly sir, I've had the privilege of knowing her for some considerable time and consider myself, if I might say so, a very good friend."

"I thought your face looked familiar. Haven't we met before?"

"Yes sir, on a number of occasions when Claire has given recitals at your church."

"Ah yes!" replied Mr Robins

"And could you by any chance be that same good friend who had a corsage delivered to her at this concert hall this evening?"

"Yes I am, sir."

117

"With the extraordinarily amorous message 'Good luck my darling, see you after the concert, I love you'."

"Yes sir, but that was a very private message solely for the eyes of the recipient," said Henry blushing.

"You seem to ignore the fact that Claire is only just twenty-one years of age and our daughter and we have a right to know if you have amorous intentions and what it is you may be proposing. We know nothing about you, apart from your name. We don't know what you do for a living, who your people are and which church you and they attend. You sound like a stranger in these parts, where exactly are you from?"

"Sir I should be happy to explain all these things and answer your questions, but before doing so I have an elderly lady with me, my mother, and I feel very uncomfortable to have left her alone and would like to bring her over to introduce her to you and Mrs Robins."

Without further ado and with a small bow as way of salutation to Mrs Robins and Claire, Henry walked away to escort his waiting mother into the group.

As Henry returned Claire was whispering to her father that Henry was English, born in London, and was not a music student but a very competent salesman in the tobacco trade, with a great future.

"Mr Robins, sir, Mrs Robins, Ma'am, permit me to introduce my mother, Mrs Chiswick." Hands were shaken all round and Rebecca engaged Mrs Robins in conversation. Mr Robins resumed his previous exchange, with Claire standing and listening.

"Claire tells me you're English. How long have you been in this magnificent country of ours?"

"I was born in Mile End, London, and my mother before me was born in the City of London in Aldgate. We came out here to join my sister's family in the fall of 1899, shortly after my father died."

"Well that's too bad about your father, too bad. As an Englishman, how do you feel your side is progressing against the Germans and against the Irish?"

"I find your question very strange, Mr Robins, something of a paradox if I might say so. Firstly, while I do have family in England I became a naturalised American citizen more than fifteen years ago. Naturally I care for the well-being of the English, but I'm first and foremost an American. Secondly the British are not fighting against the Irish and the Germans, just the Germans."

"Henry, I stand by what I said. The newspapers reported that English soldiers were killing and massacring Irishmen in Dublin up to two months ago. I read in the press that thousands of people had been killed. I repeat my question, how do you feel your side is progressing against the Germans and against the Irish?"

"Sir I think you're attempting to upset and provoke me. You were wrong in seeking my opinion as an Englishman, since I've been an American citizen since 1900, which is all my adult life. You're equally misinformed concerning the 'Easter Dublin uprising',[11] that I think you must be alluding to. As I understand it there were some five hundred casualties amongst British soldiers, police and civilians and fortunately only a very small proportion lost their lives. There was no massacre reported in any of the newspapers I read. I believe trouble flared when a number of armed, so-called Irish patriots decided to use guns and bullets to supplant the ballot box and take several government buildings by force."

"In my opinion a man who takes up arms to defend his country is a 'patriot', not a 'so-called patriot', as you describe him," said Mr Robins, antagonistically.

"Sir, this is mere semantics. A man who defends his country against an invader from without is certainly a patriot. But a man who has the legitimate option of using his vote in a ballot box against an opposite number who is not an invader and takes up arms instead is anything but a patriot. A better description might be to call such a man a rebel, an anarchist.

"Here, in the USA little more than fifty years ago, a number of misguided 'patriots' in the southern states attempted, in a similar manner, with guns, shells and bullets, to change the rules established by the majority, when Abe Lincoln became the Republican president in 1861. They used guns to fire on Charleston's Federal Fort Sumter to usurp the federal government and this led to the bloody confrontation that we call the American Civil War.

"In Gettysburg, not sixty miles from here, in three days of armed conflict, in 1863, fifty-one thousand of this country's finest men and youth, both from northern and southern states were senselessly cut down and killed and many thousands more maimed. That sir is my definition of a massacre. A senseless bloodbath caused by the leaders of these men, who you would define as patriots and the president Mr Abraham Lincoln quite correctly called rebels. At that time President Lincoln was your political leader and not mine, for

119

my grandparents were British subjects of Queen Victoria.

"One day the Irish will have the independence they seek and richly deserve, but their quest must be patiently and legitimately progressed through the ballot box. Legitimate law must always be upheld. It's a fact however that many a brave Irish regiment, more than 200,000 fine gallant soldiers, as I've heard, are fighting with the British army in France, attempting to push the German invaders back into Germany. Might I add that the present fighting on the battlefield and in the trenches of the Somme in France this month has seen horror and carnage that beggar's belief.

"I read that on the first day of the Battle of the Somme, there were more than twenty thousand killed and forty thousand wounded and maimed on the British side and a similar number on the German. At the end of a week of conflict these numbers had almost trebled with a gain for the allies of an advance of about one mile. Hundreds of thousands of the young men and youth of Europe marched wantonly to their nemesis, destroyed by politicians and incompetent military leaders. That sir is my definition of a massacre. Senseless criminal acts on the part of leaders who jump to guns to resolve policy, rather than diplomacy. Every one of us, man and boy of every nation, should be weeping and consoling his neighbour and not arguing about such things."

"No need to get so hot under the collar young man. What's happening in Europe is no real concern of ours in America. President Wilson says, 'Death and destruction on the scale we see in Europe is too big a price to pay for victory.' He has pledged to keep us out of this crazy European conflict and when he seeks re-election I hope you'll bear that in mind, when you and your friends cast your votes.

"Claire tells me you're in the tobacco business, in sales, and doing rather well by all accounts. How do you view your prospects?"

"That sir, isn't entirely my prerogative to say. My employer, I believe, thinks highly of my industry and skill. I used to be involved in the manufacture of cigars here in Baltimore and he had the confidence to permit me to act as his sales representative, working mainly on a small salary and commission and I might say the remuneration is now proving very rewarding indeed."

"I must say you're a presentable young fella, even though you're an Englishman. You're direct, candid and with a degree of modesty that I like in a man. How old did you say you were?"

120

"I'm twenty-seven years old sir."

"Excellent, and I suppose you would like to date our Claire."

"Yes sir. Have I your permission?"

"I don't see why not Henry, providing you realise that as a student she needs to be home early to get a good night's sleep. Do you live near here?"

"As it happens my mother and I live just at the far end of North Howard Street, just a short walk from the Peabody, but we're looking to move to a slightly larger apartment as soon as we can locate one in the same neighbourhood."

"Then I take it that in that part of town, you attend St Patrick's Catholic church."

"No sir, we don't."

"Well isn't that the parish church in your area?"

"Yes sir, I believe that may be so, but we don't attend St Patrick's."

"Well which church do you attend?"

"We don't attend a Catholic church."

"Well holy mother of God, don't tell me you attend the Emmanuel Episcopal Church on Cathedral and that you're Episcopalian."

"No. We simply don't go to church sir."

"You don't go to church! Why ever not? Don't tell me you're not a believer."

"No sir, we most certainly do believe in God."

"Thank heavens for small mercies. Then why ever don't you go to church?"

"We're of the Jewish faith and attend our synagogue."

Mr Robins' jaw slackened momentarily, his eyes stared in disbelief. The sherry glass Mrs Robins was holding slipped from her hand, crashing to the ground, shards of glass splintering everywhere, as she overheard the words Henry had just spoken.

Mr Robins' demeanour changed, as though struck by a double lightning bolt. Without further ado he grabbed his wife's arm, and called, "Claire, your mother isn't feeling very well. See how pale she looks, she feels it's too close in here and we're going outside to get some fresh air, right now, so come along my dear."

Claire simply stared, her bottom lip quivering, her eyes welling up with tears, as her parents moved rapidly, without any further explanation or farewell, towards the door. Mr Robins, noticing that Claire had not moved, turned.

121

"Claire, didn't you hear me? I said your mother isn't feeling at all well. The three of us are going out to get some fresh air, straightaway, so come along, my dear."

Rebecca took hold of Claire's hand, briefly pressing it in commiseration, murmuring, "Claire you must be brave. The hyenas I spoke about never sleep. They roam unfettered, everywhere, and for you, my biblical 'Ruth', poor girl, it's only just starting."

Claire, with a slow despairing look at Henry, followed her parents out of the room.

"Claire, wait, come back," called Henry, his voice, heavy with emotion as he watched her following after her parents in such distress.

"Let her go Henry. She has to find the inner courage whether with you or by herself to speak as an adult to her parents. Claire has to make them understand that she will always be their daughter, but she's no longer their little girl. She must show them and make them realise that she's matured into an adult, the fine woman you've chosen to make your wife. In the brief time I've spoken with her I know she'll make her point. After that it must depend on the good common sense of her parents. Which will they value more? Their daughter's continued love and affection, or will they lose it by a too stubborn adherence to religious belief and dogma that they cherish more dearly. I've made my choice and now you'll wait and see if they're found wanting. Come Henry, it's been quite an evening. It's time to escort your mother home."

Chapter 15

London December 1999

I checked my incoming emails daily, anxiously searching for any response to the email I had earlier dispatched. Later that week I received the response for which I had been waiting. The reply was from someone called Margaret. By sheer serendipity, from what I could determine at this stage, I had managed to find great uncle Henry's granddaughter. She had given me her full name and the naval academy town of Annapolis in which she lived in Maryland. In a relatively short space of time I had located her telephone number, and we were speaking on the phone.

There followed a lengthy conversation in which I first identified myself, assuring her that this was not some kind of hoax. After a further exchange I was able to convince her that we really were related. I was able to tell her what little I knew of her grandfather's English background and to clarify that I was in the process of creating a Chiswick family tree with a mutual cousin. I further explained that we had been exploring our family's roots and attempting to find out what had happened to my great grandfather's youngest brother Henry, who seemed to have disappeared in America. We were also anxiously attempting to locate one or more of the descendants of each of my great grandfather's siblings and in particular descendants of his youngest brother Henry.

She explained that her grandmother had told her that her first husband had come from London at the turn of the century and believed that he had brothers in that city, but had no further information. She believed that with her grandfather's death some seventy years ago the Chiswick family name had died out. She exclaimed that she was very pleasantly surprised to learn that this was not the case and would like to learn more about her grandfather's family.

After a time she agreed to send me through the internet a short synopsis of whatever she recalled her mother telling her about her

123

grandfather and grandmother together with a list of the names of her children and cousins with the town and year in which each were born. In return I agreed to send her a family tree of the descendants of her grandfather's brother's, who were completely unknown to her.

A few days later, the following document arrived, as Margaret had promised, through the internet.

From: Margaretwildingmd@aol.com
Sent: 12 December 1999 11:48:54
To: alfchiswick24uk@hotmail.com
Subject: Henry Chiswick

My mother was born Rebecca Chiswick in Baltimore on 24 March 1917, the first child of Henry and Claire Chiswick, and she believed that she was named after her father's mother whom she never met. She frequently spoke to me of her father, whom she idolised, and of his longing to visit his family in England. She shared a special memory of a gift of a piano that was sent to her parents as a wedding gift from her father's family in England, and which, more than any other possession, her mother treasured. She never recalled a day when her mother, a gifted pianist, did not play the piano; her favourite pieces were by J.S. Bach. Her mother also taught her and her younger sister on this same piano. Her description of my grandfather always demonstrated a great deal of pride and respect for his warmth, compassion for others and intelligence. He was a clean-shaven handsome man, of medium height, a good provider and while he was alive they lived very comfortably. Her parents were very well suited to each other and always appeared to be happy in each other's company. After his death and during the great financial depression, life became a struggle.

My grandfather's and grandmother's marriage was not accepted by either family because of their religious differences. He was Jewish and she was Roman Catholic. Their parents objected to their interfaith marriage, the single cause of much unhappiness in an otherwise happy

124

union in a home in which there was warmth, love, kindness and music.

My mother told me that her mother had explained that it was because of this rejection they never knew their grandparents, aunts, uncles and cousins. Initially she recalled occasionally seeing one of her father's sisters and one or two cousins, but they disappeared from the scene when she was very young and no contact had ever been made again. I believe the girls never met either set of grandparents. The only family they knew were their stepfather's family, the Collins.

The girls were not raised to worship under any specific faith, but believed in God and in his love and goodness. They both grew up with a great deal of knowledge and respect for both the Jewish and Christian faiths. Both my mother and Aunt Henrietta were very mild mannered and gentle women. They were small, graceful and very pretty. While my mother seemed to maintain her reserve, Henrietta was quick with a smile and a hello. I've been told that they both strongly resembled their father and Henrietta's personality most closely resembled that of her father.

Although I was born many years after he passed away, I always felt I knew him through my mother. My grandfather passed away when my mother was about twelve years old. I believe my mother identified the illness he experienced as a brain fever. I think it may have been encephalitis.

My mother often told me that her mother had been so deeply in love with her father that she was not able to look at another man for some years after his death. She felt that her mother had married her stepfather to provide security and comfort, more for her children than herself. Her stepfather had three children and once he arrived on the scene they were able to enjoy and live a more comfortable life again.

My mother Rebecca died in 1996, while my grandmother Claire died in 1960. My mother married twice. In her first marriage, which ended with the death of her husband in 1950, she had two children. She married again the following year and had two further children, and I am the

125

eldest in this second marriage, and have four children, a son, my eldest and three younger daughters.

My mother's younger sister Henrietta moved to New Jersey after her marriage. She and her husband had three children, a son and two daughters. She has passed away, although I am uncertain when, since we lost touch with this part of our family after Grandma Claire passed away.

Chapter 16

Baltimore July 1916

Leaving the Peabody Institute, Claire reluctantly and tearfully followed her parents, with Henry's call, "Claire, wait, come back," reverberating in her head. She hurried through the pleasant warm evening air, just behind her parents, who were angrily talking to each other. She chided herself for not defying her parents. A lifetime of cultured obedience to parental authority was not to be reversed so readily. She felt she should have stood her ground, next to her husband. She wondered why Henry had not held her back to make a stand in defiance of her controlling parents. At least Henry had had the courage to tell his mother and she had disgracefully simply capitulated. However talented, she still lacked the courage at this stage of her development and maturity to oppose the will of her elders. Now it was her turn to show her metal, to prove herself worthy of being Henry's wife.

As they stood on the doorstep of their home waiting for the butler to admit them, Mrs Robins turned to Claire, all thoughts of her daughter's talented performance relegated by the post-concert revelation of her Jewish friend.

"When we get inside, your father and I want to have a few words with you, my fine young lady. In the sitting room right now, if you please."

Entering the house, Claire rushed up the staircase in tears, her mother calling after her.

"Claire! Claire, come down this instant. I said we wanted to speak to you in the sitting room young lady. Come down this minute!"

Unheeding, she sped into her bedroom, slamming the door and throwing herself in impotent anguish on her bed.

A few minutes later, there was a knock on her door. Receiving no reply there was a further knock.

"May I come in?" enquired her father.

"No, I'm resting."

"Resting or not, I'm coming in. We're going to have to talk."

Opening the door Claire's father entered the bedroom to find his daughter's face tear streaked and puffy, angrily looking at him resentfully from her bed where she lay fully clothed. Realising that this youngest of his offspring was suffering from some sort of stress following her performance he advanced into her bedroom, pulled up a chair and sat next to the edge of her bed.

"Claire my darling we really must have a talk."

Claire belligerently stared fixedly ahead.

"I can see you're upset about something, but it was most discourteous of you to ignore your mother when she called you."

"Father you humiliated me in front of all my friends," said Claire, having learnt that the best form of defence was to immediately go on the attack. "That was unforgivable and you embarrassed me."

"Claire, you've been less than frank and honest with your mother and me. It was bad enough to think that you had befriended an Englishman, especially when eighteen months ago your mother had specifically told you that we were unhappy with that friendship. Now to suddenly discover that he's a Jew came as a bombshell. It was all too much."

"What if he is English, what if he is a Jew? He's a fine, sensitive and honourable man."

"That's not what we're discussing. It's well known that these Jews have always been devious schemers. There are many millions of fine American, Catholic, young men out there for you to date and befriend, any one of whom would be more acceptable to us."

"Father that's not the point. Henry is my friend. Why can't you accept my judgement in such matters?"

"Claire you may not have looked at yourself as closely in the looking glass as others see you, but you've become a very beautiful and eligible young woman. You're of an age that very soon, some young impressionable fellow will sweep you off your feet and come grovelling at my door to ask for my permission to marry you. Perhaps your mother and I have made a cardinal mistake in allowing you to continue with your studies instead of finding you a suitable partner and marrying you off as we did with your sisters when they were sixteen and seventeen."

"Father, I love you very dearly and I want to please you and mother, but I want to choose my own friends."

128

"I'm trying to explain to you that you're no longer a child. At your age any young man who you befriend is likely to become a suitor. It's imperative therefore that you mix with and meet the right sort of eligible bachelor."

"Precisely what sort of young man is your idea of an eligible suitor for me?"

"Our preference would be somebody whose family we know and who could provide you with a home and keep you in the style to which you're accustomed."

"Father I don't want someone to keep me as part of his home or cocooned in his household. Times have changed. As you said I'm no longer a child. I want to choose my own friends and my own husband. I want someone who'll treat me as an equal partner and not as part of his goods and chattels to demurely sit home as some kind of brood mare to raise a host of children."

"Claire, you're tired and overwrought. Don't make me regret having given you an education."

"Father, I want you to tell me precisely what it is that you find so objectionable in Henry."

"To begin with he's a Jew. They're all tarred with the same brush, all wanderers, either usurers, peddlers, shopkeepers or tailors, dispersed by God over the face of the earth as his punishment for their crucifying his only son. That's an end to the matter. There's nothing more to discuss."

"What if he weren't a Jew? What if he were to convert to become a Catholic. Would that then make him more acceptable?"

"Possibly yes, but I'd have to give that some thought, maybe even discuss this with my friend Bishop O'Connor. On the other hand why should this young man wish to convert and take the holy sacrament simply to be your friend? It would only make sense if he had some ulterior motive. That would be typical of the scheming Jew we've all been warned about in church."

"Father were he a convert to Catholicism, would he be acceptable to you as my friend?"

"Most probably yes."

"So you're saying his only impediment, purely and simply, is that he was born a Jew?"

"Claire, are you thinking of this young man in any romantic sense?"

"Father, I choose not to answer that question."

"I see. I wasn't born yesterday my fine young lady. Now I understand the situation. I sense you imagine yourself to be in love with this young man. Well if that's the case I forbid you to have any more contact with him until I've discussed this possible conversion of your friend with Cardinal O'Connor. As I've said, even if he were to convert I'm not certain that he would be the kind of suitable husband for you that your mother and I would envisage. After all there would still be the problem that he's English and of course there would be his family, none of whom would we find in the least acceptable."

"I'm tired father and I need to undress, wash and get some sleep."

"Goodnight Claire. Remember what I've said. I want no blasphemer as your friend, or a possible son-in-law. I forbid you to see him until we can determine whether he can be converted and admitted into our true Catholic faith."

With that he bent forward, kissed Claire on the forehead and turned and left the room as she responded,

"Good night father."

Mr Robins descended the stairs, where his wife, who had been waiting anxiously to learn of his talk with their daughter.

"What did she have to say for herself Charles?"

"My dear, I think we'd better discuss this in the privacy of my study."

Mr Robins led the way followed by his wife. Once seated within the confines of the study with the door closed, Mrs Robins reiterated. "Now Charles, what did she have to say for herself?"

Mr Robins related to his wife the discussion he had just had with Claire, concluding with, "Bridget, I fear that we may have a problem on our hands. She's known this man for well over eighteen months, as far as I can tell, and I think she sees him as more than a casual friend. I think she may even believe that she's in love with him or some such romantic nonsense. Infatuation is possibly all it is, but we must be on our guard."

"Charles, did she say she was in love with this man?"

"Not in so many words, but reading between the lines that's a possibility."

"Charles, I know precisely when I met him. It was at a carol concert the first week in December the year before last. We returned here and I spoke to Claire, the little minx, about him and

130

she said at the time she'd known him for three months and she'd invited him to the concert because he'd never heard her sing or play the organ."

"That being the case it seems they've known each other at least twenty months. She asked if I would have any objections to her befriending this man and I explained that I had many objections, first and foremost because of his Jewish religion. I then agreed that if he were to convert I might see this friendship in a more acceptable light."

"What do you propose we do about this Charles?"

"Bridget, I gave her no firm undertaking that we would find him acceptable even should he convert. I did however tell her that I'd discuss the matter with Bishop O'Connor as soon as I could and I expressly forbade her to meet with this fellow again until I gave my express permission."

"I think that in addition to your speaking to the bishop, we should arm ourselves with another bow. I'll make it my business to speak with some of our friends and see what can be done to have a few eligible young men pay her a little more attention. Do you think we should consider sending her away anywhere for a few weeks to avoid any possibility of her disobeying your instruction?"

"No, I hardly think that will be necessary. She has her coursework at the Peabody and she's always shown herself to be a diligent and obedient daughter. Providing she sees that we're genuinely consulting with Bishop O'Connor and that we're not placing a permanent ban on her friendship, pending those discussions, then I think we may be able to keep this thing under control. Remember she's been forbidden to have any further contact with this young man until I've discussed the possibility of his conversion with the ecclesiastical authorities."

The following morning before leaving the house Claire's father called her into his study where he spoke to her. He reiterated that he would not hear a further word about her friendship with Henry pending the outcome of his discussion with Bishop O'Connor. She was forbidden under the direst of penalties to ever see or communicate with the young man again, until such time as discussions had been progressed to determine how he might proceed upon the path of conversion. She was also warned that were he to convert they *might* consider lifting the ban. This was not to be construed as any guarantee that he would then be acceptable to them as a future marriage partner for her.

In spite of these warnings, Claire continued to deceive her parents. She constantly saw Henry and frequently visited Rebecca in whom she found an amazing ally and friend. Claire and Henry decided to keep to their timetable of revealing the truth to Claire's parents at Thanksgiving, although there seemed little to be gained in postponing the confrontation that was bound to take place.

True to his word Mr Robins made an appointment to visit the bishop. An interview was arranged for eight in the morning, two weeks later. On the appointed day Mr Robins announced to Claire that he was leaving to keep an appointment that very morning with the bishop. He walked the short distance from his home to the bishop's house, which was the diocesan office situated immediately adjacent to the Basilica of the Assumption of the Blessed Virgin Mary.

Although he had met the Bishop on a number of occasions and referred to him as a friend, he had never previously been into the renaissance-style building. He was ushered into a suite by an elderly lady in nun's habit who escorted him in. The large central desk before a wide partly open window in a very spacious room duly impressed him. The window, partially framed with draped deep red velvet curtains on either side, allowed the bright golden rays of the early morning sunlight, reflected from the trillions of otherwise invisible minute floating dust and pollen particles, to slant in at an acute angle, streaming in from the quiet of the cloistered garden outside.

Bishop O'Connor was seated in a high-backed maroon velour upholstered chair, writing at his desk as his visitor entered. The bishop slowly set down his pen, carefully blotted his writing, and rose in greeting, holding out his arm for the supplicant to kiss the ring on his extended hand. Following the normal formalities of greetings and compliments Bishop O'Connor indicated that his guest might be seated on one of the pair of finely carved chairs facing the writing table and enquired how he might be of assistance.

"Your grace I must compliment you on the tranquillity and beauty of your office. Totally unlike mine at Bethlehem Steel."

"Perhaps Mr Robins were you to install a cloister outside your window rather than a steel rolling mill you might achieve some similar calmness."

They both laughed as Mr Robins replied, "I doubt very much

132

that our shareholders would permit us to do that. We're working at full capacity, producing more and more steel than ever before, mainly for the allied ship-building war effort. Production's at an all time high and we're all simply working flat out, round the clock. I should imagine that there would be a horrendous outcry, greater than the noise from ten rolling mills, from England and from Prime Minister Asquith and his Welsh magician of a munitions minister Mr Lloyd George should we cease production, even for a day."

"Yes this European carnage is dreadful and there appears to be no end in sight to the conflict."

"I mentioned that we're working at full capacity and endeavouring to increase our production of steel. At the rate the allies are sustaining their shipping losses, we will never be able to replace the tonnage sunk."

"Is that really so?"

"Your grace may be aware that there was a clash between the British Royal Navy Grand Fleet and the Imperial German High Seas Fleet in the North Sea just two months ago between the coasts of Norway and Denmark at what is now being described as the Battle of Jutland'.[12] It's said that the battle was inconclusive. The British were stated to have lost one battleship, one cruiser, five destroyers and reported seven thousand men drowned. The Germans lost less than half that number together with three capital ships, not to mention damage on both sides to other fighting ships and injuries to men. One can but imagine the quantities of steel needed to build more warships and to replace sunken merchant ships."

"On the face of the tally you've given, one would hardly consider such a dreadful battle inconclusive. What a horrendous loss of young lives, ten thousand of God's children slain and drowned and scores more bereaved families left to mourn. Surely this was a decisive victory for the devil, in addition to a German maritime victory?"

"Your grace, one might believe so from the figures, but the naval outcome was rather different. With my Irish descent, I candidly admit that I've little love for the British. One must however give credit where credit is due. The British are known as bulldogs for their tenacity to fight when involved in battle. Nowhere more is this so than in their naval heritage and tradition. Any and every opponent knows historically that should they tackle the Royal Navy at sea, it's always a fight to the finish, no matter what the odds.

"These British warships do not capitulate. Surrender is absolutely not in their naval vocabulary. The Germans are aware that unless these British ships are blown out of the water, they carry on fighting even beyond the last shell. When out of ammunition their British opponent is as like to resort to ramming rather than surrender. The German fleet slunk back to the safety of their harbour in Wilhelm-shaven under a blanket of fog and poor visibility at night, leaving the North Sea and the oceans to Davy Jones and the Royal Navy. That's hardly the action of a victor. The victors lost more ships and men, but their action and fortitude in 'the field of battle', so to speak, was completely decisive. The losers retreated away to be holed up in their port. Only the German submarines dare to sneak out, hidden and submerged beneath the waves. I doubt very much that we will see the German fleet daring to venture out again to defy the Royal Navy. I hate to admit this as an Irish American, but all credit to the daring and tenacity of those British sailors. In a naval battle I'd rather have them with me than against me, no matter what the odds."

"My son, thank you for your assessment of the naval situation as you perceive it. May God in heaven and in his infinite wisdom, have mercy on the souls of all those young sailors and comfort their sorrowing families.

"Before we go further you mentioned that you enjoyed the tranquillity and beauty of this office. Very few are aware of its existence outside the Holy See. You of course know that Baltimore also has one of the world's finest conservatories of music. I've heard that your daughter's a very promising Peabody conservatory student, who's played the organ with great charm and accomplishment in many of our churches. I've yet to hear her perform, but I'm reliably informed that a major delight lies in store when that time comes."

"It's very generous of you to say that your grace."

"Did you know Mr Robins, that Baltimore has a number of other significant firsts and bests? In the field of medical excellence there is the Johns Hopkins Hospital. Were you aware that surgical gloves were first introduced more than a decade ago at that very hospital and that the world's foremost physician William Osler, now knighted and living in England, was its chief of staff until quite

134

recently? We also have the Maryland University Hospital, the first medical faculty to be established in the USA. In men of letters there was Edgar Allen Poe and now we have Mr H.L. Mencken. In this very building in which you are seated, designed by Benjamin Latrobe in the Renaissance revival style of architecture, completed in 1821 after twenty years construction, you have the very first Roman Catholic cathedral constructed in the USA. I could go on, but I digress. Time is speeding by and we both have very busy schedules. I'm certain that you've visited me for more pressing personal matters than to have me give you an account of the excellent facilities available in our city. How may I help you?"

As briefly as he felt able Mr Robins explained the situation. His youngest daughter Claire had been associating with and had seemingly formed an attachment to an English naturalised American Jewish male whom she had known for more than a year and a half. Once he had completed his summary of his perceived problem, the bishop pondered for a few moments and then spoke.

"My son, I do not feel that this presents any insoluble problem. You're fortunate in having an intelligent obedient daughter who is prepared to listen to and be advised by her parents. I must admit that with our swiftly changing environment such rectitude is rapidly declining. Should there be any US involvement in this European conflict, in spite of all that our politicians say to the contrary, then we may well see a further slide in moral standards.

"We all have an inviolable duty to save every individual's soul from purgatory and damnation by encouraging that person to make a genuine conversion to our true faith. I need to emphasise that in the case of a mature adult we need to be convinced that this is a sincere and proper desire, and not simply an expedient for some ulterior motive or gain.

"God wishes to be adored by all people, and while we as his ministers agree with this principle, we are in no doubt that there is only one path to his eternal truth and salvation. This is through our Lord Jesus Christ, and his one true holy Catholic Church."

"Your grace, could you give me any indication how we might proceed in this matter?"

"My son all that needs happen is that you contact your own parish priest. He will then give you an appointment to interview the individual seeking conversion. A timetable of instruction will then be arranged, usually requiring, under normal circumstances, some nine months to a year of tuition and study. Following the successful completion of the course, baptism will be arranged, the Holy Sacrament can be taken at communion, and confession can be undertaken. A baptismal certificate will then be presented to the supplicant, and the individual will then enjoy all the rights of belonging to the mother church together with the usual incumbent responsibilities. Such an applicant can then be married and buried under the Church's auspices."

"Your grace has been most helpful. It now remains to determine whether or not the supplicant is genuine and to proceed accordingly."

Taking his leave, Mr Robins later that evening saw his daughter and confirmed all that had been discussed with the bishop.

"Claire you may see your friend on one single occasion, and solely to acquaint him with what I've discussed with Bishop O'Connor. Should he wish to proceed further you can advise him to seek a parish priest of his choosing. You may then only see him again once he has renounced his Jewish faith and become a true believer. I'll require you to let me know when you see him, and his response to the advice to convert. Do you understand, and agree to what I've said?"

"Yes father, but I fail to understand why I can't see him until he has finished a conversion course which will take nine months, or more."

"Claire those are my conditions, and they're not negotiable. Should you not agree then I might need to consider sending you off somewhere, far away from the influence of this man."

Claire agreed, and told her father that she would be able to see Henry within the week.

Henry had rented and moved into the larger apartment that he had promised his mother some weeks before the embarrassing episode at the concert and now lived on the third floor at 825 North Howard Street, less than half a mile from Claire's home. Rebecca wanted to move out of the apartment to live with her daughter Annie and her husband and children in order to give Henry the opportunity to set up home with his wife, but Henry would simply not hear of it. He explained that until Claire had her parents' approval they would not be living together as husband and wife. He and Claire wanted Rebecca to continue living with them. Rebecca must understand that she should consider their home as her home, as long as she desired.

When Claire next met Henry, the following afternoon, as she customarily did each day beneath the monument in Mount Vernon Square, she again tackled him on the subject of conversion as they sat holding hands and talking.

She told him of her father's recent conversation with the bishop and the agreement that her father would lift the ban on her seeing him once he'd converted. Henry pointed out that were he to agree, there was the prohibition that they should not meet for upwards of nine months or more, which was totally unacceptable. Furthermore, there would be no guarantee that her father would accept his proposal of marriage to his daughter, and last, and most importantly, he felt that it would be dishonourable of him to embark upon a course that his conscience told him was wrong, and morally unacceptable to him.

"My darling I must be as honest and candid with you as it's possible to be. For some considerable time I've had great reservations and doubts concerning the very existence of God and I must now tell you that I no longer believe in a deity. I completely renounce and reject any concept of a God. I think you might consider me to be a Jewish atheist. I believe in my Jewish traditions, which are marvellous, and priceless, but without believing in God. In the past four weeks I've been following news reports of the Battle of the Somme raging in France. I have English cousins and former childhood chums fighting and dying there with the British Expeditionary Force. It's reported that more than twelve per cent of the male population of France, Germany and Austria capable of bearing arms have been killed in the war so far. Both Axis and Allied armies have chaplains and pray to the same God. I tell you candidly this God is a sham. A horrendous myth devised by my early ancestors.

"If there is a God tell me Claire, or better still, tell the mothers, tell the wives and widows, tell the grieving children and orphans of the slain and maimed, tell the heartbroken, tell them how a God could permit this awful pain, this suffering, this butchery."

"Henry, darling, I can see how terribly upset you are, and you've every right to be so, but I can't explain the majesty and infinite wisdom and working of God's mind."

"Claire these are just meaningless platitudes that I've heard before and you continue to hear from your priest and that you

137

repeat. There's simply no God and this has clearly demonstrated the truth to me. Give me Mr Charles Darwin's theory of evolution and the facts of scientists. I can better believe in these theories than the trickery of a God who would permit pain and suffering on the scale and magnitude being witnessed daily in France and Europe. When I hear you play Bach or Mozart I can fleetingly believe that herein lies the majesty of a God who touched the minds of these great composers and your hands to interpret their works. But to kill the children of a whole generation and say there's a God of love or compassion, this is calumny."

"Henry, I know you're angry and distressed, my darling. Each report of this horrible war upsets every one of us, but I need to convey a response to my father. What would you have me tell him?"

"Please Claire, tell your father that I simply can't accept conversion under the terms he stipulates. Tell him that I no longer believe in a God; therefore how less likely would it be that I could believe in the Son of God and a Holy Spirit. You my darling can believe as you wish, but the Somme and the trenches of France have been my epiphany and will continue to be so, every hour of every day, until this inhumane conflagration is at an end."

"My darling are you saying that you're now an agnostic and you aren't certain in your belief in God?"

"Not at all. There's no uncertainty Claire. I now recognise that I'm an atheist. I realise that we've all been conditioned. If you feed people a constant diet of potatoes once they're weaned in infancy, then is it any wonder that they would seem to prefer to eat potatoes as adults. And if we're fed a constant diet of a belief in God, from infancy, then small wonder we all believe in God when we've reached an age of reason and maturity. That is until a few of us start to awaken to the reality that we've been trained to believe in an illusion, no more real than Santa Claus, the tooth fairy or elves and goblins.

"I believe in the fine precepts and traditions of Judaism and whatever is good and honourable that any religion may teach, but I can no longer believe in a God or any form of deity that our primitive forebears devised. Their ideas were archaic at best and have no place in a modern secular society. Religious dogma of every kind, from the most primitive idol worship onwards, has possibly produced more untold human misery, suffering and death in the name and sanctity of some God than any other series of calamities.

138

And worse still, there seems little likelihood that it will abate in the years to come."

"Henry I believe in God, no matter what you say and when this dreadful killing stops, as one day it must, I'm certain you'll again accept the reality of the divine presence of God. Meanwhile, darling, please help me. What am I to tell father?"

"Tell your father I would like to call to see him to explain my position and discuss this further. Would you suggest to him that I would like to do so next Sunday, after lunch or at any other convenient time of his choosing."

"Henry if you refuse this olive branch my father is extending and don't convert, it shows how little you really love me, or care for me." With that Claire's eyes brimmed with tears as she started to gently cry.

"Claire my darling, please don't cry. No man has ever loved a woman more dearly than I love you. You must never doubt my undying love, nor must you forget that you've married me among other things because you said you saw and admired something of my true moral worth and integrity. It's for these very reasons we've avoided telling your parents of our love and our marriage and colluded to pursue this charade in order not to upset their religious sensibilities that we might more gradually gain their approval. My devotion is not just unabating, it grows stronger every day and that's why we'll continue to attempt to appease your parents in the hope that they'll come round to accept our marriage.

"My preference would be that you move in with me today and we live openly as man and wife rather than continue with this deception. Your father's olive branch is not what it seems. Let him agree to our marriage, immediately after I've converted, and permit us to meet when we wish during the months of religious education. I might then swallow my principles, or pride, call it whatever you wish, and abandon all for you my darling. I'll go through the motions and charade of conversion and belief in a deity in which I no longer believe. But what he's offering is little more than a baited trap and it's not worth my consideration. I'll continue with our pretence as long as we initially set out, but I think we're deluding ourselves."

Claire dabbed her eyes dry and bravely smiled. Being in a public space, they lightly kissed cheeks and hugged before parting, in order that Claire might rush home to speak that evening to her father.

Claire conveyed Henry's message almost in its entirety to her father and said that he would be calling to have a frank discussion with him the next Sunday shortly after lunch. Her father said that the imposition on any further meeting with Henry stood and that out of courtesy he would see her friend for a few minutes and no more, when he called.

On the following Sunday afternoon, Henry called at the Robins home to speak to Mr Robins, bearing a small bunch of flowers to present to Claire's mother. He rang the newly-installed doorbell and within seconds the butler opened the dark mahogany front door. He requested him to wait on the doorstep and closed the door. Feeling like a tradesman, his usual greeting at this house, he waited in the heat and humidity of the early afternoon, thinking to himself that at least he hadn't been requested to go round to the tradesmens' entrance. Half a minute later the door reopened and there stood Mr Robins.

Before Henry had any opportunity to offer any salutation or to say good afternoon, Mr Robins unceremoniously and without greeting scornfully announced.

"Mr Chiswick, my daughter told me that she believed you might wish to renounce your religion and become a Catholic to follow our true faith. She now tells me that you've little or no intention of doing so unless I guarantee that you may marry her once you've converted and you wish to speak to me on the matter."

"That sir is in part my position. I thought that we could come to some understanding whereby should I agree to the conversion you wish me to proceed with..."

Mr Robins interrupted him, silencing him in mid-sentence.

"Henry, your conversion is too serious to be a subject for bargaining or debate. Had you accepted the opportunity to convert to Catholicism, I would have then given serious consideration to the matter of your seeing my daughter again. Even then I could certainly not at this juncture give any guarantee of consent for your marriage. Meanwhile, as I understand it you are unwilling to convert without certain guarantees, which in all candour I'm unwilling to give. Since you will not convert I shall reiterate that I will tolerate no Hebrew in this home and I do not want my daughter to see you ever again.

"If you dare call again, I'll have the hunting hounds set on you. Furthermore, I've expressly forbidden Claire to associate with you

140

and if I thought for one moment that she was disobeying my instructions by seeing you, I'd throw her out of the house, and disown her, without a nickel. Good day to you sir and now be gone!"

With that, Mr Robins drew back within the house and with calculated intimidating hostility the door was slammed in Henry's face, leaving him standing there. Henry, holding his bouquet of flowers, wilting in Baltimore's hot, humid afternoon sun, stood momentarily in ignominious silence, not knowing what to do. He then turned slowly away, bowed and humiliated. He once more descended the white steps, his prepared words of conciliation and hopes for his future in the eyes of Claire's parents as her husband unspoken.

Within the house, Claire had been listening at the head of the stairs and had been able to clearly hear Henry's attempted words of appeasement and her father's angry, intemperate response. As the door slammed she rushed back to her room, closing the door and throwing herself on her bed where she wept in anguish and frustrated childlike despair.

Chapter 17

Baltimore Summer 1916

Throughout the summer, Claire, unknown to her parents, visited Rebecca. In much the same way in which Henry had initially grown to love and admire Claire through talking and their mutual love of music and literature, so both Claire and Rebecca slowly bonded much as in biblical times had happened between Naomi and Ruth, as Rebecca had hoped and intended. There was one significant difference. Claire felt her visits to Rebecca were almost akin to a supplicant visiting the Oracle at Delphi, such was the depth of Rebecca's knowledge and experience.

Whenever Claire visited, Rebecca would demonstrate how to cook certain traditional Jewish foods and delicacies, including chicken soup with lokshen and kneidle, in addition to the usual run of the mill fare that any English or American housewife might prepare. This was quite a revelation to Claire since she had always been shooed out of the kitchen by the cook and had no idea how to make a cup of coffee or even boil an egg. They talked about the one man whose love and affection they shared, helping each other, cooperating as a mother-in-law and daughter-in-law seldom do.

"Claire, I want to show you today how to make one of Henry's favourite desserts. You need to make a few notes recording the ingredients or you'll find yourself in a frightful muddle," said Rebecca one day. "It's called a sour cream cake. It looks delicious, tastes delicious and it's child's play to make providing you put in the correct quantities and never let on how easy it is to make. I have a seven-inch tin or loose-bottomed pan and I need an oven temperature of 350 degrees. Now these are the ingredients that I've set out on the table. Take one packet of Graham crackers, two ounces of melted butter and half a level teaspoon of cinnamon. Crush and mix the crackers with the butter and cinnamon and put this in the bottom of your tin to make a base. Mix four cartons of sour cream with one cup of sugar and one large tin of a fruit cocktail. Pour this into the tin over the base. Cook for twenty minutes."

Claire now broached the subject of the possibility that if she were to persuade Henry to agree to convert, her parents might not oppose their marriage.

"I think that it's a little late in the day to seek this as an option. You can speak to him again should you wish, I can't stop you, but I know that he would consider such a thing as a betrayal and I would most certainly support him in his attitude."

"But it would help make so many things that much easier."

"Claire, in the few weeks I've known you as my daughter, I've grown very fond of you. I've come to understand the fine qualities my son discovered in you that convinced him that you should be his wife. I'm going to try, if you have the patience to listen to me for a few minutes, to explain to you our opposition in general as Jews and my own position regarding this matter.

"I know what you want to talk about is important and we'll talk about it in a few minutes while we fix our cake. Remember Napoleon said 'An army marches on its stomach' and he might have just as easily have said 'What's on the dinner table can help make or break a marriage'. Perhaps that was the problem with his marriage to Josephine! First we'll mix this cake and pop it in the oven so that while we're talking it will be cooking. It should then be finished by the time we've talked about this proposed idea of conversion."

Within five minutes Claire had properly mixed all the ingredients and placed them on top of the crushed cracker base in the tin, which in turn was placed in the hot oven.

"Claire, we must time this for twenty minutes and we can talk as we wait. Now let me see, where were we?"

"You said you were going to explain the situation as to why you wouldn't encourage Henry to convert to my religion."

"Ah yes. Now we all believe in our one creator, Almighty God, no matter what name we give him. Our patriarch Abraham first described the one God on which the three great monotheistic religions are all based. First Judaism, established some four thousand years ago, from which Christianity evolved some two thousand years later and the Islamic faith some fifteen hundred years ago. Think of these religions as each of God's children representing three siblings, or brothers. Judaism, the eldest; Islam the youngest and Christianity the middle child. Are you following my line of thought Claire?"

143

"Yes, it's a very simple and logical concept. We're all God's children."

"That's correct. As with every family, the children are constantly vying and striving for parental attention and love, which we call sibling rivalry. It happens constantly. We have examples in the Bible of this competitiveness leading to horrendous injustices and even terrible crimes. Jacob commits larceny. He steals his older twin, Esau's birthright, from their father, the patriarch Isaac. Joseph's brothers are jealous of the coloured coat his father Jacob gives him and as an alternative to murder sell him into slavery. Worse still fratricide, where Adam's son Caine murders his brother Abel in a jealous rage. There's constant rivalry for the love and attention of the parent in every family.

"Jesus, his parents and brothers, his disciples and, during the first fifty years following his crucifixion, the earliest Christians were all Jews, with almost no exception. As Christianity started to evolve, these followers began to distance themselves from their ancient Hebrew origins. They claim that Jesus, their deceased leader, wasn't comparable to the prophets of the Bible or even a messiah, but even more important. They claimed him as the actual Son of God. They had gone one better, showing they were not merely different, but newer and better, with a New Testament. The mainstream Hebrews completely rejected these concepts.

"There can be no denial that Jesus was cruelly tortured and barbarously crucified by the Romans as were countless other patriots and zealots. To make their newer religion more acceptable to the ruling Roman conquerors, certain untruths were propounded. The worst of them was that the Jews and not the Romans killed Jesus of Nazareth, their inspirational leader. The Romans did the torturing and crucifying, but the Jews made them do it against their better judgement. This made the Jews guilty of 'Deicide' and not the Romans. The most dreadful crime imaginable, killing God's son for which not only were the perpetrators to be punished, but the whole race to which they belonged were to be eternally damned.

"The Jews telling the Romans to kill Jesus is like President Wilson telegraphing the kaiser from the White House tomorrow, with Pope Benedict XV writing to him from the Vatican in Rome telling him to stop the dreadful slaughter in Europe, to leave Belgium and France immediately and go home. He would ignore the request. It

144

just doesn't make sense. And for all those poor young men in uniform, more's the pity, it won't happen. Such untruths hardly mattered and harmed no one at the time, while the early Christians were an inconsequential minority. They were just a tiny fringe group, whose members, more often than not, were fed to the lions in Rome for public entertainment as they endeavoured to separate themselves from their Hebrew origins. Gradually and imperceptibly times and attitudes changed.

"Once the Roman Emperor Constantine adopted Christianity in the early fourth century and made Christianity the formal religion of the Roman Empire, the younger sibling rival was in the ascendancy. In early medieval times when the Christian Church had to contend with the third and youngest sibling, the Muslim faith, matters took a truly nasty turn for the worse. Islam had exploded out of Arabia into North Africa, Spain and the Middle East, conquering Jerusalem and in its turn seriously challenging its older Christian brother. Successive popes struck back with a series of military campaigns with the era of the crusades, against the youngest Muslim brother.

"Neither the Catholic Church nor the Muslims wanted to kill their eldest sibling's adherents. They simply wanted to usurp that brother's place as the preferred favoured religion in God's eyes. The way each chose to do this was the same. Convert all those adherents by persuasion, force or any means short of killing them then you have eliminated one of the contenders for God's favours, in this case the Jews, the eldest brother. And Claire, if you doubt what I'm telling you, remember the sibling rivalries in the Bible.

"There have always been the fringe fundamentalists and extremists who killed, or propagated calumny and lies that encouraged terrible violence towards Jews, but the vast majority were content to let matters rest, once the Jew converted.

"Inexorably, you will see the youngest Moslem brother will keep pushing the older brothers, in particular the more dominant Christian brother, until he in turn will become the dominant family member. In time he will strive to usurp the dominance of his older brothers. Of course the older siblings will push back endeavouring and probably failing in the attempt to stop this happening. It will take hundreds of years and however terrible this prediction, there will be no avoiding this constant rivalry with the resulting bloodshed and unhappiness that will ensue.

145

"To give you a simple illustration take the early middle ages. The Catholic Christian brother really made it tough for the Hebrew elder sibling in many, many, ways. Papal edicts encouraged the expulsion of Jews from England in 1290, from Spain in 1492 from Portugal the following year, and from France in 1350. Clear them out. Make their lives intolerably difficult. Tell them 'You can only stay if you convert.' Many abhorrent regulations governing the manner in which Jews were permitted to live were introduced. A Papal Bull of 1555 confined Jews into walled enclosures called 'Ghettos' and prohibited all occupations other than the sale and repair of second hand clothes and lending money. Jews were forced to wear items of apparel to identify them as Jews, such as a dunce's hat to humiliate them, and were prohibited from owning land, attending any centre of higher education or joining guilds. At times there were even restrictions on the numbers that could be married in any one year.

"The official papal order of the day was to denigrate, to dehumanise, to offend, to belittle. In fact anything that would hurt, short of killing. Then offer these suffering people, these Jews, the simple option of redemption. Convert to the Catholic faith, the true faith, in order to put an end to all the suffering and misery. The Moslems similarly treated their Jewish minorities with disdainful tolerance as third class interlopers. Stay a Jew and suffer. Convert, become one of us and all your problems are ended.

"Some, and who can blame them, took the easy option and converted. Many of our ancestors didn't. Unfortunately in every age in every society there have been those extremists who have mistakenly taken the law into their own hands. While Church and mosque condemned killing Jews, many hotheads considered it a duty to pillage, rape and kill those who would not convert, causing untold suffering and loss of innocent life to tens of thousands of Jews in every generation throughout the world. It continues to this very day.

"The unspeakable horrors your ancestors experienced in famine, death and displacement from their homes in Ireland seventy years ago, sadly and terribly, was little more than the Jewish people have suffered century by century for the past two thousand years.

"We don't hate our younger Christian and Muslim siblings for past indignities. We simply want them to stop bullying us now, as well as each other, that we might live as siblings, all equally

146

exquisite and loved in the eyes of God. We want to be left in peace, to enjoy our lives and to be allowed to make a fuller contribution to the rich tapestry of life we all share.

"Claire, when you ask Henry to convert, he'll tell you that we're all the children of the same God. We may have different features and names, many may have other skin colours, but we follow parallel paths towards God's grace and glory. I'm certain that Henry wouldn't make it a precondition that you follow his Jewish belief; therefore it's equally wrong that you should press him to change just for the sake of appeasing your parents. My advice to you is not to push him. I'm certain he will not do it. You should encourage him to adhere to his faith and not change on the whim of your parents. Forcing anyone to agree under duress is reprehensible."

"Mother, I've listened and I think, for the very first time, I really understand your position. I find it incredibly simple when you explain it this way.

"Thank you. I hope I've been of some help. You must realise that I've attempted to explain my position, in less time than it takes to bake our sour cream cake."

"What ever am I to do?"

"Claire you're an intelligent and exceptionally talented young woman. Nobody forced you to choose to be Henry's wife. You made that difficult decision and now three months later I tell you candidly my dear that I'm pleased you made that choice. Now you must have the courage and conviction my dear to think for yourself and fight for what you want and consider is right.

"As patiently and kindly as you know how, you need to confront your parents. No longer their timid little child, reassure them of your filial love and devotion, but you must tell them who you are. Tell them where you stand, a married woman as Henry's lawful wife. Only you can do this.

"Goodness me, we must stop talking and you must rescue our cake from the oven, before it's overcooked. Make sure you've a clear surface ready to place the tin on when you take it out of the oven and prepare some muslin gauze or something to place over it when it cools, so the flies don't get at it."

Claire did as she was bid and removed the sour cream cake from the oven.

"That looks wonderful, and it was so simple."

"If you can spare a few minutes to call tomorrow we'll have a piece with a cup of coffee. Hours of hard work and practice are needed, as well you know, to make difficult things seem simple and easy to accomplish. In the case of this cake, making it is just child's play, but you must never let on. We'll just keep it our secret. It never does any harm to let guests think that it has required hours of skilled baking."

Rebecca always insisted that after immersing her hands in water Claire should always dry her hands thoroughly and then use a glycerine and rose water emollient to keep the skin youthful and supple, particularly in wintertime.

Week after week, as they cooked and baked they would talk. Rebecca explained the term *kosher* and its biblical derivation whereby milk and animal produce needed to be kept separate, even the culinary utensils of every kind used for either of these major food products. She talked of the biblical prohibition of certain types of food including the much sought after Chesapeake Bay crabs and seafood, which were among them, and which so many of her more modern co-religionists chose to ignore.

Rebecca told Claire of her childhood in London. Her parents had three surviving children. There were two older brothers and she was twelve years younger than her second brother. Her father, a glazier, could barely make ends meet. He had been born in London and had told her that he believed his family had arrived in London from Holland shortly before he was born. In contrast with the typical girl in mid-19th-century London, she had been taught to read by her father and could also read the biblical Hebrew scripts.

Hers had been an arranged marriage. She had been compelled to marry when she was barely twenty, having met with her future husband, David Joseph, who was twenty-five at the time, just twice before the wedding. She spoke of her first child, Rachel, born in 1873 and then of a succession of miscarriages and stillbirths before the almost miraculous live births of a further five surviving children. There was her daughter Annie in 1879, Amelia in 1882, Abraham in 1883, Sidney two years later and Henry in 1889 before her husband had passed away in America. She also spoke of the terrible years of hardship before she had arrived in America and her feeling of loss that she had not seen the two sons she had been compelled to leave behind in London, since 1899.

She related how her husband had escaped from Poland. He had told her that any time after the age of twelve there was always the likelihood that boys would be conscripted into the Tsar's Russian army. During the period of the Crimean War in the 1850s military service was for up to twenty-five years duration. Parents would do all in their power to avoid having their sons conscripted, since all too often these children were never seen again.

Their parents arranged for David Joseph and his brother to leave Poland to make their way to America to join an older brother. While travelling westwards they were stopped by Polish guards at the border with Germany. The guards found money sewn into the boys' new coat sleeves that their father, a tailor, had made them for their journey. The guards, laughing and mocking them, had confiscated the money, before sending them back home to Konin.

Later that same year, and far wiser, they made the journey a second time. As they timorously approached the border crossing, they were able to hide and wait for nightfall. When all was quiet and the solitary border guard slept snugly in front of his brazier, they escaped across the frontier into Germany. In Bremen they purchased tickets at an office on the quayside and embarked on a transatlantic ship for America. The boat stopped in Harwich where they disembarked. When they attempted to reboard the ship they were turned away. It was then that they learned they had been cheated and charged for a ticket to America and sent to England. Safe, but penniless, they had somehow survived the journey. Caring for themselves and living in a tiny attic hovel, barely larger than a broom cupboard, in London's Spitalfields, they worked as tailors and grew up, two waifs, never again seeing their parents or family.

These were happy summer days for Claire as she grew to know her mother-in-law, learnt to cook and sew and enjoyed her music at the Peabody, returning dutifully to her parents every evening without revealing her full day's activities.

On one occasion while cooking, Rebecca told Claire of the derivation of her father's family name Levy. "The Bible records that Moses brother Aaron was made the chief priest. His son and male heirs thereafter became the Kohanim or priestly people. The assistants to the Kohanim, or priests were to be the Levites and likewise the male heirs thereafter inherited this function in perpetuity."

"Do you mean you can date your family line back all that way?" gasped Claire in surprise.

"There are lots of gaps, but certainly I can. Let me explain. Of the thirteen tribes descended from Jacob's children, (Joseph's sons

149

Manassah and Ephraim became the forefathers of two tribes) nine tribes (Asher, Dan, Ephraim, Gad, Issachar, Manassah, Naphtali, Reuben and Zebulon) all disappeared with the Northern Kingdom of Israel following the onslaught of the Assyrians. The remaining tribes of Judah, Benjamin and Simeon occupied the southern Kingdom of Judah of which Jerusalem was the capital city.

"The descendants of this state survived for a further century before its citizens were taken into Babylonian captivity. The Levites from the tribe of Levi were never given tribal land, as were the remaining twelve tribes, since they were always to be assistants to the Kohanim or priests. Fortunately a formidable number of them appear to have lived in the southern Kingdom of Judah.

"Following some fifty years of captivity, our ancient Hebrew ancestors maintained their identity. Most returned to Jerusalem, some remained in Babylon, a small number dispersed to become the start of a growing diaspora. Unlike those exiled from the Northern Kingdom of Israel, some hundred years earlier the survivors of the exile from the southern kingdom of Judah were able to maintain their religious identity.

"This was achieved largely through three changes that had taken place over the previous century. A considerable portion of the male community had become literate. The Bible in its earliest form had finally been written, and a tradition of weekly readings to the community had been instituted. What at the time appeared to have disadvantaged this tribe in early biblical times when portions of land were allocated would later prove a bonus in life's lottery of survival. And believe me, in almost every generation we Jews have had to learn that skill of survival time after time."

* * *

Early on the morning of 5 November Rebecca, a usually robust energetic woman, took to her bed feeling unwell. She described it to her son as feeling "just a little indisposed". Henry called his sister Annie, telling her that their mother wasn't feeling well and asked if she would keep an eye on her while he was out at work.

As she lay there in bed, she spoke to Annie, recalling her fond childhood memories of the Guy Fawkes' Night[13] fireworks she had watched in London on 5 November each year.

Rebecca ate nothing and simply sipped a little water. She asked for a heating pad to hold against her stomach, which was hurting in

150

waves of pain radiating from the centre. During the night she vomited twice. The following morning she again threw up and appeared in such distress that in spite of her protestations, Henry summoned a doctor.

The doctor arrived and, having taken a brief history, examined the patient in the presence of her daughter. He felt her pulse, checked and confirmed that she was running a slight fever. Gently he placed the flat of his hand on Rebecca's abdomen and discovered as he palpated the surface, an area of great tenderness, in the right lower quadrant. He then placed his hand in the centre of her abdomen, pressed firmly, which caused some discomfort and then suddenly pulled his hand away. Rebecca cried out in pain. Shortly after, he indicated the consultation was at an end and asked Annie to follow him. Outside the bedroom door, Rebecca was conscious of the conversation that was going on, but felt too uncomfortable to take much note, seared by the pain in her belly.

The door opened and Annie reappeared, blowing her nose and dabbing her eyes. "Mummy, the doctor says you're not at all well and you must go to hospital straight away."

"Don't cry Annie. Tell me, why did he say that?"

"He said that you have an acute inflammation in your belly and he thinks you've got appendicitis or something like that. He says that if we can't get you to hospital straight away, it could become really serious. You might even need an operation and, and they, and they can..." She could not finish the sentence a flood of tears and sobs blurring anything that she might try to say as she buried her face in her pinafore.

"Please don't cry like that Annie. I only wish I had something to ease this awful pain, it's getting worse by the minute. Worse even than when I had any of my babies."

"I'll make you another hot pad. That'll help some, until the ambulance comes. I suppose they'll take you to the Maryland General, it's far closer than the Johns Hopkins."

Annie made a hot pad for her mother and asked her neighbour to summon Henry and her husband from work, explaining that her mother was very sick and was being taken to hospital. As they waited for the arrival of the ambulance, Annie sat with her mother, holding her hand, as Rebecca, still in considerable discomfort, confided in her daughter.

"Annie, I tell you I'm terrified of the surgeon's knife. I don't

151

want him to cut me. I hope it isn't going to end up the one way journey as happened with my mother."

"Mummy, don't be silly. If the surgeon needs to operate you'll be asleep under an anaesthetic. Whatever do you mean by a one way journey?"

"When my own mother was sick, she had a fever just like me and they took her to the hospital and she never came home."

"Don't you dare say, or even think such ridiculous things. Of course they'll make you better and you'll be home in no time at all."

"Annie, I've never told you what happened to my mother. It was dreadful. She died alone, without family or friend. It was in 1884 when you were just five years old. I think you were far too young to remember her."

"Yes I do vaguely remember Grandma Henrietta."

"After she died we had no more daughters so we named Henry after her, which was the closest name we could think of that resembled Henrietta."

"I seem to recall she was a very small grey haired lady, dressed in black with a black bonnet."

"Yes, when my father died she dressed in black, what they called widows weeds. In those times widows dressed that way and she never wore any other colour after he died. It was a dreadful fashion. I think Queen Victoria may have started it, after her husband Albert, the Prince Consort died. As I was saying she was a widow and lived by herself. I think it was in 1884. Your brother Alfred was about one year old at the time, when she developed this fever. I remember the doctor was frightened that it might be smallpox. I'd four young children to look after and couldn't visit. They wanted to put her in isolation, but there weren't any isolation hospitals."

"Where did they take grandma?"

"They took her by ambulance to an isolation ship on the Thames just below Greenwich."

"That was a long way to travel from Spitalfields."

"All the people and the authorities were terrified of these outbreaks of fever. Thousands of people used to die and they tried to isolate any one they suspected of having smallpox. I don't think she had smallpox. I didn't see her the day they took her away, but nobody I spoke to saw any blisters or pox marks on her skin, but she still died.

"They used to take people by horse-drawn ambulances to a house

152

in London Fields. There they stayed for a time until the hospital steamers arrived. Then the health authorities took them by boat down river to the hospital ships.[14] If the journey didn't kill them and the cold on those cockroach and rat infested boats didn't get them, they might recover and be sent to a nearby farm that they called a convalescent hospital."

"Did she recover?"

"Mother died, may she rest in peace, after she'd been there two weeks. There was no one with her who she'd have known, poor woman, since she was in isolation. The death certificate didn't mention smallpox. It recorded her death was due to enteric fever."

"How did she come to have enteric fever and what is it?"

"I don't think we really know how she caught it. It usually comes from drinking water or eating food that's been contaminated by some of the germs that produce that illness. It's another name for typhoid, the same thing that killed Queen Victoria's husband Albert.[15] Anyway, it's my guess that somebody may have been using river water for drinking or cleaning pots and crockery. Drinking water was taken to the ships in large casks, filled from some wells close by. They didn't have any piped water. Whatever the cause, many of the poor folk who were taken to those hulks didn't survive the journey, or the conditions, including my poor mother."

"Let's not be so morbid. You'll go to a clean modern hospital, with a good fresh water supply. The doctors and nurses will make you better and you'll be home in a few days."

"Annie when we get to the hospital, don't leave me. I'm not as brave as I pretend to be. Promise me you'll hold my hand. I'm so terribly scared. I'm no heroine, please don't let me die alone."

"Mother, don't be so morbid."

"I brought you into this world, gave you life, and nurtured you when you were small and helpless. In return the only thing I ask is that you promise me if they can't make me better you'll at least be with me and hold my hand and look after me when I leave. Promise me, then I know I won't be afraid of dying alone."

"They'll make you better and I promise I'll hold your hand, but right now I'm just going to put a towel, some soap and a clean nightdress into a bag for you, so we can be ready when the ambulance comes."

"Remember, you promised me. I do wish it would come soon, this pain is getting worse in spite of this pad you made me."

153

"They'll be here any minute now and we mustn't keep them waiting."

A little later that morning, the horse-drawn ambulance drew up in the street at the kerbside outside the Chiswick apartment. Its arrival attracted a number of small children, who stood on the sidewalk watching and gawking. In considerable pain and emotional distress, Rebecca was taken, on a canvas stretcher, held by two robust male medical attendants, down the several flights of concrete steps to the waiting ambulance. Once secure within, she was rapidly driven to the Maryland General Hospital, close by on the 800 block of North Howard Street, accompanied by her daughter and son-in-law.

Waiting in the hospital anteroom, with its all-pervading odours of antiseptics wafting in from wards and corridors, they were visited in the mid-afternoon by the attending Maryland University Hospital surgeon. In hushed tones he explained that their mother's condition had become worse since her arrival. He feared that a gangrenous appendix had caused peritonitis to set in and her condition was too grave to risk surgery. He explained that they should not give up all hope as sometimes the infection in the abdomen became walled off into an abscess, which could later be drained, but that the next twenty-four hours would prove decisive.

The hospital rules allowed visiting for one hour from two to three p.m. for two visitors only on Saturdays and alternate afternoons during the remainder of the week. The following day was not a visitor's day, but two relatives would be permitted to remain in the waiting room, since the patient's condition was considered grave. In spite of Annie's protestations they would not bend hospital rules to permit her to sit with her mother at the bedside as she wished.

Early the next morning, after making his hospital rounds, the surgeon again visited Rebecca's family anxiously waiting in the cramped and cheerless waiting room. He explained that their mother's condition was in crisis. With a raised temperature and increased pulse rate, he feared they must prepare themselves for the worst. The patient had a generalised peritonitis, for which there was no known cure.

Rebecca, a gentle lady, appeared aged and drained, moaning to herself in her white metal-framed hospital bed. With sunken veiled eyes, cheekbones protruding from her suffering face, her skin as

154

she lay there, was hot and dry. She was dehydrated, with parched lips and tongue, a rapidly reducing shadow of her earlier self. Suffering the agony of her belly pain, she lay in her hospital bed, alone as she had feared most, moaning quietly with each laboured breath. Close to the door to the ward, a mobile cotton screen isolated the area from the other patients. Her grieving family were permitted to visit briefly that afternoon, only two at a time. Later in the evening Rebecca fell into a toxic coma, which appeared to give her some relief from the agonising pain in her now distended abdomen.

In the early hours of the next morning her rapid but diminished pulse weakened and faltered. It rallied fleetingly as though uncertain how to proceed as it irregularly transmitted her frail heart beat one last time, then stopped. Her blood pressure plummeted. She gasped for breath momentarily once, then again and then no more as her once invincible heart, chastised by unseen microbes and toxins, capitulated. Her indomitable spirit, now wearied by disease and humbled by pain, took refuge in flight, as it journeyed throughout eternity to the bosom of her ancestors, free at last from further hurt and torment.

The night sister, seated at her desk, with its small night light in the middle of the ward, expecting and then noticing a change in the patient's stertorous respirations, stood up. Efficiently and confidently she walked across the large darkened ward to check her patient's condition behind the screen, her starched uniform rustled as though a gentle zephyr were following in her wake. She parted the cotton curtains and examined the patient. She felt for the patient's pulse. Finding none and noting the fixed dilated pupils, confirming life had silently drawn to a close, she gently closed Rebecca's eyelids. Next, as she had been trained, she tied a bandage under the chin to support the jaw, removing the pillow to permit the body and head to lie flat. A few minutes later she recorded in her ward book in black ink: "Nov 8. 1916. Monday 02.15 Patient Rebecca Chiswick ceased breathing. No pulse. Duty surgical intern informed."

She then proceeded briskly on her way to inform the deceased's sleeplessly waiting family. There followed the staccato reverberating sounds of the nurse's shoes, heel sole, heel sole, and the sound from her uniform like a soft breeze though the trees, as she progressed rapidly along the darkened, polished stone corridor.

155

Shortly after in the waiting room there came the muffled wailing cries of the bereaved and the repeated stifled sobs "Mother! Mother!"

The following Tuesday morning, 9 November, dawned cold and clear. In the raw heartless day, forever emblazoned into the minds of her children, Rebecca was interred less than thirty-six hours after she had passed away. Henry, her closest male relative, tearfully sobbed as he recited *Kaddesh*, the traditional Aramaic Jewish mourning prayer for the deceased while he and his sisters following the interment sat *Shiva* in their rendered garments, the time-honoured seven day period of mourning. This was held in Annie's home, where, seated on low stools, they were visited by relatives, neighbours and friends, including Claire, who expressed tearfully to Henry and his sisters how she felt she had lost not just a mother-in-law, but a remarkable mentor who had shown her compassion, warmth and friendship from the very moment she had learned of her marriage.

A solitary small *Yartzeit* candle burned every day that week in each of the homes of Rebecca's children, to remind each of her family, not that they needed reminding, of their irreparable loss. Thereafter on the anniversary of their parent's death, for one day, a *Yartzeit* candle would burn for twenty-four hours, that being the ancient Hebrew tradition, for remembrance and respect.

Chapter 18

Baltimore November 1916

Claire, her July marriage concealed from her parents, lived at home and continued her studies. To all outward appearances, although somewhat quieter and less communicative, she was the same talented, dutiful and deferential daughter the Robins had always known, leaving daily to attend the Peabody Institute and returning home to practise in the evenings. She never revealed her daily visits to her mother-in-law and clandestine meetings with Henry, lacking the courage to confront her parents' wrath with the truth of her deceptions without having the support of Henry by her side.

She had told her parents of the death of Henry's mother and of her intention to see Henry to offer her condolences, but had been forbidden to do so, nor even to write a condolence note. Needless to record, she continued to disobey and mislead her parents, as the young are often wont when interests of the heart are contrary to parental advice and wishes.

Claire had however changed. Stirring deep within, the seeds of her love for Henry had coalesced in an indissoluble union. She noticed how she seemed to be nauseous in the mornings and had, on several occasions, thrown up. She was losing weight while the waistband of her skirt seemed, without washing, to have either tightened, or shrunk.

She confided these happenings to Henry, who realised that they could no longer postpone telling the Robins, in particular, and the world in general, that they were husband and wife. It was decided that since Claire's parents would not permit Henry to enter their house, and since it would be unseemly to attempt to force his way into the Robins' home to meet her father, he and Claire would have to confront them together the following Sunday, as they left church. The unarmed ambush, for that is what it amounted to, was planned and brought forward to two weeks before Thanksgiving. The confrontation could no longer be postponed, lest Claire's condition should unintentionally reveal itself.

The following Sunday morning, as arranged, Henry entered the church and seated himself on one of the empty rear pews until the conclusion of the service, going over in his mind and rehearsing what he intended to say to Claire's parents. As the concluding hymn was sung and the last words of the priestly benediction intoned, the congregation started to file out. Claire, as she had arranged with Henry, walked more rapidly ahead of her parents down the centre aisle. As she hurried she opened her purse and cautiously removed its only metallic object, a simple gold wedding band that she carefully placed over her left ring finger. Wearing her wedding ring for the second time in public and which she had resolved never again to remove, she dutifully took Henry's arm that they might exit together ahead of her parents. Once outside, Henry and Claire turned to face the Robins on the sidewalk as they left the main entrance and turned in the direction of their home. Henry cleared his throat, standing with Claire, barring their further progress, and began.

"Good morning Mr Robins sir, and to you Mrs Robins Ma'am, I've something rather important I'd like to say to you."

"Out of my way young man, we've nothing we wish to learn from you or your kind and would you kindly disengage yourself from our daughter."

"Mr Robins, I insist you must and will hear me here, in the street outside this house of God, since you'll not hear me in your home."

"By heavens, I'll not be spoken to in this manner. I've no intention of listening to anything you've to say now, or at any other time, so would you unhand my daughter immediately."

"Mr Robins..."

"Step aside, and let us pass, or must I summon help?"

"I would have preferred to speak to you in a more reasoned manner..."

"Not another word, I say. Remove your hands from my daughter, right now and get out of our way."

"Mr Robins, I've no other way of telling you. The plain and simple fact is that Claire and I are married..."

"What did you say?" roared the irate father.

"Claire and I are husband and wife and have been so these past four months."

"Claire, tell me this just isn't true. Surely you haven't deceived

158

and lied to your own parents?" Mr Robins spluttered, glaring at his daughter.

"Father," exclaimed Claire, now holding up her left ring finger for her parents to observe the simple gold matrimonial band, "we were married on the fourth of July last and..."

Her father interrupted.

"You married this Englishman, this non-believer, this Jew?" His voice rose incredulously, "You mean you defied me, in spite of all that I've said and taught you? The Bible tells us his people murdered our Lord and Saviour. They carry forever the guilt of this act and are eternally damned. Damned in the eyes of God and all mankind. Don't you understand, he's damned to burn in the pit of hell? We can have nothing to do with him and that must now apply to you if, as you claim, you're his wife. If you married him, then you're no longer any daughter of ours."

"But father, you're being cruel and besides which you're wrong. Whatever despicable things may have happened nearly two thousand years ago has no possible bearing on Henry or his family today. How could it have, nearly a hundred generations, later? It just doesn't make sense to pursue an unfounded vendetta for all eternity. In any case it most probably never took place that way and..."

Her father brusquely overrode her protestations, shaking visibly with rage as he bellowed, "I'll not tolerate this, nor listen further! He's contaminated your thoughts with this vile Hebrew poison and you've been deceitful and lied to us. Go, collect your clothes right now and leave our house this instant. Neither your mother nor I want anything more to do with this man. If you've been foolish enough to dishonour yourself, to become his wife, then this will apply to you as well."

Clinging tightly to Henry's arm she pleaded desperately, "Father, mother, we're married. We were married legally according to Maryland state law. I'm expecting a child next April and I thought this news might give you some pleasure and soften your hearts towards us."

With these words she burst into tears, hardly hearing as her father venomously spat out his final insult.

"Apostate! Devil's whore! Out of our sight. You're no longer any daughter of ours!" He rushed with his wife headlong through the crowd of onlookers who stood in astonishment as they witnessed insult hurling, feuding relatives amongst one of their community's leading families.

Henry tried, while shaking with humiliation and anger, to console Claire. Together, both in tears, now depressed as though bereaved, they walked slowly past the gathered gawking congregants, back to Henry's apartment, the unhappiest and most recent victims in a never-ending line of those suffering man's intolerant inhumanity and bigotry to his fellows.

*   *   *

Claire was absolutely devastated and bereft. Henry spent the rest of the day attempting as best he could to comfort her in her grief, hardly knowing what best to do to console her. With his mother no longer on the scene and his sisters less than enthusiastic to have a Catholic sister-in-law, he had no close relative or female friend to call upon to assist him. Claire would not eat or drink and sat at the table staring, lost in grief over what she perceived as the unreasonable behaviour of her parents.

Neither Henry nor Claire realised that an invisible transformation had been taking place slowly and imperceptibly within Claire's emotional persona. Having commenced with her agreement to marry she was rapidly approaching the final stages of an impressive psychological journey no less epic than the metamorphosis that transfers the earthbound caterpillar into the colourful airborne winged butterfly. Since her marriage to Henry, she had been transferring her attentions, both mental and physical, from her pampered affluent lifestyle to the exposed tip of the iceberg of poverty. With Rebecca's death, she sadly identified the loss of a true friend who had revealed greater depths of understanding and a sense of goodness than she had perceived even in her own mother.

This elegant young mother to be was developing emotionally from an intelligent talented child with little insight into her own immaturity towards her parent's control, into a graceful and intellectually resourceful woman of passionate kindness and sweetness. The trauma of Rebecca's death and the antagonism of her parents towards her husband and now herself on the flimsiest illogical pretext had now pushed her through the final metamorphic transformation. With her slim elegance and poised talent, she had now attained a rich dimension of emotional maturity, passion and self-assurance.

160

Suddenly she seemed to awaken and spoke through a fresh but silent cascade of tears. "Henry, my own father called me unimaginable names. He called me a whore." Henry placed his arm round her shoulders and rested her head on his chest to comfort her again, as he had been doing periodically since they had returned to their apartment. Gently kissing first her hand then bending his head to kiss her head and then lower to her tear-dampened cheek, he gently responded.

"Darling, I don't think he really meant what he said, it was just that he was taken by surprise, off his guard, and he was very upset and angry. I think he was more upset at our apparent deception than anything else."

"Henry, he said some awful things to you as well. What unimaginable wickedness does he see that could make him say such things? He condemns you outrageously for the accident of your birth. That's totally monstrous and illogical. I know I deceived them wickedly, but I meant no harm by it. I just thought it would give me a little more time to help me open their eyes to the see the fine qualities I perceived in you."

"Darling, as a boy I was quite used to having to defend myself when called names. A few more, whether from your father or anybody else, are of little consequence. My earliest memory was being told by father to shout back at those children calling me names, 'Sticks and stones may break my bones, but names will never hurt me!' But in reality Claire, in spite of yelling back in defiance, it was always upsetting. It did hurt. It always hurt emotionally, deep down. It always stuck in my memory afterwards for months and months. Even as I speak of these things, I can recall some of those horrible events years later, when I was no more than knee high to a grasshopper, being insulted and teased by the other boys.

"I had to fight every day in the orphanage over some trivial injustice including name-calling. If you didn't stand up for yourself, the other kids sensed there was a weakness and they would probe that Achilles heel more and more, making life a worse living hell than it was. I always had to fight back, even when a boy was bigger and stronger and I knew I would lose. I wasn't brave or anything like that. I just had to send a loud clear message to the other boys. They had to know that I would stand up for myself whatever the cost and then they stopped name-calling, pushing, shoving, fighting and bullying me. It was easier for them to pick on

161

some other poor waif, who was too timid to give a proper account of himself.

"What I can't and won't tolerate is anybody treating my wife in that manner. Had it been anyone other than your father I assure you I'd have taken him to task in a way that would have made him remember his manners when next speaking to a lady in general, or particularly to my wife."

"Henry, whatever imagined crime my father considers I've committed, and no matter what he says, you must promise me that regardless of the provocation you'll never use violence against him. He's my father and we're taught to honour our parents."

"Claire, he's spoken to me in the most derogatory manner on three separate occasions and I've held my peace. I've always treated him with respect because he's your father. But be in no doubt. I've committed no crime that warrants that he or any man should be crude or disrespectful towards you, the sweetest woman I know. If he speaks to you again in such a manner, then I'd certainly show him the error of his ways with a sound thrashing."

"Please Henry, I don't know what we've done to deserve this, but we must never ever descend to that level. Better by far that we should move to another town, to avoid all contact, than we should even think of behaving in this manner. You must promise that you'll never contemplate violence towards my father; I should die of humiliation and shame."

"Very well, I promise, but I think it's best that we write a letter to your parents explaining our point of view and our reasons for our clandestine marriage. We must see if we can persuade them to understand our position and try healing the vast gulf that's opened between us."

The letter, diligently written by Claire and Henry to Claire's parents later that day was delivered by hand the following morning. It was returned through the reception desk at the Peabody, unopened and unread with the simple message in her father's handwriting on the envelope 'Return to Miss Claire Robins, address unknown'. Claire was compelled to give up her studies at the Peabody Institute at the end of that term, at Christmas. A promising young career, destined to have given pleasure to many hundreds in years to come, was now extinguished, since no further financial parental assistance for fees was forthcoming. A far cry from previous year's Yuletides when her parents and Henry were all so proud of her performances.

That Christmas there was a small concert at the same church where Claire had given her successful recital two years earlier. Claire performed two Bach organ pieces *The Toccata and Fugue* and *Sheep May Safely Graze* but although her latest recital was extremely well received, the absence of her parents at the performance removed a considerable portion of her pleasure from the occasion. These Christmas concerts could never again be the same for her.

* * *

A wedding gift, from Henry's more affluent brothers in London, could not be sent across the Atlantic, due to the war that raged in Europe and the threat to shipping from the German navy. Instead, Henry received a generous pre-paid voucher from them, with which to purchase a piano of his choice at Stewarts, the Lord and Taylor's store in downtown Baltimore. Claire helped choose an upright piano, since this would take up less room in the confines of her new more modestly proportioned apartment. It proved to be a veritable liferaft to Claire as it enabled her to practise as she awaited the arrival of their first child. It became her most treasured possession and seldom did a day pass that she did not put it to use, expressing through its keys, pedals and strings the whole gamut and range of her emotions throughout the years.

* * *

On 24 March 1917, Claire was safely delivered of a fine healthy daughter, whom they happily named Rebecca. As was customary in the Jewish tradition, she was named after a recently deceased relative to perpetuate the name and spirit of that loved one. In this instance Henry's mother, who in spite of her initial opposition to their interfaith marriage had been so magnanimously kind and supportive of her children, for which Claire remained eternally grateful. Henry delivered a letter by hand to Claire's parents, telling them of the birth of their granddaughter. He knocked on the door and gave the letter to the butler, stating that he would wait for a reply. He waited at the closed door for fifteen minutes, but no response came. He walked away, embarrassed to have been foolish enough to wait for a response that he realised, deep down within, would never be forthcoming. This blessed event, the birth of their firstborn, received no acknowledgement of any kind from Claire's parents, sisters or family; not then, not ever, further marring Claire's otherwise happy marriage to Henry.

Chapter 19

London January 2000

On 31 December 1999 there were celebrations, partying and magnificent firework displays across each of the world's time zones, either bidding farewell to the old or greeting the new millennium.

There is the old story of a glass standing on a table into which wine is poured. Depending upon the person's psychological attitude, a pessimist will see a half empty glass of wine, while an optimist will see the same glass half full. In my case it was overflowing and didn't really matter, since well before millennium midnight, I was completely sozzled. My wife later had to help me to bed, since my half glass was somewhere between glass number eleven and twelve, not to mention a couple of shorts in between.

Of the firework displays my wife told me that she judged the Sydney Harbour Bridge display to be the finest, a suitable beginning to a new millennium, while Mayor Ken Livingstone's London Thames spectacular was something of a damp squib.

The realisation that the world's computers had not all simultaneously gone down on 1 January 2000 encouraged me, a few days later, once I had really sobered up and recovered from an almighty hangover, to plunge into the internet to explore the 1930 US census records which were being made available to the public.

I had decided that we should endeavour, with the help of the 1930 US census, to trace the progress Henry and his family had been making, and their whereabouts at that time. It took several weeks before I was able to trace Henry Chiswick and when I did I was, to put it mildly, absolutely astounded. I found the following very brief entry.

US Federal Census April 1930.

Address: the Baltimore Hospital for Mental Diseases. Baltimore MD
Henry Chiswick aged 42 yrs. Divorced.

To my shocked disbelief I had found my great Uncle Henry, aged forty-two, a divorced man in a mental hospital. It was surreal, like a Salvador Dali painting, with its distorted bent clocks and timepieces.

I pondered what might have happened in their marriage and where his wife and children were at that time. This new information was completely at variance with anything I had expected following my conversation with Margaret Wilding and the email she had sent me barely eight weeks previously.

I hastily telephoned Janet and excitedly told her of my discovery, which seemed at odds with the story received from Henry's granddaughter, of her grandparents' years of alleged harmonious domestic bliss, brought to a conclusion only by Henry's untimely demise.

"It's most peculiar. According to Claire's daughters their mother married some years after the death of their father. They told their children how happy the early years of their childhood had been. They idolised their father and all was apparently well for them and their mother up to the time of their father's death. They had never known either set of grandparents, aunts or uncles, except one aunt, who lived in the next apartment block, because it was said that everyone had ganged up to ostracise them because of the intermarriage. But divorce and remarriage – little wonder great uncle Henry ended up a nutcase in a mental hospital," I expounded.

"Well things like this happen in the best regulated family circles," responded Janet. "A little fling or two on the side, followed by divorce and then the big cover-up, it happens very often. The odd family skeleton locked in the cupboard to maintain an outward show of respectability."

"But how could she, why should she, hoodwink us like this?"

"Alf, don't be so damned naïve. It happens all the time in every family sooner or later. Every family has one or more black sheep in every generation. The remainder of the family are astonished, sometimes titillated, but generally everyone's ashamed and so you get the big cover-up and denial."

"They spoke of the terrible hardships during the years of the depression. It was so bad that there was often no food in the home and Claire had to take in washing and needlework, with which her daughters needed to help, and to give piano lessons. At one time she had some cleaning job in the church. Life was extremely hard.

166

Seemingly out of desperation Claire later remarried and that's as far as I've pursued the story," I said.

"Well it hardly measures up to the 1930 census facts you've just found. Whatever happened to Claire after the divorce?"

"I've tried to find Claire on the 1930 census, but she's completely disappeared. I wondered if you might have any suggestions to make."

"If you can't find Claire, it may have been because she remarried and changed her name, or perhaps she went to live abroad," said Janet.

"She certainly remarried, but where she may have lived afterwards is a mystery."

"Alf, while Claire may have changed her name there are still the two children identified in the 1920 census, and for all we know there might have been more in the following years. We know at least one of Clare's grandchildren lives in Baltimore so it's a pretty reasonable bet that she also continued to live there. Have you tried looking for them in the census?"

"No, but I'll certainly follow it up as a lead when I have a little spare time."

* * *

A few days later on the internet, I checked the census record for Baltimore, and filled in the search criteria for Rebecca Chiswick. Within moments the information appeared on my screen.

US Federal Census April 1930.

Address: 945 Fayette Street, Baltimore, Maryland
Andrew Collins, aged 38 yrs head of household.
Occupation; Attorney at Law.
Claire Collins aged 38, His wife, housewife, music teacher.
His children Andrew Collins Junior, aged 14 yrs, scholar,
Edward Collins aged 11 yrs scholar and
Robert Collins aged 5 yrs.
Rebecca Chiswick aged 13 yrs., scholar, and
Henrietta Chiswick 10 yrs, scholar.

There seemed little doubt. I had found Claire Chiswick, now Mrs Claire Collins. Henry's divorced wife was living with another man, an attorney at law, as his wife, probably in very comfortable circumstances, in Baltimore in 1930 with her children. Her former husband, my great Uncle Henry, languished at the time in some sort of mental institution. Some wife he turned out to have married! Some marriage!

It was understandable that Claire wished to conceal her divorce, since in that era divorce was considered a shameful failure and disgrace. However, how was it that a teenager such as Claire's older daughter Rebecca wasn't aware of the happening? Was it that she knew and that she aided and abetted her mother in the cover-up, when her mother divorced the father she allegedly idolised?

In retrospect, how simple it had been. What a web of deceit we had now uncovered. There was still a little more information that was needed to solve this puzzle. So typical of life, somehow each time we appeared to have resolved one problem it seemed another had magically appeared in its place to tax our ingenuity.

Henry was certainly not dead. There was no indication as to *when* he had been hospitalised though, or when the divorce had taken place. We still had no way of knowing whether, like Claire, he had remarried or had further family. There was likewise no indication as to the type of mental illness from which he was suffering.

Was his illness something temporary, such as might have been due to an addiction to alcohol, or depression, or was it a permanent problem such as paranoia or schizophrenia? Furthermore, was the divorce a *consequence* of permanent mental illness, or had he suffered some form of severe mental or nervous breakdown *following* his divorce? With so many questions to be answered, would we ever learn the real truth?

I telephoned Janet, told her of my discovery and suggested that we meet to review how we were going to establish what had become of Henry Chiswick, since the information we had received from Claire's granddaughter was patently inaccurate. Why had she lied to us in this manner? After all, her grandparents must have passed away many years ago and what harm would there be in being forthright and truthful?

Perhaps she had not lied. Was she repeating some form of disinformation provided convincingly by her mother, aunt and grand-

168

mother over many years to conceal something that was considered disgraceful? Some shameful event in that era of time that needed to be kept secret? If so, did we have any right to invade their privacy, digging up long-buried secrets? Most intriguing of all, what was this important secret and could we ever find out?

Chapter 20

London 2000

Our next meeting was held at my home. We went straight to the computer and logged on to the US Social Security Death Index. We programmed in the name Henry Chiswick and waited. Within a few minutes we were provided with a list of close on seventy-five names. It took very little time to scan down the list to eliminate those who were either too young or too old, or who had died outside the parameters of the ten years from 1925 to 1935 that we had arbitrarily set. Finally we were left with a Henry Chiswick whose last residence was Baltimore and whose date of death was September 1931.

"That could well be our man," I said excitedly.

"You're probably correct, but we must have some corroboration."

"Fine, all we need do is to apply to the Baltimore Department of Vital Statistics, Death Registry department, pay the required fee and request that they send us the death certificate. Then we'll know if we have our man."

"That might simply be a waste of time and money. The Social Security Death Index didn't say he died in Baltimore, it merely stated his last known residence was Baltimore. He might have been travelling in the US or abroad at the time or living somewhere other than Baltimore when death occurred."

"Then what do you think we should do?"

"I've a hunch that your first suggestion will establish if this is the Henry we're looking for, but there are a number of other options."

"All right, fire away."

"Not so fast, you tell me what else we might do – after all, this is a learning curve for both of us."

"Well there are a number of other possibilities I can think of. The best bet would be obituary notices. We could communicate with the local Baltimore newspapers, or any local paper with the same religious affiliation to the deceased, to see if there were any obituary notices for Henry Chiswick in September or October 1931.

If there were, we might be able to recognise the names of members of his family. An alternative would be to communicate with the hospital mentioned in the 1930 census to enquire if there are any records that exist relating to Henry Chiswick and if they give any indication of his next of kin, or his date of death."

We opted to contact the Baltimore Department of Vital Statistics. We discovered that an application had to be made by completing an official form and submitting a fee of $3.00 if we were collecting the certificate in person, otherwise a stamped addressed envelope would also be needed. We were able to obtain the certificate within three weeks and realised that we had the death record of my ancestral great Uncle Henry Chiswick. In more recent times we learned that some states would only provide a certificate with the cause of death obliterated, while other states simply refused to provide any certificate at all.

Death Record
Deceased: Henry Chiswick.

Date of Death: 15 September 1931. Date of Birth: 1 May 1889.

Born: London England. Father: David Joseph Chiswick, Mother: Rebecca.

Death occurred: As an inpatient at the Maryland Hospital for Nervous Diseases, Baltimore MD.

Cause of Death. 1) Bronchopneumonia.   Duration: 4 days.
                2) Post Viral Encephalitis. Duration: 5 years.

Surviving Spouse: N/A. Divorced. Occupation: Cigar Salesman

Death reported by: Claire Collins.
Relationship to Deceased: Former wife.

To fully unravel the mystery of Uncle Henry we decided that it would be helpful to obtain one further piece of information: a copy of the documentation relating to the transcript of his divorce. We decided that if we could determine when Claire had married Andrew Collins, we would then be able to look back a few months earlier, a year, or two at most, in our search for the divorce papers. Janet again turned up trumps. She explained that she had a very good friend working on a sabbatical in Washington DC and would simply send her an email asking her to assist us by going into the First Street Library of Congress to search for the marriage certificate.

To my amazement I had a phone call later that week from Janet telling me that she had just received an email response from her friend, confirming that Claire Chiswick and Andrew Collins had been married in church, in Baltimore, on Sunday 24 June 1928. We could hardly credit the ease with which we had been able to gather this information simply by searching in the right place.

We learned with a single telephone call to the Baltimore City Hall that divorce indices were available and in which department in that huge building the divorce records were located. We were courteously informed that, "If you know the exact year of the divorce, you can arrange to do everything via email and use your credit card to pay us for our trouble in sending you the information." We hastily sent off our email request, with the names of the divorce litigants and the suggested date of divorce using the parameters covering one year, from June 1927 to June 1928.

Divorce in those days was seldom seen as an option in an unhappy marriage, which meant there were very few divorces on record. Within minutes we had provided credit card information for payment and received the information that we needed. We read with growing excitement details of the divorce proceedings in January 1928 in the city of Baltimore. Involuntary separation had been given as grounds for the divorce since the parties had lived apart without interruption for two years: one year prior to the husband's illness followed by his year in hospital. The divorce was uncontested and custodianship of the children was given to the mother, Mrs C. Chiswick, whose attorney was a Mr A. Collins. A guardian *ad-litum* represented Mr H. Chiswick, who, on grounds of ill health, did not appear in court during the proceedings.

This really would have been the end of our quest, except I realised I would be travelling to Washington DC at the end of March for a business meeting and found that my schedule might be arranged so that I could spend a couple of hours in Baltimore, *en route* to the Baltimore Washington International Airport.

I phoned Margaret Wilding and made arrangements to meet her at the Harbour Court Hotel, overlooking the picturesquely renewed Baltimore harbour. She said that she would be delighted to meet her new-found English cousin and would like her eldest son to accompany her, since he was nearer my age and might have far more in common.

Chapter 21

Baltimore Maryland March 2000

We met as arranged for a snack lunch at the Harbour Court Hotel in downtown Baltimore's Light Street, since that was all my time would permit. Nicholas, a fellow of about my age and Margaret's eldest son accompanied her.

We exchanged the usual exaggerated courtesies, and each extolled how delighted we were to meet cousins where there had been no direct family contact in more than a hundred years. I must admit that I felt something of a glow of personal achievement to realise what Janet and I had accomplished and I was genuinely really pleased to meet them.

I opened my black case, which I kept with me in the flight cabin, and handed Margaret a wrapped gift containing a silver picture frame with a picture of myself, Laura and little Edward. Deep down I still felt a little miffed that Margaret had been a party, although hopefully unknowingly, to the deception and cover up concerning my great uncle, her own grandfather Henry, even though she had never known him.

Our waitress arrived and we each ordered sandwiches and coffee. Mine was a toasted Tuna sandwich on whole wheat bread. I shall never cease to wonder at the variety of breads available that restaurants offer throughout the whole of the United States, for a simple sandwich. When it arrived I could barely conceal my amazement at its awe-inspiring size. There appeared to be more than sufficient for a small family, not to mention the constant refills of hot coffee at no additional cost, unlike most catering establishments in Britain.

I produced photographs of my family that I had brought with me to show Margaret.

"Here's a photo of my father Edward and his father, my grandfather Paul. Paul's in military uniform because it's the last picture grandma had before he was killed in North Africa. This one's of my great grandfather Alf Chiswick. They say I look quite a bit like him, but I don't see the similarity other than the scant mop of hair. He was your Grandfather Henry's older brother, who more than eighty years ago sent the wedding present of a piano to his youngest brother."

"I don't have any photographs of my grandfather," said Margaret, after closely studying the photos of my Grandfathers Paul and Alfred.

"I've seen photographs of my mother and aunt in their teenage years and believe there's a slight facial likeness with your great granddad, Alfred Chiswick."

Margaret in turn showed me pictures of herself and her family who were all total strangers so far as any likeness was concerned. I explained that I intended to give her a copy of the family tree, but before doing so I needed to ask her some questions, to which she readily agreed.

"You recall you sent me an email letter telling me that your mother Rebecca stated her parents were a very happy couple and that only some considerable time after her father died had her mother Claire, your grandmother, remarried."

"Yes I certainly do, and I brought a copy along with me as you asked."

"You also told me that both sets of grandparents opposed the marriage and for that reason your mother and her sister never saw either set of grandparents, aunts and uncles."

"Yes, sadly that is perfectly correct; my mother never saw either set of grandparents."

"Well I think it's time that we dealt with one or two misconceptions on your part. To begin with when your mother was born there was only one, not two, sets of grandparents opposing the marriage and refusing to see the grandchildren. Henry's father David Joseph, your great grandfather and my great-great-granddad died, we believe sometime before 1899, and his mother Rebecca in 1916, at least six months before your mother was born, which tends to imply that Claire's parents were the ones who were so strenuously opposed to the marriage."

"Oh I see. I just hadn't realised."

"The next difficulty relates to the information you gave me concerning your mother's parents' marriage. I found that your grandfather was a patient in the Maryland Psychiatric Hospital and that your grandmother divorced him and remarried while he was alive."

"Now wait Alfred, you're completely wrong and that's patently

175

untrue. I remember my mother distinctly told me that her mother and father had a wonderfully harmonious relationship as she personally remembered it and that Claire only remarried after Henry's death. My Aunt Henrietta said much the same thing on a number of occasions."

"Margaret, I'm not in a position to dispute what your mother told you, but I can tell you that her parents were divorced and I've written evidence to that effect."

"Alfred, that's a lie, a downright falsehood and if the hospital has told you that, I shall write to them seeking an apology, and if one is not forthcoming I shall sue them for libel."

"I think," said Nicholas "that you're upsetting mother. I don't like your attitude with this line of questioning and I think that you should stop right now."

"Let's hold our horses," I said, raising my hands in mock surrender. "It's neither my intention, nor wish to upset you, Margaret, nor you Nicholas, nor anyone else. I simply have an enquiring mind and would like to get to the truth of something that happened seventy years ago. I didn't say the hospital communicated this information."

"Then I shall instruct my attorney to serve an injunction on whoever disseminated such falsehoods about my family," Margaret said, clearly very upset.

"There's truly nobody for you to sue," I replied.

"On some conjured up written evidence, you're making false allegations that are upsetting mother and unless you desist, we'll have to leave this lunch meeting," interjected Nicholas.

"Nicholas, your great grandfather Henry, your mother and you are part of my family. Although we've never met before today, we're all family and we're all on the same side. My great grandpa, my namesake, and your great grandpa were brothers. I'm simply trying to clear up a mystery, a seventy-year-old mystery, and I thought you or your mother might be able to help. My information comes from three impeccable sources. I'd like you to take a look at copies of documents that I've brought with me before any of us says another word."

I rummaged through my case as rapidly as possible and retrieved a green file with the papers I had brought with me. I carefully removed the copy certificates, each enclosed in its own transparent polythene envelope, from the file, producing from my small

176

audience a look of as much surprise as a conjurer might have witnessed when unexpectedly producing a couple of rabbits from an empty top hat. I set the documents on the table, inviting Margaret and Nicholas to examine them carefully.

"Here they are, in the order in which I first saw them. As you'll see the first is the April 1930 US federal census, which shows that Henry aged 42, at that time living in a mental hospital, was a divorced man. The second is a copy of the 1931 death certificate of Henry Chiswick. It shows that at the time of his death, he was a divorced man and that Claire was the informant and stated that her relationship was that of his *former* wife. The third is a transcript of the divorce petition of January 1928."

Margaret and Nicholas looked at the documents. After two or three minutes had elapsed, Margaret was the first to look up. She almost whispered.

"Oh my heavens, I really can't believe my eyes." And sighing deeply, she continued, "All these falsehoods. After all these years! I just can't believe this! Whatever does it all mean?"

"I think Margaret that every family has the odd skeleton or two in a locked closet. Skeletons that we forget about because they're painful reminders of something in the past that we wish had not happened, or of which we might have felt shame and embarrassment, and this is one such closet we've inadvertently opened. I'm truly sorry to see that I've caused you this distress.

"In genealogical research these things tend to happen from time to time. Before we condemn anyone, we have to consider a number of possibilities. Laws and attitudes change with time. An illegitimate birth, or cohabiting when unmarried, even divorce, were terrible sins up to forty years ago and would be concealed, whereas not today. Perhaps your grandmother eradicated these unpalatable truths and intended revealing them at some later date when her daughters were older and mature enough to understand. Then possibly through some illness or memory lapse, or even lacking the courage to disillusion her family, she omitted to do so. There could be a number of other possibilities. Can you think of any that might have applied to your grandparents?"

"Alf, this has been a great shock and upset to me. All my life I believed totally all my mother and Aunt Henrietta had told me and now they're neither of them with us any more and there's nobody left to ask."

177

"Did anybody ever drop a hint or clue as to what really happened, that might help unravel this mystery?"

"No. None that I can possibly think of."

"Well, it does no good to wake a sleeping dog, is the old saying," said Nicholas.

Margaret added, "Alf, it was amazing to have been able to link up with grandfather's family, something I've wanted to do over the years, especially after Grandmother Claire passed away, since we never knew her family or grandpa's. With my illusions shattered I wonder now what I've achieved with this. As the Bible tells us, in Ecclesiastes, 'In much wisdom is much grief, and he who increases knowledge increases sorrow'."

"Margaret, I'm sorry to see you distressed like this. It was never my intention to cause you or Nicholas any upset, but I must disagree with that Ecclesiastes thing. It's certainly not a philosophy that I could ever accept. I believe one should always seek knowledge and truth. Sooner or later some good, somewhere, will always come of it. As Keats famously said in his 'Ode on a Grecian Urn', 'Beauty is truth and truth beauty, that is all ye know on earth, and all ye need to know'."

As I quoted Keats I thought to myself: *my Harrow English literature master would have been proud to hear me spout something like that in my concluding statement. Just shows how a good education can occasionally be of some help.*

I looked at my watch.

"Good heaven's, it's late, we've been chatting longer than I realised, just look at the time. If I'm to catch my flight I really must run. Margaret, I'm going to leave you this updated copy of our family tree. Maybe if we think long and hard enough we might come up with some ideas that could explain the mystery that surrounded your grandparent's divorce. Do let's keep in touch, and if you ever visit London do look me up, there's a huge family waiting to meet you."

Having paid for lunch, and with handshakes and farewells at the end of our brief meeting, I hurriedly took my leave. I arrived back home the following day, delighted to be reunited with my wife and family. The day after that, I telephoned Janet and recounted my meeting with our American cousins and the mystery that still remained.

Chapter 22

Baltimore September 1926

The previous year Claire and Henry had been house-hunting, to find a home with a yard or garden in which their growing daughters could play and perhaps keep a rabbit or some other pet. Claire had found a suitable house in a good newly-developed neighbourhood in Ellamont Road, Ashburton, a prosperous Baltimore suburb, and had arranged with the realtor to return with her husband for a further visit at the weekend.

While showing them the house it came to light during a conversation concerning neighbourhood school and church amenities that Henry was Jewish. There was a hurried conversation between the realtor and the vendor. The realtor turned and explained, "I'm awful sorry folks, but ah've jest been informed thet this here vendor has decided to withdraw his home from the market an' is not intendin to proceed with the sale. There seems like there's little purpose in viewin' this darn house any further an' the vendor has jest requested thet we all now leaves his property straight away."

Once outside, the realtor escorted them back to his car as, flustered and embarrassed, he attempted to explain the situation to an incensed Henry and Claire.

"This here area's not restricted in any way, but residents in the area hev a good neighbour's policy an' hev agreed amongst there-selves not to sell on any account to Negroes, or Jews, an' I didn' knows how you were Jews, cause yew don' seem like it. Yew look's like very fine people to me," he explained. "Yew awl see it's like this. These good people are worried thet once one family moves in, others of their kind'll follow and they jest don't want to live next door to no black folks or Jews. They'll move out an' the more folks moves out, the more property prices an' real estate values'll spiral downwards in the neighbourhood. Yew ken understand why they feel this way an' if yew lived here I know'd yew'd feel this way yourselves. I ken show yew some real pretty homes in other areas of

179

the city right now, where I know yew awl won't have no difficulties. What d' yew say?"

"I say," replied Claire, her anger mounting as the realtor spoke, "That these prejudices are dreadful. If these people are our fellow Americans, then they're from some other planet, because they certainly don't come from the same mould as George Washington, Thomas Jefferson and our nation's founding fathers. The signatories of our Declaration of Independence wrote of life, liberty and the pursuit of happiness, and nowhere, but nowhere, is there any precondition that this may only apply to those who are white and Episcopalian, excluding Jew, black, brown or whoever. My husband and I feel that we wouldn't demean ourselves by living here among such alien neighbours, even if you gave us the house for twenty dollars! This would not be a suitable environment in which to raise our children amongst such bigotry. We'll stay in our apartment and make do, thank you very much, as we are."

"Ahm awful sorry yew feel this way ma'am."

"I would be obliged if you would now simply stop talking to us with these horrible platitudes and take us back to North Howard Street, straight away."

* * *

Henry purchased a smart secondhand black Hudson automobile, instead of a new home, replacing his old Model T Ford, which he had used to carry samples during the week and for trips into the countryside with his family at weekends when weather permitted. He was a good salesman, business was booming and he travelled far and wide to earn his growing commissions. He planned that as his fortunes progressed they would be able to make a European trip the year after next.

Life with Claire had certainly been good for Henry. His main disappointment was that he had been unable as yet to save sufficient to make the journey back to London to visit brothers and unknown nephews and nieces who had never met him or his wife and daughters. He had been saving and was determined that one day soon he would take Claire, Rebecca – now ten – and Henrietta Ruth – now six – to visit his family and show them the many famous places he had known as a child: the Tower of London and its ravens, Tower Bridge and Buckingham Palace, St Paul's Cathedral, the fourth on the same site and the tallest building in London when completed in

180

1710, the architect Christopher Wren's masterpiece, with its organ which Mendelssohn once played. To hear the sounds of that immense bustling city, the hub of a great imperial empire, see the autumnal fogs, smell the acrid fumes from tens of thousand smoking chimney pots – all this was planned for the future, a dream that was to be rudely and cruelly unfulfilled.

Claire was still deeply in love with Henry and he with Claire. Happy and content, they filled their home with love, music and harmony as they had planned. Their daughters were an amalgam of their parents, but said to be more like their father in facial appearance and temperament. Both were bright students and very adept at playing the piano under Claire's expert tuition. They had also inherited their mother's ability to sing and sang in their school and local church choirs. Claire regularly played both in church and in her husband's synagogue whenever a special occasion such as a wedding warranted it, the additional income being saved for summer camp for the girls.

The only blight to Claire's happiness was the unrelenting attitude of her parents so that her daughters never knew a grandparent in spite of her attempts at birthdays and Christmas to contact them. Her sisters and their families had sided with their parents, which meant that her children knew no Robins family aunts, uncles or cousins. She sent cards, notes and messages at every opportunity, always trying for the sake of the children to build bridges of reconciliation. Regardless of her every endeavour the result was always the same and Henry repeatedly advised that she should desist, since each rebuff caused additional stress and unnecessary sadness.

*　*　*

The first Sunday in September, Henry came down with a runny nose, sneezed several times that morning and felt he had a slight fever. His limbs ached, his temples throbbed with a headache and he felt a little nauseated and generally indisposed.

"A mild chill, I'll stay in bed for a while and shake it off by tomorrow," he announced to Claire and the children, who were disappointed that he would be unable to take them out for the barbecue he had promised.

As the day advanced his headache became progressively worse. Henry claimed the light hurt his eyes and Claire, not unduly concerned, pulled down the blinds to darken the room. The sound

181

of the children playing seemed incredibly loud and later became unbearable. By late afternoon the headache was of such intensity that Henry cried out in pain. Cold compresses that Claire applied to his brow and the ingested aspirin hurriedly purchased at the pharmacy by Rebecca on her mother's instruction gave Henry little respite and caused him to throw up.

In spite of his protestation that he would sleep it off and be fine in the morning, Claire was beside herself with worry. Fearing that this might be the precursor of the dreaded poliomyelitis, which was endemic every summer, she sent Rebecca to summon the local doctor to come to their apartment as soon as possible. Before the doctor arrived it was very clear to Claire that Henry had become drowsy and seemed to be unable to respond coherently when she spoke to him. He appeared to speak as though inebriated, although no spirits or alcohol had passed his lips, which greatly increased her anxiety and worry.

The doctor arrived and after a few minutes spent questioning and examining her husband announced that he was showing symptoms of a meningeal irritation and that a neurologist should be consulted and preferably he should be admitted to one of the isolation wards at the Johns Hopkins, where he could be examined more thoroughly and observed for a day or two. Early that same evening Henry was transferred to hospital, Claire remaining at home with the children, assuring Henry that she would visit him on the morrow and hoping above hope that in this seeming confused state, he would understand and recall what she was saying to him.

The following morning with the children in school Claire visited Henry in the hospital with her sister-in-law, Annie. To her dismay she found, by looking through a window, that Henry was being barrier nursed in isolation.

The duty resident was called. He explained that clinical examination and initial tests indicated that her husband was suffering from encephalitis, an inflammation of the brain caused by a viral infection. He said reassuringly that while there was no cure, such infections were usually self-limiting and treated with good general nursing care most patients made a good recovery within a matter of a few weeks, particularly strong healthy adults like her husband.

"But my husband seems to be sleeping even while the nurse is turning him."

"That's because he is deeply asleep. The infection causes an acute inflammation of the brain, which swells within the skull and frequently causes a loss of consciousness for a time."

"How long will it last?" enquired Claire with ever mounting anxiety.

"In my experience certainly many days, possibly two to three weeks at a minimum," came the reply.

Confused and shocked with worry, Claire permitted Annie to lead her back home to ponder how best she could eke out the savings they had at their disposal before Henry would be fit to return to work, since there was no health insurance or sickness benefit. When he was not working, both his salary and bonus ceased and were he to be absent from work for too long his job would likewise vanish.

It was only some weeks later that Claire slowly realised that while she had enquired repeatedly when Henry would recover; she had omitted one essential question: she had never asked how fully would he recover.

As the days turned into weeks and the weeks gradually became months, the economic plight Claire faced was a major concern, but hardly her only problem. The children asked repeatedly, when is daddy expected home and when could they visit him?

Claire was now allowed to visit and sit with Henry, although only three times a week, for one hour each visit, but no children were permitted. Henry had lost weight, his skin no longer hugging his frame. His eyes remained closed as his comatose state continued. Claire, relieved initially that Henry was not suffering from polio-myelitis, did not know sufficient of this other malady to ask whether or not there might be any residual incapacity or intellectual impairment. She just believed that he would reawaken as after any prolonged sleep and resume his normal activities. When would he reawaken was a question that remained unanswered. The neurologist explained that this prolonged period might be due to brain damage that might result in some impairment of his mental faculties and of his physical prowess.

Little did Claire realise that fate, that malevolent sister of misfortune, had set in train the destruction of all her future hopes and innocent dreams for her family.

When visiting, Claire sat and held Henry's hand, speaking of her love and that of the children, of how desperately she and they missed him, of the week's events, of happenings, but never mentioning her urgently increasing financial worries and difficulties.

At times she brought a book of poetry to read to Henry, just as he had read to Claire in the earlier years of their courtship, their favourites being Longfellow's *Hiawatha* and Matthew Arnold's *Sohrab and Rustum*.

Henry's family helped out with what little money they could spare and the shortfall was made up from the sale of the Hudson automobile and the little Claire could earn, using her classical musical talents, giving music lessons and occasionally playing at a church service or wedding. She moved to a smaller apartment. Her shopping bills diminished, because she and her daughters ate more frugally, she more meagrely than they, as her continuing weight loss revealed. She had even undertaken to launder some of the church vestments and linens in return for a pittance, since the church considered such drudgery to be a noble calling, a reward in itself.

Henry regained consciousness after almost four months. His illness had largely deprived him of the use of his right arm and leg. He was unable to utter more than monosyllabic words, which apparently made little or no sense and most seriously he seemed unaware of where he was and showed no recognition of Claire or his sisters.

Week after week through the winter, the biting winds blew in off the Atlantic shore, as Claire trudged backwards and forwards through the packed snow and ice to the hospital. As spring arrived and with repeated further discussions with the doctors, realisation was dawning for Claire. She started to fully comprehend what she had been able to observe for herself over the weeks since Henry had regained consciousness. The encephalitis had wreaked permanent physical damage on Henry and had virtually destroyed every vestige of his once fine intellect. His gaunt emaciated face and dishevelled appearance reminded her of the Henry she once knew, but in all else he was a husk, an empty shell, physically and worst of all mentally.

He had sustained damage to his nervous system that would not only make it impossible for him to ever resume work, but worse he would never be able to be cared for at home, in a domestic environment. He was unable to recognise or communicate with her. The doctors informed her that there was now nothing more that they could do for her husband to assist his recovery and that he would be transferred at the end of the week to the Baltimore State Mental Hospital.

184

With his transfer to the Spring Grove Maryland State Mental Hospital in Catonsville, Claire would now have further to travel to visit. She spoke to the doctors at the new hospital, to Annie to any friends who might listen. Her nightmare was never ending. She had lost weight, her face was lined and drained with worry; she had become a widow in all but name.

She wailed silently at night, smothering her sobs and cries in the bed sheet, lest the children hear her. Crying night after night and willing herself to sleep, desperately praying and wishing this nightmare might end. Wishing and praying her love, her Henry, restored to health might again, as in times past, hold her in his arms, embrace, protect and comfort her. Might again call her his darling Claire. Might walk and frolic with her and the children once more in the park. Might again give her one further posy of violets. Might yet again read the poetry, long into the night, they so enjoyed together.

"Henry, I need you, we want you," she repeatedly murmured and only the stillness of the night remained, as drained emotionally, sleep offered some brief but only temporary respite, for in the morning her terrible problems remained. Through her mind kept flowing the words of a different Henry, Henry Wadsworth Longfellow: "There is no grief like the grief that does not speak".

Chapter 23

Baltimore September 1927

By summer's end, Claire had gradually realised that her life had become like a driftwood boat on a vast pitiless expanse of ocean. Her daughters were passengers with her. They were drifting helplessly without sail or power, the elements indifferent to their plight, slowly succumbing to thirst and hunger. She must somehow regain the initiative and with it redeem her own sense of direction and self-respect. She resolved upon a course of action that horrified her, but about which she felt she had no alternative. She must take charge of her own life before it was too late. To this end she decided to consult an attorney as soon as possible.

Claire had learned that Andrew Collins, an old school friend, had some years earlier set himself up as an attorney in a law practice at 445 East Fayette Street, three blocks east of the North Calvert Street court house. She had not seen him since high school, but had been told that he was well thought of and his law practice was very successful. So it was that she made an appointment to consult him the following week, in the early afternoon of Monday 5 September.

At the agreed time she arrived at a large red brick house, the first floor approached by a set of impressive wide stone steps and balustrades topped by a gleaming, frequently polished, brass handrail on either side. She climbed the steps, rang the front doorbell and waited. Within a matter of seconds a smartly dressed young woman opened the door and having identified the caller, invited Mrs Chiswick to accompany her past a large staircase, leading to upstairs living accommodation, into the spacious ground floor law office of Andrew Collins.

Following a brief wait in an outer reception area, she was courteously asked by the same young lady who had opened the door, who she later learned was Andrew's secretary, "Would you care to follow me please?" and was ushered into a large, well appointed office with two leather lounge chairs facing a desk, behind which Andrew was seated. On the desk were framed pictures of a woman with two young children, a separate picture of three young boys, an ornamental inkstand in front of a large central blotting pad and to one side a telephone. As she entered, Andrew rose and politely offered her a seat, saying, "Claire, How nice to see you after all these years, how are you?"

The secretary standing to one side asked, "Would you care for a little refreshment, perhaps some iced tea, or coffee?" Following Claire's response of, "Yes thank you. Iced tea would be most refreshing on a hot day like this," she disappeared to prepare the refreshment.

"Are you still playing the piano? I remember you were really good with the classics and seemed to win all the end of year piano competitions."

As they awaited the arrival of the tea, they briefly continued their exchange of pleasantries as Claire looked round the room. Along one wall were shelves of red and brown legal books, embossed with gold lettering, stretching from floor to ceiling, while behind Andrew's desk was a plethora of framed certificates and diplomas. In one corner stood a tall long-case clock, whose brass pendulum glinted as the reflected sunlight caught its repeated brief transit behind a narrow ornamental wood and glass door.

Before she had an opportunity to explore further, the secretary returned with two glasses, which she placed on the desk before Claire and Andrew. She then withdrew, closing the office door, leaving only the sound of the ceiling fan swish, swish, swishing as it revolved overhead and the pendulum clock quietly ticking in the corner behind her chair.

Andrew enquired more formally, "Claire, how can I help you?"

Before she could utter a single word, tears began rolling down her cheeks as though a small damn had burst, the droplets leaving irregular grey circles on her summer dress where they fell, as she searched urgently in her purse for her handkerchief. Haltingly between sobs, and dabbing tears from her eyes, she then began to narrate how Henry had been struck down by his unexpected illness and all that had happened in her life, in the twelve months since then.

At the end of her account Andrew exclaimed, "Oh my heavens Claire, you poor girl! I had no idea that you'd been experiencing such problems. You most certainly have my sympathy. Tell me, how

187

can I help you? Can I lend you some money; you can always pay it back later whenever you feel you're able."

"Thank you, but no. I'm not here to borrow money from you Andrew. I'll not conceal the fact that I'm sorely in need of money, but that's not my reason for coming here today to see you."

"Then how else can I help you?"

"Andrew I need your help both as a friend and an attorney. As a friend because I haven't the wherewithal to pay you any fee at present and as a lawyer because I need your legal help."

"Let's not worry about the money side of things for the moment Claire. In what manner can I help you legally?"

"Andrew, I despise myself for saying this, but I must have a divorce. Can you help me?"

"If that's what you really want. You do realise that there's a great stigma attached to divorce? I'll do my best for you, but you'll discover that polite society will be very antagonistic and the Church will certainly not accept this course of action. On what grounds do you wish to proceed?"

Silently sobbing, she sniffed, vainly willing her tears to stop, telling herself she needed to be strong and resolute.

"Andrew, I no longer have a family I can turn to for help. I married against my parent's wishes. I married Henry in a civil marriage, which wasn't solemnised in any church. Since Henry was taken sick in September last, life has been an indescribable, unrelenting, nightmare, a disaster greater than I can bear alone and with which I can no longer cope, no matter how hard I try.

"I've worked all the hours that the good Lord has given me, to support my daughters and myself. I must also make time to care for my children and visit my husband. I stand in line shopping. I cook, clean our home, prepare lunch boxes, scrub, wash, mend, sew and a host of other domestic chores. The little I earn giving music lessons and any other work I can find is simply not enough. I just can't make ends meet, no matter how hard I work, no matter how hard I economise.

"What little savings we had, were long ago completely used up. I've had insufficient money for food and necessities. I've barely had anything to put in the children's lunchboxes for some weeks and now at times they go to bed hungry. No matter how hard I try to cut back, our circumstances grow worse. I've very few choices open to me and I realise I can't go on like this, I truly can't. Society penalises me unfairly for being a woman. Womens jobs are all menial and underpaid, and I'm deprived of the right to earn my own livelihood with which to support myself and my children without the financial assistance of a man."

"Has your husband no family who could help you?" enquired Andrew.

"Henry has three sisters living here and two brothers in England. The elder brother in England, I believe, has become quite wealthy, but contact was lost after his mother died in 1916, and neither I nor Henry's sisters have any idea where he might be living now. His three sisters each have large families and are also struggling financially. They do give me a little help from time to time, even without my needing to ask, but insufficient for our real needs and I can't live off their charity like this indefinitely.

"I wasn't brought into this world to be a parasite. I was always told that I was born with a unique musical talent, to give pleasure to others, to help lighten life's burdens through the gift of music and I'm failing. I've failed miserably, in everything I thought possible. I feel like an empty box and I've, I've..." Claire cried again into her handkerchief, before she was able to continue. "I've lost all my self-esteem. I have thought long and hard about my options. I might just get by with full-time work. I would only be able to earn about half the wages of a man doing the same job, if that, providing I placed my girls in an orphanage and only visited my husband on Sundays. But Henry's harrowing experience in an orphanage, when he was a child in London, was sufficiently vivid that I can't inflict this upon our girls. I can't degrade myself either, to walk the streets like the painted harlots, poor wretches, who we see standing and strolling round the harbour. The only other choice I have is that I must file for a divorce and when free again, urgently seek a man who will be understanding enough to marry a divorced woman like me, with children and who will then help support me and my children."

"I can understand the depths of your predicament. A woman, alone with young children, simply can't survive without assistance from her family. As you've explained the situation to me Claire, would I be correct in believing that your husband has lost his intellect and reason through this dreadful illness?"

"Yes."

"And is there any likelihood that he'll recover?"

189

"No. Unfortunately that's the dreadful state of affairs. The doctors at the Johns Hopkins and at the Maryland have all told me that there'll be no further recovery."

"Then would I be correct in assuming that any petition for divorce would be uncontested?"

"Henry wouldn't and couldn't contest the proceedings. He's unable to understand anything that's said to him. He's neither able to recognise me or anybody else and these indispositions are permanent."

"In that case Claire we can proceed with an application for an uncontested divorce, providing your husband's doctors are able to provide the court with reports confirming all that you've just told me. The next question is, on what grounds are you seeking this divorce?"

"I just don't know the legal grounds. I've heard that marital infidelity is one such reason and non-consummation of a marriage is another, neither of which would apply in my case. I don't believe that failure to gain approval of ones parents are grounds?"

"Quite right. If a failure to obtain full parental approval before marriage were grounds for divorce, then very few marriages would survive for any time and divorce would be rampant," replied Andrew, laughing and at last drawing a smile from Claire.

Andrew stood up, walked over to the shelves of law books and rapidly reached for one of the heavy red leather volumes, with its embossed gold lettering, which he took down. Returning to his desk he sat down, opened the legal tome, leafed through the pages and then announced, "Here we are. The Maryland state statutes provide grounds for divorce after one year if your separation is mutual and voluntary. I'm certain your grounds do not come within this category. Desertion for one full year, by one or other party, is a possibility. Your husband has deserted you, but again this might be seen as a constructive desertion, since he had no choice when being confined to hospital, which might render this line of reasoning invalid.

"Insanity provides grounds for divorce. There is a requirement that the individual needs to have been confined in a mental institution for three years. This would provide the most telling grounds for your divorce, but it does mean that you would need to wait a further two years. There is an involuntary separation clause, where the parties live apart without interruption for two years, which would require that you wait a further year."

"Andrew, our circumstances are difficult enough as it is. If I had to wait a further year for divorce proceedings to be justified, then I don't know how my daughters and I would ever survive as a family. We're almost destitute now, as it is, and it would be absolutely impossible."

"Leave this to me Claire. Give my secretary the names of the doctors who have cared for Henry and the hospitals to which they are attached and I promise that with their reports I'll find adequate legal grounds to be able to file for your divorce straight away. We might need to suggest that Henry left the matrimonial home some months before his illness, in order to justify grounds of involuntary separation. Would you be willing to say this should I be unable to find alternative grounds?"

"If I'm left with no alternative, then of course I must agree."

"It may not be necessary, but providing you're in agreement with this strategy and since Henry would be unable to contest any statement you make, it's likely that this would be our safest route to ensure a speedy divorce. By bending the rules a little here and there we might achieve a greater good, providing I have your cooperation and discretion."

"Of course."

"I'll also need a fair amount more information from you, as soon as possible, but none that you'll find too onerous. I'll then be in a position to represent you as a petitioner in your divorce proceedings. We'll file your papers in the county court and then we'll need to serve a divorce petition on the respondent."

"Who is the respondent?" asked Claire.

"That's the other party; in your case, Henry. An uncontested divorce will become absolute within two to three months. I can virtually promise you that in all likelihood you'll be free to remarry early in the new year, so you can make whatever plans you need accordingly. Normally we would have to consider which of the parents would have custody of the children, but in view of Henry's continuing indisposition I'm certain the court would agree that this responsibility would devolve entirely upon you as the mother."

"Andrew, I don't know how to thank you. Will you be able to wait a year or two for your money?"

"Claire, don't worry on that score, I can wait forever and you can pay me whenever you're able. If you wish you can repay me in

191

kind. I've a piano upstairs that is tuned, but unused and children who've yet to learn to play some musical instrument or other. Perhaps when you've time you might consider providing weekly lessons for my two older boys.

"I'll need several hours of your time, meanwhile, to make your deposition so that we can write up your divorce petition. Perhaps you can check with my secretary so that we can do this as soon as possible – the sooner we start, the sooner you'll have your divorce."

They both stood up, Andrew walked round his desk, shook Claire's hand and opened the door, with the parting words, "Goodbye Claire, it was good to see you after such a long time, even under these difficult circumstances. If everything goes according to plan, I believe you'll have your divorce by the end of January."

Chapter 24

Baltimore September 1927

At the weekend of the first anniversary of Henry's illness, following her first visit to her attorney, Claire found Henry in bed in his small, starkly whitewashed, bare bedroom, which had been allocated off the main ward, when she next visited him. The main ward was intimidating. Huge and white, there were row upon row of metal beds spaced along its length, each bed separated from its fellow by a small bare bedside locker. Along the width there was a narrow walkway of little more than the width of a bed and then the foot of the next bed spaced as the previous row. At the head of the metal bed head was another bed, pointing the other way, with a total of eight beds across the width of the ward. In this manner the ward accommodated seven or eight score of beds. It reminded her of a giant odorous sardine box, devoid of any humanity or warmth, smelling constantly of unwashed bodies and stale sweat.

Henry had been assigned to the minute side ward because of his severe physical incapacity and it was here that Claire sat with him as he lay still and mostly unmoving in his bed. She held his warm but unresponsive hand, recalling the tenderness of his caresses the soft eloquent sound of his voice, his gentle nature.

She spoke to him quietly and earnestly.

"Henry my darling, my love, what have you, or I ever done? What bestial act have we committed to deserve to be punished in this manner? Thank heavens you my dearest are unable to see and will never comprehend how low this illness has brought you and how it is destroying your own wife and children. Each day has become a struggle against want and uncertainty and dear sweet Jesus in heaven help me, I can't continue like this any longer.

"I feel I can't live without you, but I can't survive with our babies with you like this. I can't let our children go hungry any longer. I have an unfailing duty to see that they're nourished properly. I don't care if I must accept the degradation of the need to stand in

193

line for yesterday's bread and food at the end of each day. I can barely replace the shoes on our daughter's feet; they're growing so fast, that I must accept hand me down clothes whenever I can. I can accept the burden of a convent life if I must. But I can't bear to watch our children go hungry. They hunger daily for food, and for the attention I'm unable to give them because I'm so sick and drained with worry.

"The children often go to bed hungry, they're almost starving. I'm treated like a widow. Nobody asks after you any more, apart from our little ones, and even they no longer ask me every day, as they once did. Except for me, only the nurses and doctors here know, or seem to care, if you're alive. I feel isolated and alone and frightened, because I'm so alone. I've no memories to share with any, but you, and now even this pleasure has been taken from me. Without our shared memories what am I, what do I become?

"Our daughters hunger for their father's love, and I hunger for my lost love." Dropping to a whisper, "If it weren't for the girls I'd put an end to my plight and unhappiness. I'd readily turn on the gas tap and go to sleep." Dabbing her eyes, "And Henry, don't think I haven't thought of it a score or more times, these past weeks, and it frightens me. I feel waves of helplessness, in my depression, sweep over me threatening to submerge me. I'm terrified that I might just once give in. It would be so easy. I'm teetering on the edge of a horrible abyss and I can only see one strategy. My darling I know you can't understand me, but I've reached a decision, the most pitiable decision a wife and mother can be called upon to make. It fills me with loathing and self-contempt. Those who choose not to understand my predicament will think of me as despicable, but this doesn't matter, my mind is made up. I've thought long and hard and realise to survive we have no other choice. I must marry again.

"We must divorce and then I must remarry. Yes I'll marry again, though I shall never stop loving you my darling. You have to understand I must remarry, for we can't survive any other way, I shall go mad if I go on much longer like this. I'll never be able to love another as I've loved you. I don't have any other choice. I'll see that I have no more children, but I'll give him loyalty and comfort in exchange for the support and security he can give our children and me. I must divorce you as soon as I can, because we must survive

194

and as God is my witness I know of no other way. There is no other way." Standing up and advancing to the door she turned.

"Henry you're the love of my life. You were my very first love and we were so happy in our love and sweet innocence. I promised to love you in sickness and in health and in my heart I shall always love you and be faithful to you. I shall always love you my darling, as no other. I willingly let you make me a mother to our children and now I must use any and every means possible to make a home for our children and feed them in any way I'm able, whether with or without you. I should beg your forgiveness and understanding if I believed you retained any ability to understand my desperate plight, and I pray that God may forgive me. I shall tell the girls today that you've died, that I've become a widow. I shall never tell them the truth of what I've resolved, for they're too young to understand this seeming betrayal. Should I be held to be accountable and believed wicked and contemptible then you must know that I've tried and have truly not been strong enough by myself to do what we were able to do together.

"And Henry, when that day comes when you and I shall be whole again and meet at the great reawakening, on judgement day, as I know we shall, I shall clasp you in my arms, call you husband again and never let you go. I shall let our children and all mankind know that I made a sacrifice for our children, and you Henry were the only man I ever truly loved."

She then turned, opened the door her emotional catharsis nearing its bitter end and ran sobbing from the room. Henry neither acknowledged her words, nor gave any indication that he knew she had been present.

She proceeded home slowly in a daze, not recalling anything she saw, or how she arrived back at her apartment. Sitting at the piano, she emitted a series of primeval sobs and cries of, "Henry, Henry, please forgive me. Henry, I need you. Please help me I'm so utterably miserable and alone."

Then, gently lifting the hinged black polished wooden keyboard cover, she commenced to play Bach, the music transcending any further words that she might utter, slowly pouring her grief and sorrow into the keys, which then produced the soft sonorous sounds of the music she and Henry had so often enjoyed together. She played more Bach, with its noble adagio movements, again and again, the music a comforting opiate to her anguish, a beauteous

195

poetry to her melancholy soul.

Hour upon hour, unaware of any passage of time, she played music, first of Bach, then Schumann, then the compositions of others, their music gently providing that tender balm to quieten her inner torment. She played on and on, ceasing only when her daughters arrived home from school.

"Mother, hello, mother, we're home!"

As they approached she tearfully embraced each of them in turn, again and again, telling them, "My darlings, I have just come from the hospital. Daddy has been very sick for a long, long time, and today he left us to go, to go..." and here she sobbed, "...to go to heaven. We must all be specially brave, Daddy would have wanted it so. We've all sustained a great loss and you've lost the most wonderful daddy in the world."

All three sobbed and cried until Claire announced, "My darlings, for daddy's sake we must be braver than this. We must dry our tears and say a little prayer together for daddy and ourselves." She stood with her arms round each child and together taking their lead from their mother they slowly recited, "Our father, Who art in heaven..." Then Claire said, "Now I'm going to play the 'Crimond arrangement' that Daddy liked to hear me sing of the twenty-third Psalm and you're going to help sing it with me."

She played the introductory chords and then together they sang.

"The Lord's my shepherd I'll not want..." At the conclusion, as the last chord died away Claire said, "We're going to light a single candle as Jewish and Catholic tradition requires. In daddy's religion it's called a *Yartzeit* light. Claire then lit and set a candle in a candlestick on the piano. "We'll always set it on the piano. It's the most treasured of the wedding gifts, daddy and I received so many years ago, before either of you were born. We'll always treasure this piano, and we'll play it every day, as a symbol of the love daddy had for us and that we have for him.

"Each year from now on, on the first of May, daddy's birthday, we'll light a candle in his memory to remind us of the happy times when we celebrated his birthday and he celebrated our birthdays and we will sing the twenty-third psalm that he loved so. We'll never again light a candle to commemorate the sorrowful anniversary of his death because he would always want us to celebrate the happy times in his life. I want you to promise me solemnly in your hearts that you'll always do this for daddy and me."

196

Chapter 25

Baltimore October 1927

During the following days Claire found a small two-bed apartment on the other side of Baltimore into which she and the children moved with the piano and their few remaining possessions. With a broken heart she had resolved to cut herself off from Henry's sisters and their children, fearing that through further contact Rebecca and Henrietta might learn the dreadful truth of her betrayal. Henry was still alive, and she would do anything to avoid having her children learn her abhorrent and shameful secret. Protecting herself and maintaining the finest reputation in the eyes of her children became her overriding priority.

In time, this dreadful decision and seeming duplicity would fade into oblivion once she had found another partner and married again. She was determined that Rebecca and Henrietta must never know her secret, which would follow her to her grave and beyond.

She twice attended Andrew Collins' office to make her deposition to enable him to write up her divorce petition. At the conclusion of the second session Andrew asked Claire, "Have you considered my suggestion that you give my sons a weekly piano lesson? I could pay you for the lessons and we could also write something off from my fees."

"I must confess I haven't given the matter any thought. I've been so busy relocating. But yes, of course I can find time to give them lessons. How old are they?"

"My eldest, Andrew Collins Junior, is eleven, the next one's Edward, aged nine and then there's Robert, aged two, although I think he's probably far too young for lessons of any kind."

"When would you like me to start the lessons?"

"As soon as you feel you're able. The weekend would be better as the boys like to romp and play after school. Do you think you could come here to give them the lesson? We've a beautiful grand piano that only the piano tuner uses."

"I could, but first I'd have to make arrangements for my daughters to stay with friends while I'm away."

"That won't be necessary. You could bring them with you."

"That's very kind of you, but wouldn't your wife find this a terrible imposition to look after two more boisterous children?"

"Claire, this is a large well constructed house and no matter how boisterous they might be, I can assure you that with the door closed you'd hardly hear a thing, and I'm certain that Annie would find no difficulty in coping with the influx of two more children."

"Would you mind if I tried out the piano?"

"Certainly, I've a few minutes to spare before my next client." So saying he stood up. "If you'd care to follow me, the piano is on the second floor in the music room, and I can also introduce you to Annie, if she hasn't gone out shopping or visiting."

They left the office area, Andrew telling his secretary, who was busy pounding an oversize Remington typewriter, to call him on the intercom when his next client arrived. Reaching the second floor he led Claire into a spacious, brightly sunlit high ceilinged room at the back of the house where she found a magnificent Steinway grand piano, facing a vast window overlooking the tops of distant trees.

"Claire, you try out the piano while I see if I can find Annie to brew up some fresh coffee."

Claire sat at the piano, lifted the keyboard and played a few notes to check it was tuned as Andrew had claimed. She then let her fingers glide over the keys. She was playing a Chopin nocturne when Andrew returned and he just stood, transfixed, until she had finished. With the last chords he exclaimed, "Bravo! Claire that was marvellous. We've not heard anything nearly so good since we've lived here."

"Thank you, it's always so pleasing to play in a room of this size, when one finds a magnificent piano in really tip top condition like yours."

"Could you play anything else, while we're waiting for our coffee to arrive?"

"Of course I can." Claire resumed playing and had played no more than a few bars when there was a knock at the door and in came a middle-aged lady, slightly rotund in shape with shining polished ebony skin wheeling a trolley on which was a tray. The magical aroma preceding her was given out by two steaming cups of hot coffee and a plate heaped with small dainty chocolate chip cookies.

198

"Come in!" exclaimed Andrew, and turning to Claire said, "Claire I'd like you to meet Annie, who helps me look after the boys." Then turning to Annie he announced, "Annie, this is an old high-school friend of mine from way back, heaven knows when, who's going to give the older boys some piano lessons."

Following the introductions Claire and Andrew sat on a spacious settee in front of the coffee table, sipping their coffee as Annie left the room, having received instructions to call when the intercom summoned Andrew to his next client.

"Forgive me, but I was a little taken aback," said Claire. "I had thought Annie was your wife, before she appeared."

"No. Annie has been with us as a nanny ever since Jane, my late wife, came home from the hospital with Andrew Junior in her arms."

"I'm so sorry. Did I understand you to say late wife, Andrew?"

"Yes. It's two years since Jane passed away. It was when Robert was born. It's a simple, but difficult story and I still get rather choked up talking about it. About three years ago Jane became pregnant with our third child. We were ecstatically happy and everything was fine during the pregnancy. She visited the same obstetrician who had delivered our two previous children, for her antenatal care, and everything progressed normally. Jane went into labour and we arrived at the hospital maternity unit in good time as she had done with the other two confinements. The obstetrician arrived and she was safely delivered of a beautiful little boy. Nothing could have been simpler or more magnificent.

"There had been no complications whatsoever, apart from a small perineal skin tear, which our fellow was repairing with a couple of stitches to save time as he was waiting for the afterbirth to come down. When he finished his suture, he suddenly discovered that the womb had enlarged massively and that she was bleeding, without his having realised there was anything untoward happening. That gynaecologist had been completely negligent, too busy trying to save a couple of minutes of his precious time. She lost a huge amount of blood and he had to manually extract a retained placenta. She rallied for a few hours, but she was desperately weak from the loss of blood and the shock of the procedure without any anaesthesia.

"She developed an infection and had lost the strength to fight against it. The love of my life was lost to me as she succumbed two days later from septicaemia. I could have wrung that doctor's neck

199

when he broke the news to me. Told me he and the nursing staff had done all that was humanly possible. He was inept and he knew it. He destroyed my children's happiness and mine and killed Jane just as surely as though he had plunged a knife into her heart. I simply have no recollection of the remainder of that day or of the days that followed.

"It left me numb and shocked. I was in a state of suspended animation. I had been left with a family of three boys to care for, without a mother. I had a demanding law practice to manage, or to attempt to manage. Inwardly I wept every day, never daring to show others the tears I kept imprisoned within. I cried in self-pity and anger, never heroic enough to reveal to the outside world the awful emptiness I felt inside. At night I could cry openly as I wrestled with insomnia, desperately trying for a decent night's uninterrupted sleep, banishing the dreams and nightmares that haunted me.

"I had to go through the motions of living and I have no idea what I did, or how I survived. Family and friends were kind, solicitous and understanding to a fault, but that did little to assuage my loss. Little by little, as the weeks went by, they lost patience with me.

"After six months, even my father told me that it was time for me to put the past behind me and to pull myself together. 'You should go out a little, meet people, perhaps take in a show' he advised, as though I needed this gratuitous advice. He meant well, but I think he didn't really understand that for months I had been in the depths of despair and I was simply struggling every day to achieve some outward appearance of normality. Of course I'd have liked to pull myself together, but it wasn't like a dog emerging from a river onto dry land simply shaking the water off with consummate ease. I felt that I had been clinging to a waterlogged piece of timber in mid-stream and try as hard as I might I just couldn't make the river bank and dry land. I haven't revealed these things to anyone before for fear of appearing weak and thought unmanly. I've not been able to summon up sufficient courage to tell anyone of what I've been going through these past two years. Somehow listening to you play has made it easier and perhaps more appropriate to speak of these dreadful happenings and my own inadequate feelings in response."

Drained, Andrew just sat there and Claire instinctively extended her hand to his, and murmuring, "I'm so very sorry Andrew I

200

hadn't the remotest idea, and here these past days I've been encumbering you with all my problems."

"We all have our sorrows and burdens. Seldom though, do we men ever have the courage to risk exposing what may appear to be an unmanly weakness to others. You weren't to know. We had simply lost touch and neither of us knew of the other's difficulties. Had I realised the terrible risks you ladies go through in childbirth I would have seen to it that we had fewer children, but then I suppose the risk is almost identical with each and every birth, whether it's the first or the third."

There followed a few moments of silence, Claire's hand still resting on Andrew's, which he had not withdrawn, when Annie knocked and entered to announce the arrival of Andrew's next client.

"Claire, you must excuse me. However much I would like to stay talking and listening to you play, I must go," said Andrew softly as he stood up.

"I'm sorry to have burdened you with my recent difficulties, it was completely unintentional. Somehow you must have touched a sensitive release spot and it all came tumbling out. I promise not to let that happen again. Please continue playing on the Steinway if you wish, I'm sure it enjoys a master touch, or," laughingly, "should it be mistress?"

"By the way I shall need you to come back in a couple of days when the paperwork is ready for your signature." As he reached the door to exit from the music room and Claire's presence he turned and smiling, "Perhaps if you arrange the time appropriately with my secretary, we can have a spot of lunch together. I guarantee it will help restore some of that lost self-esteem you were telling me about, and we can talk about the less traumatic events in our lives."

* * *

Claire's divorce was finalised at the end of January and became absolute three months later. Claire was an intelligent talented woman and Andrew found her absolutely captivating, particularly when she sat at the piano keyboard. Andrew realised how vulnerable Claire was following her divorce and fully understood her need for the comfort and security of a man. They had much in common from their youth, with shared memories and values. He realised he needed a mother for his growing children, particularly

201

his younger sons, who seemed happy and content with Claire and her daughters, and he needed the warmth and comfort that a wife could bring into his life.

On a number of occasions he invited her to join him for dinner, to accompany him to the theatre and to partner him when he attended professional functions. Andrew had invited Claire and several close colleagues with their wives to dinner on Easter Sunday. Following their meal, they proceeded to the music room to talk, over a glass of port, many of the men smoking cigars. Two of the guests entertained the others at the piano. Claire, who had been assisting Andrew, then volunteered in her turn to entertain. She played two pieces on the piano, making the evening a more resounding success.

Andrew offered to escort Claire home and once the last guest had departed, he seized his opportunity to propose marriage, which proposal Claire was pleased to accept on three conditions. Firstly, that he would never ever reveal to her children that her former husband was still living and would assist her in propagating the story that she was a widow. Secondly that he must never raise any objections to her visiting Henry in hospital, whenever she wished. Thirdly that while they would have a normal conjugal relationship, he must never ask or expect her to have more children. Andrew willingly agreed to these preconditions. Warmly they embraced and then spoke of how best to break the news to their children. They later set a date for their marriage in June and each decided they would favour a simple church wedding.

Each first of May, Claire continued to light a candle for Henry, which she set upon the piano, as she stood with her growing daughters as they, by tradition, sang the twenty-third psalm with the Crimond music. Never were they to know of their mother's remorse and guilt, for with Andrew Collins a new and brighter chapter had opened in their lives.

In June 1928, in a modest church ceremony, Andrew and Claire were married, the church never having recognised her earlier marriage to a non-Catholic. The need to record that she was a divorcee was therefore omitted from the marriage register and certificate. Both Claire's daughters now had a new father and Andrew's three sons a new mother.

Chapter 26

Baltimore September 1931

During the second weekend of September 1931, Claire had made her usual visit to Henry. His condition had remained largely unchanged save that, unlike Oscar Wilde's Dorian Gray, his appearance had aged exponentially faster than his underlying goodness would have warranted. In spite of the presence of a small, shielded electric fan, he still suffered from the residual effects of the late summer heat and humidity in his colourless bedroom cubicle.

Claire had noted on her earlier visits that he had a persistent cough. Although the staff had previously reassured her that there was no cause for concern she noted that it had become worse and was again reassured by the male nurse in charge that there was no cause for alarm.

Three days later she received a telephone call from the hospital telling her that Henry's condition had deteriorated and that he now had a bronchopneumonia, which the staff were powerless to treat other than with general nursing care. She hurried to the hospital, where she found Henry in a state of unconsciousness, breathing rapidly and soaked in perspiration. Under her supervision Henry was bed bathed and his sleeping attire changed and Claire sat with him for much of the remainder of the morning.

Later she left, and called on her former sister-in-law, since Annie had no telephone, to tell her in person of her brother's deteriorating condition. She climbed the stairs and rang the doorbell of the apartment. Annie opened the door and in some unconcealed astonishment said, "Oh it's you. What's brings you here?" She made no attempt to invite Claire in, nor demonstrated any sign of pleasurable recognition.

"Might I come in for a few moments to talk to you?"

"Well if you must."

"No, it's all right. I shouldn't have come unannounced. I can

203

speak to you out here just as well. I've just come from seeing Henry at the hospital."

"I didn't know you even visited your ex-husband or cared for that matter." Claire ignored the slight and continued

"He's running a fever and the staff tell me that he's developed bronchopneumonia. It's very likely that he might not pull through and I thought you'd like to know as soon as I knew."

"Well that's very nice of you for letting me know. I didn't know you cared about him any longer as his ex-wife."

"Annie, I could try to explain once again that I had no option but to divorce Henry, but I don't some how feel you're prepared to listen to me, or to understand."

"You're damned right I'm not prepared to understand. You married my brother when both his and your family were opposed to the marriage. Your family for all their money and position threw you out and it was Henry's family that accepted you. Then at the slightest hint of trouble you chucked him over like some discarded broken doll."

"Annie, you've completely distorted the true facts and deep down you know it."

"Claire you married my brother for better or worse and in sickness and in health and within a year of his illness you were busy seeing attorneys and arranging a divorce so that you could marry some rich lawyer."

"Annie, it wasn't like that at all. I'd been reduced to penury. I used to walk five miles to save a quarter on trolley fares when I visited Henry. Two and three times a week in the winter when it was five below. I did the same in summer when it was sometimes hot enough to fry an egg on the sidewalk. I even drank cups of hot water to save a few pennies on tea whenever I could. I was almost destitute and had nothing more to economise with. I couldn't let my children go hungry any longer. Condemn me if you must but I chose the only way to save my family as a family. I divorced Henry in order to remarry, because at the time I was desperate. But at the time, as God is my witness, I had no inkling *who* I'd marry."

"Rubbish, you could've asked me and Amelia for money. We'd never refused you in the past."

"Annie, you've a selective memory loss. Of course you gave me money and I was grateful for the little help you and your sister could give me, but you had no more to spare, or to give me. With

204

what little pride I had left I couldn't beg, or would you have had me sell my body to the dregs of humanity round Baltimore harbour?"

"The facts speak for themselves. Your behaviour was despicable. You're a schemer and a liar and you divorced and ditched poor Henry for someone with money. I wonder how you can face your children when you've done that to their father."

"Annie, I've not come here for an argument. You're never going to see my point of view, nor do you seem in the least bit prepared to understand, or remember my hopelessness and desperation at that time. But all that's in the past, It's finished. I may have divorced Henry, but morally I consider him my husband and I always shall, whatever you might think. I came here today, in friendship, which you reject, and so I do so now merely out of duty to tell you of his deteriorating state of health. It's very likely that Henry may shortly succumb to this infection. Should that be the case, I'll make all the arrangements with the funeral home that dealt with your late mother's funeral and have them organise the interment at the same Jewish cemetery, where Rebecca, may she rest in peace, was laid to rest. Furthermore I intend to pay for all the funeral expenses. Since you've made it patently obvious that you don't want to speak to me, I'll leave it to the undertaker to communicate with you if and when the need arises. Goodbye Annie."

Without further ado, Claire turned and inwardly shaking with emotion, walked away. As she did so the door to Annie's apartment closed with a resounding slam of 'good riddance'. She returned to her home and no sooner had she entered than the dreaded telephone call came from the hospital. Henry had succumbed to his infection and passed away. Claire arranged with the hospital superintendent that she would be returning to collect the medical certificate and explained that she would immediately contact the appropriate funeral home to make all the necessary arrangements for the funeral to take place the following day, according to Jewish custom. Before leaving for the hospital she telephoned Andrew at his office to explain all that had taken place.

The following morning witnessed the remnants of a mid-September hurricane as it swept northwards from Florida up the east coast, reaching the Chesapeake Bay as a summer storm. It faltered, blowing heavy rainclouds racing onwards to New York before teetering eastwards to disappear into the North Atlantic. Rain teemed down and diminishing gusts of wind blew with

205

periodic and reducing ferocity, tearing at tree branches and those man-made objects not securely fixed or tethered down. The detritus of leaves and branches littered the ground, mingling in the rivulets of water that flowed, coalescing into countless rivers, shallow lakes and puddles.

Late that morning a small sorrowful and bedraggled group of people in rain attire, attempting to huddle under umbrellas which were soon blown inside out, waited for the arrival of the hearse. As the sparse funeral cortège arrived directly from the Baltimore Mental Hospital into the Adath Yeshuron Cemetery grounds, the mourners slowly followed to the graveside. The mourners were Claire, Henry's two sisters, and their husbands, all of whom did their best to ignore Claire. Head covered, Andrew Collins accompanied Claire but appropriately kept discretely to the perimeter of the group and was not introduced to Henry's family. There were no nephews or nieces and no past friends attending. By tradition there were no flowers. The pallbearers lowered the simple pine coffin into the ground, laying Henry to his final rest after five years of existence following the devastation wrought by an unidentified virus upon his fine brain.

There was no immediate male next of kin to say *Kaddesh*, so this was delivered by the officiating rabbi, while in her heart Claire at the same time silently accompanied him as she intoned the Hebrew words of the ancient prayer she had learned for her beloved Henry: "*Yitgadal, v'yit ka dash shamay raba, b'almadivra chiru tay, V'yam lich malchut tay.*" ("Let us magnify and sanctify the great name of God, in the world he created according to his will").

The rabbi gave no eulogy and the service was as brief as etiquette would permit, enabling the rain-drenched participants to escape back to the shelter of waiting conveyances provided by the funeral home.

All except Claire, who stood alone, silently grieving for what appeared an interminable time. She then took from a pocket in her wet raincoat a small posy of carefully wrapped yellow primroses, with a solitary blue violet in the centre, which she had been holding carefully concealed for this moment. She bent down slowly and placed it on the grave. A token of her continued love for Henry, with the timeless reminder of the flowers he had so joyously given her those many years ago, when he had proposed marriage and they had consummated their love.

206

She could barely move her leaden feet, so drained was she emotionally, as she then softly sang, like a whisper on the gusting wind, that only she and her beloved Henry might hear, her own personal prayer of farewell to her love. Oblivious to all and everything around her, she sang from part of the requiem mass, to the melody of Gunod's *Ave Maria*, her own simple message to Henry, the first and the supreme love of her life. The rain fell in lightly diminishing droplets, with none but Andrew standing a few paces behind to hear as she sang that small part of the Latin requiem;

"*In Paradisum dedunct te angeli* (May the angels lead you into paradise)
In tuo adventu suscipiant de martyres (May the martyrs receive you in your coming)
Chorus angelorum te suscipiat (May the chorus of angels receive you)
Aeternam habeas requiem. Amen (May you have eternal rest. Amen)"

As she continued to stand motionless over Henry's final resting place, immersed in her anguished thoughts and grief, Andrew stepped forward and without speaking gently took her by the arm, leading and assisting her back to their car, out of the rain.

Henry's sisters only sat *shiva* for the remainder of that day in Amelia's home, and not the traditional seven days. Claire was neither invited nor expected to join them. She was no longer welcome as a family member. She had, in their opinion, moved 'beyond the pale'. Henry had died, but the plague of bigotry persisted. It continued to flourish, in every facet of life. The hyenas Rebecca warned Claire of were alive everywhere in every race and culture.

A small obituary announcement was placed in the *Baltimore Hebrew Weekly News*, but no one informed his London family. Contact with their brothers had been severed involuntarily following Rebecca's death in 1916, and so Henry's family were unaware of his demise. Within one generation there were none in England who would even recall his existence, while in the US there was only his widow and daughters Rebecca and Henrietta.

That evening Rebecca and Henrietta dined with Andrew and his sons, their adopted family, in the dining room in Fayette Street, enjoying the usual conversational banter that flowed across the dining table. Claire had announced to the children, through her husband, that she had a headache and must be excused. She rested, devoid of appetite, in her bedroom, unable to face her daughters that day. Her secret was permanently safe with Andrew, the one person in her family who knew, and she silently sobbed herself to sleep, again recalling the other Henry's words, "There is no grief like the grief that does not speak."

Rebecca and Henrietta were totally unaware of the funeral. They were never told of the event, always believing that their father had died in 1927.

Chapter 27

London March 2005

Over the years that followed, I was able to complete most of the genealogical task I had set myself in 1999 following the birth of our firstborn child Edward. I traced descendants of every child of David Joseph Chiswick, the sisters and brothers of my namesake, my great grandfather, Alfred. It required some considerable time and a prodigious amount of luck and help from others. It was a really formidable undertaking but looking back, both enjoyable and challenging.

By checking on the internet at www.1837online.com, I was able to access the 1861 UK census to discover the decade in which my earliest Chiswick ancestor had first arrived in the UK.

He was David Joseph Chiswick (Chiszyk), my great, great grandfather. In 1861 I discovered that aged fifteen and giving his occupation as a tailor, he was living in a room at 23 Church Street, Spitalfields, London, with a younger brother. In this the same year the Russian serfs were first given their freedom, while on the other side of the world that horrific conflict, the American Civil War had just started. David had in all probability fled, no more than a year or two earlier, a mere child, to escape from czarist tyranny in Poland, racing westwards, accompanied by a younger brother. The prize that he attained was a life of religious freedom, toleration and liberty in England, for himself and in time his descendants, many of whom emigrated further west to that other great bastion of liberty, the USA.

Having discovered and been able to communicate with one or more present-day descendants of each of David Joseph's children, I set about attempting to finalise my genealogical task by discovering where each was buried and their cause of death. I identified the terminal illness of David Joseph and Rebecca and their six children and in which town each was buried. I was then left with one small missing piece of the puzzle. I knew in which town and cemetery Henry had been buried, but could find no marker of any kind. The remaining mystery to resolve was precisely *where* Henry was buried.

Search as I might, with what little skill and fortitude I possess, I have to date been unable to find the stone marking Henry Chiswick's grave in Baltimore. Had I been able to find the grave I would have placed a small pebble on the headstone to indicate, by tradition, that a family member had visited the deceased and had recited a small prayer. Perhaps a stone was never placed to mark his grave, or possibly I have temporarily exhausted my genealogical run of luck. But wherever my Great Uncle Henry's final resting place might be, as Claire sang that day at his funeral, "*Aeternum Habeus Requiem*. May he truly rest in eternal peace."

Amen.

Notes

(1) Spitalfields is now part of the London borough of Tower Hamlets, immediately to the north of the Thames and the old walled city. The name originated from St Mary's Spital, a medieval hospital founded in 1197 in fields adjacent to the north-east boundary of the city of London. Following the devastating 1666 fire of London the area was built up and a market established. The area has always attracted newly-arrived immigrants, commencing with the Huguenot French silk weavers in 1685. Bounded to the north by Shoreditch and the south by Aldgate, it is traversed by two major roadways, Commercial Street and Whitechapel Road. In the Whitechapel Road bell foundry the famous Philadelphia Liberty Bell was cast in 1751 with its famed biblical Leviticus quotation, "Proclaim Liberty throughout all the land" to commemorate the fiftieth anniversary of William Penn's 1701 constitution for Pennsylvania, the forerunner of the US constitution.

(2) Louis Cheslock (25 September 1898–19 July 1981) Composer, teacher, violinist and author, began teaching at the Peabody Conservatory in 1916, a year before his graduation. He remained a dedicated teacher at the Peabody for sixty years until his retirement in 1976. In 1916 he became the youngest member of the Baltimore Symphony Orchestra. Present at the inaugural concert, he continued as a violist with the orchestra for twenty-one years, becoming the concertmaster. Born in London, of Polish Jewish parents, he arrived in Baltimore by way of Quebec in 1901 where he lived and worked. In 1964 he was awarded an honorary Doctorate of Musical Arts by the Peabody. His remarkable eight-volume *Stamp Collection with a Musical Connotation* was left to the Peabody Museum. His younger brother, Saul Cheslock, studied violin as one of his Peabody students from 1926 onwards.

(3) George Peabody was a wealthy self-made businessman and banker who donated funds in 1852 to establish the first musical college of its kind in the United States. Known as the Peabody

Institute it opened in 1866 in Mount Vernon Place, overlooked by the Washington Monument in the heart of the city of Baltimore, and is today part of the Johns Hopkins University. Born in 1795 in Danvers Massachusetts, Peabody left school aged eleven and fought in 1812 against the British. He amassed one of the largest financial empires of the nineteenth century and was a director of railroad companies, banks and the company that laid the first transatlantic cables. He moved to England in 1827 and settled for a time in London, where he became the first of only two Americans to receive the Freedom of the City of London. (The second was General Dwight D. Eisenhower, later US president, 1952–60.) The Prince of Wales, later King Edward VII (1901–10) unveiled a statue to him in Threadneedle Street, the City of London's financial centre. In 1867 he received the US Congressional Medal. In 1862, to help house the city's poor, he established a huge charitable enterprise, the Peabody Trust, which still flourishes to this day. Among his many charitable works in housing and education he established a teacher training college in Nashville, now part of the Vanderbilt University. He died in 1869 and was temporarily buried in Westminster Abbey. His funeral was attended by Queen Victoria, the Prince of Wales and Prime Minister Gladstone. He was later buried in the Massachusetts town of his birth, renamed Peabody, in his honour. Eloquently summarising his attitude towards education he wrote in a letter to his nephew: "Deprived as I was of the opportunity of obtaining anything more than the most common education, I am well qualified to estimate its value by the disadvantages I labour under in the society in which my business and situation in life frequently throws me. Willingly would I now give twenty times the expense attending a good education could I possess it. But it is now too late for me to learn and I can only do to those that come under my care as I could have wished circumstances had permitted others to have done by me." In Spitalfields George Peabody established his major London Peabody Housing Trust, providing homes for the poor

(4) Bethlehem Steel: the Pennsylvania Steel Company established a steel mill and shipyard at Baltimore's Sparrow Point in the mid 1880s. In 1916 this was purchased by the Bethlehem Steel Corporation (thus named from its origins in the village of

Bethlehem, Pennsylvania in 1863). Under the chairmanship of Charles Schwab, a protégé of the Scottish steel baron Dale Andrew Carnegie, Bethlehem Steel became the largest and most profitable steel mill in the USA. It specialised in the production of structural steel, used in bridge and skyscraper construction, and armour plating, used in ship construction and repair. By the end of 1945, some 20 per cent of American warships were built from this steel. It also produced cannon casting, making some 33 per cent of all US military gun castings. Bethlehem Steel was the largest employer in Baltimore during both world wars and became immensely profitable during those and other periods of major military conflict and construction.

(5) Robert Bruce (1274–1329), Scotland's Earl of Carrick was frequently in conflict with the English, attempting to regain independence for Scotland. Following a series of unsuccessful battles he fled for his life. Dispirited and hiding alone in a cave, he watched a spider trying to spin a web. Each time the spider failed, it simply started all over again, until after many attempts it succeeded. Inspired by this observation, Bruce returned to battle again for Scottish independence. He inflicted a series of defeats on the English, thus winning him more Scots supporters and eventual victory at the Battle of Bannockburn in 1314 against the English army of King Edward II. He was then crowned King Robert Bruce of Scotland, an independent sovereign state. The story serves to explain the maxim that every young British school child is taught: "If at first you don't succeed, try, try and try again".

(6) Nurse Edith Cavell, born in 1865, the daughter of a pastor living in Swardeston, Norfolk was nurtured in the great English nursing tradition of Florence Nightingale. A patriot, and humanitarian, she was an exceptional woman who established a nursing school in Brussels in 1907.

With the outbreak of hostilities in August 1914 she had continued her nursing care, as a member of the Red Cross, treating any and every wounded man who came to her nursing home, from either side in the terrible conflict. She had, however, assisted and concealed upwards of some 200 young English, French, and Belgian soldiers in her care to escape north into neutral Holland to avoid capture by the occupying

213

Germans. The Germans considered this treasonous behaviour.

She was arrested, interrogated, and readily admitted her guilt in harbouring these wounded combatants and aiding their escape. At a court martial she was declared guilty, and was executed by a German firing squad as a spy, in late October 1915, in spite of public opinion calling for a commuted sentence. Her words the night prior to her death were that "One should hate no one, but love all." The German medical officer present at her execution wrote. "She was the bravest woman I ever met, and was in every respect the heroine her nation considered her. She went to her death with tears in her eyes as the blindfold was put in place, but with a poise and bearing which was impossible to forget."

Executing a nurse, who was certainly not a spy, was a public relations disaster for the Germans. Following her execution, Allied military recruitment doubled in the winter months, and in the USA was a major factor in encouraging them to side with the Allies in 1917.

As a testament to her courageous humanitarian behaviour as a nurse, a statue was later erected in central London, just north of Trafalgar Square, at St Martin's Place. On the plinth her last words read "Standing as I do in view of God and Eternity, I realise that patriotism is not enough. I must have no hatred or bitterness for anyone." In Canada a mountain peak was dedicated to her name.

(7) Battle of the Somme: just fifty miles from Paris, the German advance of the previous years had halted in the plain of the River Somme. To consolidate these gains, the Germans installed lines of trenches and fortifications in great depth. They next attempted to force a breakthrough to Paris at Verdun to the south. In February 1916, a ferocious battle ensued, as the Germans attacked the forts guarding Verdun. The French held on tenaciously and to relieve the pressure on the French army an offensive was planned by a combined Anglo-French force under the British General Haig, assisted by the French General Foch, further to the north in the region of Peronne, where the River Somme changes direction from flowing north to flow westward. The clash of titans commenced on 1 July 1916 and ended on 18 November. On both sides more than four million men were involved in this single battle.

The Germans sustained a loss of one million men killed, injured and captured, while the Allies' loss was marginally greater. There were three distinct phases in the battle. In the first day alone, the British sustained sixty thousand casualties, of whom twenty thousand were killed. By 18 November the greatest gain of land had been an advance by the Allies of four miles. In September there first appeared a new vehicle. Officially termed a heavy armoured car, combatants called it a 'tank'. At the end of 1916 the Germans had gained more land in the first years, but with their failure to take Verdun and the immense losses at the Somme, a military victory seemed impossible. The continued siege of Axis ports by the British naval blockade produced immense food and material shortages. The German military had then begun to realise that battling against the French and the British they would never win what had become an immense war of attrition.

(8) Gregorian calendar: the Venerable Bede, in about AD 700 is believed to have been the first to date the years we currently use from the birth of Jesus. The Roman King Romulus, in the seventh century BC developed a ten-month solar calendar with 304 days, their year commencing with the spring or vernal equinox, i.e. when the length of the day and night are exactly the same. The months, which we easily recognise today were:

(March) *Martius* named after Mars the god of war.

(April) *Aprilis*, based on the latin to open.

(May) *Maia* the goddess of spring and growth.

(June) *Juno* the goddess of wisdom and marriage.

(July) *Quntilis* which was later in 44 BC renamed *Julius* after Julius Caesar, who modified the calendar to provide a 365-day year.

(August) *Sextilis* which was renamed *August* after Augustus Caesar.

September, October, November and December were named after the Latin roots for seven, eight, nine and ten. Later in the seventh century BC the Roman King Numa Pompilius increased the year to 354 days by including two new months between December and March. These were

(January) *Janus* named after the two-headed god of gates and doorways and (February) *Februarius* the month of expiation. The Julian calendar remained in operation in the Christian

215

world for some sixteen hundred years until 1582 when Pope Gregory the thirteenth issued a papal edict amending the calendar to correct minor deficiencies in the Julian version by removing ten days from October in 1582, and abolishing leap years in years ending with 00 but including a leap year if the year ending in 00 can be divided exactly by 400. Only Catholic countries made the change at that time. Protestant countries followed some years later. England and America adopted the modified calendar in 1752 when eleven days were removed from the calendar as Wednesday 2 September 1752 was followed by Thursday 14 September 1752. Russia and some Eastern European countries changed in 1918.

(9) Fort McHenry: Fort Whetstone had earlier been built to defend the approaches to the city port of Baltimore and was renamed Fort McHenry in honour of George Washington's Secretary of State for War. On the night of 13 September 1814 the defenders had successfully withstood the British Admiral Cochrane's naval bombardment in the war of 1812, after his forces had sacked and burned the city of Washington. Inspired by seeing the Stars and Stripes colours still flying over the fort the following morning, Francis Scott Key, a Washington attorney and poet, wrote a poem, 'The Star Spangled Banner', which he set to an old English drinking song 'Anacreon'. The flag in question was of huge proportion, just over a quarter the size of a football pitch, and when flown from its masthead could be seen at a distance of some eight miles. It was the second version of the flag, containing fifteen stars and fifteen stripes. The remains of this flag are in Washington's Smithsonian Museum. After 1818 the American flag returned to its original thirteen stripes, with a white star on a blue background added for each state in the union. The states of Kentucky and Vermont had been the additional states represented in the Fort McHenry flag. Any additional state joining the union from then onwards had an additional star added to the flag on 4 July.

(10) The Peabody Institute, in its earlier years, had no concert quality organ. Students were taught and practiced on instruments in nearby churches. In the North Hall, a smaller concert hall seating an audience of a hundred and fifty persons, located above the Friedburg Hall Auditorium, an organ manufactured in Cleveland Ohio by Holtkamp was installed in 1998.

The North Hall was then renamed the Griswold Hall in honour of Leith Symington Griswold, who studied piano at the Institute between 1926 and 1936 and whose descendants donated funds for the Hall's restoration and the installation of the magnificent 'Holtkamp Organ'.

(11) The Easter Uprising of 1916 was a pivotal event in Ireland. Before the Uprising, few in Ireland openly supported the fifteen hundred rebels who participated in this armed rising. The rebellion was ruthlessly and rapidly suppressed with a loss of some fifteen hundred soldiers and civilians. Courts martial summarily tried and executed some twenty ringleaders of the insurrection. After the 1916 Uprising, those involved achieved the status of heroes.

(12) Battle of Jutland: the major naval battle of the First World War took place in an area of the North Sea, some sixty-five miles west of Denmark in May 1916. At the outset of the First World War in August 1914 the British had the world's largest and most powerful single naval fleet. As in earlier wars the British instituted a naval blockade of enemy ports. The Germans had been increasing their naval size and strength in an attempt to compete with the British and by the outbreak of war possessed the world's second most powerful modern naval force. Submarines and smaller craft regularly left German ports but the larger German warships remained unwilling to venture out. The British Grand Fleet under Admiral John Jellicoe sailed periodically into the North Sea, sweeping through that part of the ocean in search of any adversaries. On one such occasion the Fleet sailed out on the morning of 30 May 1916. They were unaware at the time that the German High Seas Fleet, with almost all its heavy warships, was about to set out under Admiral Reinhold Scheer, for its first major sortie since January 1915. The German navy intended sailing northwards in the direction of Norway, hoping to find and destroy one of the smaller groups of Royal Navy ships that frequently patrolled that area. At four a.m. on 31 May the German High Seas Fleet left port, sailing for Norwegian waters. Each fleet was, at the time, unaware of the presence of the other. On each side, small, faster, lighter vessels scouted many miles ahead of the larger cruisers, behind which came the heavy dreadnoughts and battleships with their massive guns. At two-

twenty p.m. contact was first made between light cruisers of each side but each were unaware that the main battle fleet of the enemy was some miles behind. Part of the British fleet engaged the German warships while a group under Admiral Beatty attempted to sail between the enemy vessels and their base, to cut off any means of escape. The main action between the heavier ships lasted some two hours that evening as the German fleet attempted to escape south, back to port, having realised the strength of the British fleet opposing them. With nightfall and mist, sporadic action continued between lighter craft, while the German fleet made good its escape back to port. The following morning, apart from wreckage, there was no sign of any of the German fleet and the Royal Navy remained in control of the North Sea. The British lost six cruisers and eight destroyers. The Germans lost a battleship, six cruisers, six destroyers and a submarine, with many more badly damaged on both sides. Both sides claimed victory. With similar numbers of vessels lost and more German vessels severely mauled, the British remained at sea to maintain their blockade while the German navy concentrated on underwater warfare, with their capital ships remaining, bottled up, in port. Immediately following the engagement the Germans were far more economical with the truth than the British. In spite of German claims and propaganda at that time, this was one of the greatest British naval victories, second only to those fought by Admiral Horatio Nelson against the French.

(13) Guy Fawkes Night celebrates the failed attempt in 1605 of Robert Catesby, assisted by Guy Fawkes and a few Catholic supporters, to blow up King James I and all his ministers at the opening of Parliament, with barrels of gunpowder which were hidden in the basement of the Parliament building. Prior to each opening of Parliament since 1605, 'Beefeaters' search the crypt of the building. British children celebrate this anniversary with bonfires and fireworks on 5 November.

(14) Hospital Ships in London:
Sir Roland Hill, the man who in 1840 started the world's first uniform penny post, tried to establish, with the Metropolitan Asylum Board (MAB), a smallpox and fever hospital in Hampstead, some three miles from the centre of London, and another in Fulham. The public were opposed to smallpox and

218

fever hospitals anywhere close to where they lived as the death rate from smallpox was in excess of 30 per cent at that time. During an 1881 smallpox epidemic, the MAB arranged for three huge old wooden ships to be anchored together in Deptford Creek just below Greenwich in the lower reaches of the River Thames. These were converted into floating wards, to accommodate hundreds of sick patients who might be suffering from smallpox or any infectious illness, where they might be isolated to prevent the spread of infection. Nurses, all of whom had to be single, and vaccinated against smallpox, staffed these floating hospitals. These ships were in use until 1902. Two of these hulks were large wooden warships, the *Atlas,* built in 1860, and the *Endymion,* built in 1865. The *Atlas* was for the male patients and was linked by a walkway to the *Endymion,* which was for staff accommodation, administration and kitchens. A third ship, an old paddle steamer, the *Castalia,* linked by a walkway to the *Endymion,* provided accommodation for women. A paddle steamer ambulance service, started in 1884, conveyed patients and supplies from three piers in London to the hospital ships.

(15) Prince Albert, the husband of Queen Victoria, succumbed to typhoid fever in 1861. The queen had a magnificent memorial built to him in 1876 in Hyde Park, opposite the Royal Albert Hall, north of Exhibition Road. Recently renovated, it is well worth a visit and close inspection.

* * *

E-mail locations
  www.Ancestry.com
  www.EllisIsland.com   www.jewishgen.org/jri-p
  www.1837online.com   www.jewishgen.org

Yiddish and Hebrew Words

Chutzpah – sauciness or cheek
Maven – an expert
Lockshen – a pasta, like linguini
Kneidle – a small dumpling
Shiva – Hebrew for the number 7. The days of official mourning
Shlamiel – a fool
Tzures – trouble.